DATE DUE MAY 06

9-20-06			
11-7-06			
11-22-06			
5-10-08			
4/16/15			
GAYLORD			PRINTED IN U.S.A.

Blessing

**Also by Deborah Bedford
in Large Print:**

A Morning Like This

This Large Print Book carries the
Seal of Approval of N.A.V.H.

Blessing

Deborah Bedford

Thorndike Press • Waterville, Maine

Published in 2006 by arrangement with Harlequin Books S.A.

Thorndike Press® Large Print Christian Historical Fiction.

The tree indicium is a trademark of Thorndike Press.

The text of this Large Print edition is unabridged. Other aspects of the book may vary from the original edition.

Set in 16 pt. Plantin by Elena Picard.

Printed in the United States on permanent paper.

Library of Congress Cataloging-in-Publication Data

Bedford, Deborah.
    Blessing / by Deborah Bedford.
        p. cm.
    ISBN 0-7862-8442-0 (lg. print : hc : alk. paper)
    1. Tincup (Colo.) — Fiction. 2. Miners — Fiction.
    3. Large type books. I. Title.
    PS3602.E34B57 2006
    813'.6—dc22   2005035099

To those who long to find
peace and protection.

To the ones who know it is
not their own power, but the Father's,
that makes things work for the good.

As the Founder/CEO of NAVH, the only national health agency solely devoted to those who, although not totally blind, have an eye disease which could lead to serious visual impairment, I am pleased to recognize Thorndike Press★ as one of the leading publishers in the large print field.

Founded in 1954 in San Francisco to prepare large print textbooks for partially seeing children, NAVH became the pioneer and standard setting agency in the preparation of large type.

Today, those publishers who meet our standards carry the prestigious "Seal of Approval" indicating high quality large print. We are delighted that Thorndike Press is one of the publishers whose titles meet these standards. We are also pleased to recognize the significant contribution Thorndike Press is making in this important and growing field.

Lorraine H. Marchi, L.H.D.
Founder/CEO
NAVH

★ Thorndike Press encompasses the following imprints: Thorndike, Wheeler, Walker and Large Print Press.

Acknowledgments

To Meme and Papaw,
Dale and Marjorie Holt, who showed
me how to make Tin Cup my own.
I love you.

To Joan Marlow Golan,
who has encouraged and
given wise counsel during this project.
Thank you for giving me the opportunity
to turn this, the work of my hands,
which I had meant for the world,
into a story that glorifies the Lord.

Chapter One

❧

Gunnison County, Colorado — 1882

"I don't want this town to be called Virginia City anymore!" Alex Parent hollered, banging his cup on the podium. "Every town this side of the Mississippi is called Virginia City. The confounded postal service is dropping off mail from back home everywhere else but here."

All 103 people in the audience agreed with him at the top of their lungs.

"That's right!"

"Yep!"

"You're right, Parent," someone else bellowed. "There's a Virginia City in Nevada and another one in Alder Gulch, Montana and another one . . ."

"So . . . we aren't Virginia City anymore," Parent hollered at them as he pounded the podium. "Who are we gonna be? We've got to discuss this and make a motion and get it down in the town records right."

For a minute, nobody said anything.

Alex Parent fidgeted, shuffling through his papers. "Well, somebody say something. We've got to have a name for this town. Come on. Let's have ideas."

One hand rose in the crowd. The hand belonged to Uley, a youngster who'd come from Ohio four years before to work in the Gold Cup Mine.

"Yep, Uley? What is it, son?"

"I think," Uley said, in a timid voice that, if anyone had thought about it, sounded a touch too high-pitched for a boy of his age, "we ought to select a name that tells people something about this place. Remember last month, when that fellow from New York got off the stage on Alpine Pass? While the driver stopped to change horses?"

Of course everyone remembered. They'd been talking about it in town for weeks.

"The fellow went to the spring to get a drink," Uley said, telling the story over again, just in case somebody hadn't heard it. "But he wouldn't drink out of that rusty tin cup they keep up there. So, George Willis pulled out his Winchester and shot off that fellow's derby, then made him drink six cups of water."

Hollis Andersen took up the story. "And

10

when the newcomer tried to get back on the stage, Willis said, 'You're too good to drink out of a cup that was good enough for hundreds of thirsty men. That cup's been sitting on that rock for five years, and you're the first skunk to pick it up, refuse to drink out of it and throw it into the bushes. If I ever see you in these parts God made for men — and not your kind — I'll shoot lower and put a hole in that thick head of yours. Savvy?'"

Everybody in the place started hooting.

Parent banged his cup against the podium again to quiet the roaring crowd. His efforts came too late. People were laughing, clapping each other on the back. "Silence," Parent shouted. "Silence!"

Silence did not come. Somewhere in the back, somebody bellowed, "It's got to be Tin Cup! Tin Cup! Tin Cup!"

Every man in the meeting room took up the cry. "Tin Cup! Tin Cup! Tin Cup!"

Parent knew he had to preserve parliamentary procedure. "I move we name this town Tin Cup! Do I hear a second? We have to have a second!"

"I second it!" Uley's hand lifted above the crowd. "Tin Cup is perfect!"

"Any discussion? If there's no discussion, I've got to call for a vote." Parent

11

banged his cup yet again. "I've got to call for a vote!"

"Vote!" they all shouted. "Vote! We want to vote for Tin Cup!"

"All in favor." Parent did his best to count hands, but that proved impossible. "All against."

In the end, he found it easier to tabulate the nays and subtract them from the number attending the meeting. It worked out — on paper — as one hundred votes cast in favor and three votes opposed.

And so, this town would change its name. When the paperwork was completed, the officers of Virginia City would sell their rights and seal to the new town for the price of two hundred and fifty dollars. "Tin Cup, Colorado, it is — one hundred to three," Parent shouted.

Hats flew in celebration. Stetsons. Wool caps. Bowlers. Even a beret or two. Every hat flew except one. Uley's. Despite the excitement, Uley stood still, hands propped on hips, hat very much in place.

"Here we go again," Hollis Anderson remarked. "All of us are gonna end up at Frenchy's Place — alone — when we ought to be having a gathering with womenfolk."

"We can have a party," Charlie Hastings

told him. "We'll just get half the men to wear aprons and we'll *pretend* we've got ladies in this town."

Uley wanted to throw her woolen hat into the air. She wanted to let all her curls underneath tumble out and give away her secret. But she was stuck. Stuck like a pine marten gets stuck when it climbs down somebody's chimney and ends up in somebody's wood stove.

"You going up to Frenchy's?" somebody asked her pa.

Samuel Kirkland glanced at Uley sideways, the way a mule glances when it's unsure of its footing. "Don't think so, Amos. Uley and I've got to get home. Tomorrow's going to start early."

"Aw, Sam," Amos said. "It'll start early for everybody. Come on over and keep the celebration going."

Uley said nothing. A Christian young lady did not enter a place like Frenchy's, a man's place, without having her reputation sorely tainted. But what did it matter, anyway? With the deception she was playing on the whole town, she had no right to be counting anyone else's sins. As long as she and Sam lived in Tin Cup, nobody would know her as a genteel young lady. Things had already gone too far for that.

"Come on, Sam," Amos urged her pa. "It'll be hard work in the mines tomorrow. Tonight let's cut loose."

Uley could tell by the way he glanced at her again that her pa wanted to go.

"You should come, too, Uley." Amos clapped her on the back. "They're gonna start a poker game up there at ten. It's about time a young fella like you learned to hold his own in a gambling den."

"No thanks, Amos."

The raucous crowd funneled through the doorway, then fanned out onto the street, heading toward Frenchy's, the most popular of the town's twenty saloons. *That was certainly a subject a Christian lady shouldn't know about,* she thought, somewhat grimly, as she watched her pa get swept up in the throng. *Gambling dens and saloons.*

Uley walked toward the little house where she and her father made their home. The cob-worked cabin on Willow Street suited them much better than the crude shanties most of the miners had pieced together in the hills. She knew her pa had purchased the pretty little place in town because he wanted to do right by her.

"Hey, Uley!" Marshal Harris Olney called out as he passed by. "Why aren't you over at Frenchy's with the rest of them?"

She thought before she spoke, and consciously pitched her voice lower. "That's not a place I enjoy going."

"Wish everybody else thought that way, too," Harris shook his head jovially. "I'll be up all night."

Uley figured the marshal probably *never* got a decent night's rest. People worked hard all day long in the mines, and at night, when you'd think they'd be exhausted and ready to sleep, they came out to carouse in saloons that never closed, celebrating a few nuggets of gold — which were usually gone by sunup. *Oh, Father. It seems like nothing I could ever do would change this place.*

As she hurried up the street, Uley heard a slight sound to her left. The sound wasn't much, just a pebble skipping across the dirt. She glanced up, couldn't see into the shadows. Something about being here alone this time of night with everybody else down at Frenchy's made her adrenaline flow.

Just suppose she'd come upon a mountain lion.

Just suppose she'd come upon somebody up to no good.

Just suppose.

Uley didn't miss a stride. As she rounded the next corner, she spied a stranger standing at the edge of the darkness.

"Hello," she said to him, an unreasonable fear knotting her stomach.

He nodded without answering. As she passed him, all she caught was a glimpse — a black leather vest, legs long as a stallion's, a dark felt Stetson, a glint of moonlight reflecting in his eyes and in his hands.

A glint of metal.

Uley stopped three paces past him. The stranger was holding a gun. She turned to see him step out into the pale moonglow to take his aim.

This man, all black leather and legs, with a shadow for a face, was going to shoot the marshal in the back!

Uley didn't take time to think. She didn't take time to cry for help. She sprinted toward the man, mud muffling her long strides. She took a racing leap and sprang at him.

She hit him full tilt and heard his breath rush out of his lungs. The gun pinwheeled out of his hands. He grunted as he went down.

She fell on top of him and pinned him. She clamped her arms firmly about his neck, not about to let him go.

He tried to throw her off. She clung to him like the mountain lion she'd been afraid of moments before, her attention riveted to his neck, the only part of him small enough to hang on to.

For the first time in her life Uley offered thanks for her muscles, which were honed to do the same job as any man's. She fought for breath. "He's tryin' to shoot Olney! Somebody get over here!"

She heard feet pounding in her direction. *Thank You, Father. Oh, thank You, thank You, thank You.*

The man beneath her cursed again and said, "Now I'm going to get tried for murdering Harris Olney, and I didn't even get to kill him."

"You hold still." She glared down at him. "You don't say anything." She realized he was staring up at her now the way a man might stare at someone dead. His eyes got as big around as silver dollars.

He gasped, "You're a *lady.*"

Holding him down did not frighten her, but this did. He'd found her out. Uley let go of his neck, grabbed her head and, sure enough, the cap had flown away. Her hair hung in sodden, muddy ribbons around her neck.

She looked alternately from the man beneath her to the woolen cap lying upside down in the mud.

Every fellow in Tin Cup would arrive within seconds.

Uley made a fast decision. She figured the stranger would get away, but she had to get her hat on. She leapt off of him, grabbed her hat and shoved the muddy tendrils beneath it.

The stranger lay in the precise spot he'd landed. "You're just a *girl!*"

His words made her mad. Here she sat in the muck, a full-grown woman, strong enough to take him down, nineteen years old, well into marriageable age. How dare he call her just a *girl?*

She locked her arms around his neck again.

She couldn't think of anything worse than this, having someone find her out after all the work she'd done in the Gold Cup Mine. Just now, the only thing more humiliating than being a woman would be having them all find out she was one. "You don't tell anybody, you hear me?" She waggled a tiny, clenched fist at him. "You don't tell anybody, or I'll give you what's coming myself."

The horde of men from Frenchy's flocked toward them. The stranger didn't move his glinting eyes from her own. "Okay. Yes, ma'am."

By early morning, it was all over the new town of Tin Cup that Uley Kirkland, one of the most spry young fellows in Tin Cup, had apprehended a man trying to murder the marshal. Everyone talked of a hanging. They couldn't hang the scoundrel, though, until Judge J. M. Murphy came back from visiting his daughter in Denver.

All day, fellows clapped Uley on the back and talked about a trial. Others deemed the stranger should just be shot. After all, sidearms had kept the law in the valley for a long time before Harris Olney ever wore his star.

As Uley worked alongside her pa at the Gold Cup, she found herself wishing somebody would shoot the murderer and end this entire contemptible affair.

If the stranger died, her secret would die with him.

But then, she reasoned, that wasn't quite true. *She* wouldn't be dead. *She* would still have to live with it.

Oh, Father, wishing somebody dead is not what I should be thinking, either. What a vile sinner I am!

Around lunchtime, word filtered out that

the stranger, Aaron Brown, was registered up at the Grand Central Hotel. When Uley first heard his name, she and her pa were working side by side as timbermen in shaft eleven. Uley knew this work almost as well as her father knew it, how to square off the lumber with a broadax, how to chink the fittings so that the joints stayed watertight in the shaft. "Don't you go worrying about Aaron Brown," Sam told her. "You did a good job last night. I'm proud of you. That criminal will be dead before we get our next paycheck."

But what if Aaron Brown talked before then? What if he sat on the back of his horse right before they hanged him and shouted, "Uley Kirkland is a girl! Uley Kirkland, who has cut timber right alongside you and who you've invited to play poker in gambling dens and who you've talked to about all sorts of private fellow things, the one who tries to talk to you sometimes about the Lord and His ways, is a *girl!*"

How can you live one part of your life hanging on to the truth when the other part of your life is a lie?

They would likely hang her, too, right beside him.

Uley'd certainly fooled these men. If

they knew who she really was, they'd get all tongue-tied and red in the face and flustered. She and her pa had only deceived them for propriety's sake, a necessary little white lie so she could come West and they could stay together. Uley had not known that a small deception could carry such a heavy weight.

All day long, she could only think of a man in jail named Aaron Brown. All day long, she could only think that he knew her secret.

He knew.

By the time she'd finished her day's work, she figured she knew what she had to do with him. As soon as the four-thirty whistle sounded, she headed to town. She walked right into the jailhouse and sat down.

When Harris Olney saw her, he about pumped her arm off. "Uley Kirkland," he said, grinning. "If it weren't for you, I'd be six feet under today. Thank you, son."

"You're welcome, Marshal." Uley paused. It was time for her to save herself. "I came by wondering if you'd do me a favor."

"Anything I can do for you, I'll do it. You're a fine young man, Uley. I'll always do you favors. I'd especially like to see you happy today. What is it?"

"I'd like to see the prisoner."

Harris furrowed his brows, sending deep creases alongside his nose. "Why on earth would you want to do that?"

For one brief moment, Uley faltered. "It . . . it was dark outside. I really didn't get a good look at him. I thought I'd just like to see who I tackled by the light of day."

Harris thought about it a minute. "Well." She could see him hesitating. Of course, she would be the one to testify in court and convict him. "Odd request, it is. But I *did* promise you a favor." Harris hoisted an iron key ring off a peg. Then he led her through a door and pointed to one of the cells. "He's right over there. You stay as long as you want. Holler at me if he gets ugly."

She saw the stranger sitting on the stained blue ticking of his cot, his knees spread wide, his feet planted firm. His muddy brown Stetson lay upside down beside him.

He didn't see her coming. He'd buried his face in his hands.

"Hello."

He lifted his head and gawked up at her, eyes wide with surprise. In the daylight, she saw they were blue.

"I came to see how you were doing."

"I'm doing dandy." He didn't stand up. "Just dandy."

"Looks like it."

Aaron Brown appeared younger than she'd thought last night. She figured him to be somewhere in his thirties. He didn't look as mean now, either. He just looked sad.

A shock of chocolate-brown hair hung down over his forehead like an arrowhead. He plopped his elbows against his knees and let his clasped hands hang down between them. "You ever going to get tired of looking at me like I'm some kind of animal caught in a trap?"

She shook her head. "No." He wasn't really bad to look at. If he hadn't been the sort of person to creep into town and go after the strong arm of the law, she might have given him a second glance. She amended that thought. Even though he *was* that sort of person, she gave him a second glance.

"So you're Uley Kirkland," he said softly. "*Miss* Uley Kirkland."

"That is correct."

Imagine it. He knew she was a woman, and he treated her like one. If a murderer could be respectful, then Aaron Brown was. It wasn't the way he spoke to her, exactly, but the way he kept his eyes on her. She'd never before seen anyone peruse her with such respect, such open amazement. But then, she'd never before taken a flying leap at anyone, either.

She remembered why she'd come. She leaned closer to the bars to take care of the task at hand. "Judge Murphy's due back from Denver next Tuesday," she told him. "You'll be off this world by Wednesday morning."

"I'm painfully aware of that."

She leaned in even closer. "Since you will be gone off this world then, and it is absolutely no concern of yours, Mr. Brown, you must promise me you'll tell no one about the horrible fact you discovered last night."

He knew exactly what she was talking about. "When you lost your hat."

"Yes."

"Good grief," he said, sounding mildly exasperated. "Here I am fixing to hang for murder, and all you're thinking about is covering your own hide."

"Yes."

"And I didn't even get the chance to go after Olney."

"You would have, if not for me."

He cradled his banged-up brown Stetson in his palm as if he'd just tipped it to her. "Now, you don't know that, do you, ma'am?"

It was the most amazing thing, conversing with him. For the first time in four years, she didn't have to pretend. "You never would have gotten out of this valley alive."

"However I had to go," he said, "I *did* figure on taking Harris Olney with me."

She shook her finger at him. "You must promise me, Mr. Brown."

When he rose from the cot, she examined his frame. He was lanky and fairly thin. She'd known from grappling with him how he'd tower over her. He reached through the bars and gripped her wrists. "Your secret is safe with me, Miss Kirkland. I will face eternity next Wednesday with your secret well hidden within my bosom. I will die happy to be the only one knowing that the person who apprehended me and upended me in the dirt was a mere slip of a girl."

She didn't know how she felt about promises from somebody who'd pulled a gun to go after a man. But she'd learned enough about the male species to know they'd risk losing everything before they'd risk losing face in front of others. She turned to the other matter at hand. "I am not a slip of a girl," she said. "I am a *woman,* Mr. Brown. A full nineteen years of age."

"Oh," he said, taken aback at last. Even so, he didn't release her wrists. "I do see what you mean."

When he eyed her again, she saw him taking into account the nubby sweater she wore, and her woolen knickers, covered with mud from working the mine. She saw him surveying the shock of dusty red-brown curls poking out beneath her apple hat. "You are the most unusual woman of nineteen years I have ever seen."

"I'll thank you to let go of me," she said, her green eyes remaining level on his own.

He dropped his hold. "Why are you deceiving everyone, Miss Kirkland? And how are you hiding it so well?"

She wasn't about to let him lead her onto this subject. "I came for your solemn vow, Mr. Brown."

"You received that last night when you threatened me with your fist."

"Very well," she said, smiling a bit. "We understand each other. Good day, Mr. Brown."

Chapter Two

Well past moonrise, well after Uley's pa had drawn the curtains and extinguished the oil lamps, Uley removed the dirty woolen cap, dusted it off against her leg and began to pull the pins from her hair. Her hair fell in huge rolls against her shoulders and down her back.

Uley slipped open the top bureau drawer and extracted the beautiful silver brush that had once belonged to her mother. She began to count brush strokes as she worked the tangles from the strands. Five . . . six . . . seven . . .

So Aaron Brown wanted to know how she did such a good job of hiding her womanhood, did he?

Thirteen . . . fourteen . . . fifteen . . . sixteen . . .

She supposed that was about the most embarrassing thing of all — that she could hide it so well. Her own body rebelled against her. She was small, just like her ma, her waist barely nipping in. She supposed

27

she'd look more womanly if she had any earthly idea as to how to don a corset.

Thirty-one . . . thirty-two . . . thirty-three . . .

Her mother's name had been Sarah, one of the prettiest names Uley had ever heard. It sounded the same way she remembered her mother, patient and gracious, always ready to break into a song. One of Uley's only memories was hanging clothes on the line out back of the Ohio house, running through the wet, billowing sheets with her arms outflung while her ma hummed *What A Friend We Have In Jesus* through the wooden pins she held between her teeth. It wasn't easy for a girl to get along in the world without a ma. There were so many questions to be asked that could not be answered by anyone except for a mother. About that first warm stirring in your bosom when a handsome young gentleman let his eyes linger. The proper way to thread the laces through a corset. The only place she might seek answers to these feminine mysteries now was from the hurdy-gurdy girls at Santa Fe Moll's place. Occasionally Uley passed one of them in the streets, Irish Ann or Tin Can Laura and Big Minnie and Wishbone Mabel. Oh, Uley heard the fellows in the mines talking about these girls, all right!

She took her frustration out on both hairbrush and hair.

Seventy-nine . . . eighty . . . eighty-one . . .

The only other Tin Cup woman Uley knew was Kate Fischer. Aunt Kate, a slave before the Civil War, had escaped her master, leaving a husband and a child behind. Now she ran Aunt Kate's Hotel and Boarding House. Her customers made their own change, because Kate Fischer didn't know how to count money or weigh gold. She always dressed in simple calico, with a white apron billowing out over her massive chest like a ship's sail.

Ninety-seven . . . ninety-eight . . . ninety-nine . . . one hundred.

Uley stood and slipped the silver hairbrush back into the bureau drawer. She examined herself in the moonlight that filtered through the curtains. Even in the muted glow, she saw glimmers of color in her hair.

For one brief moment, she let herself dream. She pretended she wore petticoats that swished around her ankles, that her hair remained loose, swinging free. For a brief moment, she allowed herself to imagine what it would feel like to get gussied up, strap on delicate undergarments, pinch her cheeks till they were pink. She'd walk right into that jailhouse and say, "See, Mr. Brown? I am not a slip of a girl. I am a woman."

She braided her hair, slipped wearily beneath the handworked quilt and hugged her pillow in frustration. Although she tried to reason that she'd made this choice for a selfless reason, deep inside she knew that hadn't been the case. Five years ago, her father had given her what she wanted, a chance to come with him to the rich goldfields of Colorado, instead of staying in Ohio with her aunt and her prissy cousins. When Aunt Delilah had warned her things might become difficult, Uley hadn't understood her reasoning. She'd been so innocent at fourteen, so sure of herself, so certain the charade wouldn't have to continue for long.

She hadn't bothered to pray about it the way Reverend Henderson said. She'd been perfectly willing to take this adventure into her own hands. She bunched the pillow tight against her face and stared up at the pine planks above her. *Lord, would my life have been different if I had asked You?* Hadn't it been worth everything, she wondered, to stay in Tin Cup with her pa?

It was interesting, Aaron decided as he lay on his cot and examined the patterns in the fresh pine overhead, what a man thought about all night long when he knew he was going on to eternity. He wasn't thinking of pearly gates and golden streets. His main thought, as he lay there seeing pictures in the pine knots, was to write Beth a letter so that she'd know his fate. He was thinking it was a shame he had to die for Beth to find out that she'd been right.

At three in the morning, he stood and banged on the metal bars of his cell. "Marshal!" he shouted. "Marshal! I need to write a letter!"

The man who answered his call was an elderly gentleman Aaron had never seen before. "You hush that racket. You're going to wake the dead."

"I'm going to *be* the dead," Aaron said. "This is about the last chance to make noise I've got. I need to write a letter."

The old guy shook his head. "Can't help you. Marshal left me in charge here. Don't have any paper for you to write on, and I can't leave. How do I know you're not trying to escape?"

"I can't very well escape," Aaron said dryly. "I'm in a jail cell."

"You're the first one we've ever had locked up in here. I'm not about to let you get away."

"I have stationery and writing supplies with my belongings at the Grand Central Hotel. If you could just send someone, Mr. —"

"Pearsall. Ben Pearsall. Can't do it. Ain't anybody around to send. You'll have to find somebody to get your stuff and post it for you tomorrow. The mail only comes in and out on Mondays and Thursdays."

Aaron sat down on the creaky cot, defeated once more. Things sure hadn't gone his way these past few days. He didn't know anybody in town who he'd trust to go through his room and retrieve his belongings.

Ben Pearsall pulled up a stool and straddled it, apparently pleased to have somebody to talk to in the wee hours of the morning. "You know, you're crazy," he told Aaron. "The reason everybody turned out at the election down at Pettengill's Drug Store and voted for Olney for marshal was because he told them he wouldn't arrest anybody. Olney's said all along the marshal's duty is to give the town the *appearance* of law and order. The mayor told him the day he got his star that the first

32

person he arrested would be his last. And that's *you,* Mr. Brown. Olney didn't have much of a choice, since he was the one you were holding a gun on."

Aaron looked sour. "I guess not. I guess me and Uley Kirkland didn't leave him much of a choice at all."

"Uley Kirkland," Ben said. "Now there's a fine young man for you. But I can't figure out why that kid ain't started growin' whiskers yet. You ever seen Uley's skin close up? It's as soft as a baby's. 'Course, I imagine Uley would slug me senseless if he ever heard me say that."

"Yeah," Aaron said, unconsciously rubbing his elbow. She'd jumped on him like a wildcat and knocked him to the ground, and parts of his body were still smarting from it. "I reckon Uley would."

Pearsall scooted the stool backward. "Got to get back up front. Wouldn't want anybody to think I was talking all night to a criminal." He tipped his hat. "Been nice conversing with you, Brown."

Aaron sat down hard on his cot. Why didn't Uley grow whiskers, indeed! It would be easier for a dog to turn into a horse than it would be for Uley Kirkland to grow whiskers. And, as he thought of her, he realized who could go through his belongings and retrieve his stationery from the Grand Central. Beth would have her letter after all!

Aaron knew he probably couldn't trust Uley. He also knew he could make her do his bidding. He knew the word for it. A bad, dark word. *Blackmail.* But just now he didn't have any other options. "Pearsall!" he hollered, banging on the bars again. "Get in here, will you? I know who I can send to get my things."

Uley received his message just after she arrived at the Gold Cup. "Uley! Uley Kirkland!" Charlie Hastings came shouting into shaft eleven, wagging a lantern back and forth, sending waves of light sweeping along the walls. "Old Ben Pearsall's here with a note from the marshal. Olney wants you to get down to the jail for something."

Uley groaned. There had been times during the past two days when she'd wished she'd just kept walking and let Aaron Brown go after Harris Olney. She was fast becoming a celebrity in Tin Cup, and it didn't suit her one bit.

She left the mine astraddle her bay gelding. She gave the horse his head, letting the animal pick his way down the rocks on the steep hill while she fumed. When she got to town, she looped the horse's bridle over the hitching rail and marched into Olney's office. "What do you want with me, Harris?"

Olney waved toward the back. "*I* don't want anything, Uley. Prisoner sent for you. I wouldn't have called you out of the mine, but he says he's got to see you today. Go on back."

She stomped on through, and there sat Aaron Brown, all alone behind the bars, his head bowed as if in prayer. "I'm going to lose three dollars today because you won't let me get in a decent day's work," she said.

He lifted his head, and his blue eyes were like deep, sparkling water. She figured he probably hadn't slept all night. He looked awful. If she weren't feeling so put-upon, she might even have been sad for him this morning. "You're the only person I know in this place, Uley. I need somebody to help me."

"I'm not likely to help you. I'm the one who saw you pull the gun on Olney. I'm the chief witness against you."

"I'm not looking for a lifelong buddy," he said tersely. "I'm just looking for an acquaintance who'll go up to the Grand

Central and bring me some stationery. I've got to write a letter to one person before they string me up. Old Ben Pearsall told me the mail goes out today."

"This is why you called me down from the mine?" She was torn between being furious with him and feeling halfway important because he'd needed her. This *was* his dying request, after all. Maybe it was an important letter. Maybe it was a letter to the governor to confess his crime.

"Yeah. I tried to get Pearsall to go, but he wouldn't do it. You're my only hope, Uley. Will you go?"

She eyed him. "I don't know." He stood there, grasping the bars with both hands. They were big hands and, looking at him, she wondered how she'd gotten him to the ground.

"Why?" he asked.

His robin's-egg eyes seemed twice as blue with his face so dirty.

She didn't know exactly why it happened. Maybe it was because Aaron Brown knew she was a female. Maybe it was because she'd considered her femininity so much during these past days. Whatever the reason, she felt herself blush, felt a spreading burst of heat fan her face the way flame spreads in a forest. "I don't think it would be right, Mr. Brown. Me going through your personal things."

"Uley Kirkland!" He hit the bars with his open hand. "Don't you go all prim and proper on me now. You're the one who pounced on me out of nowhere and left me sprawled in the dirt. You're the one that's got every poor depraved male in this town thinking you're one of them."

"You hush up, Mr. Brown." Her face turned even redder. "You mustn't say that."

"Oh, mustn't I?"

"No."

In the front part of the office, a door opened. "Morning, Marshal," someone said.

"Morning, George," they heard Harris say. "Where'd you go last night? I saw your horse. You missed some mighty fine guitar picking at Ongewach's."

"Wasn't tryin' to miss out. Was having some fun of my own at a poker table."

Uley Kirkland and Aaron Brown's eyes met.

He wouldn't start on this story, they both knew, if he had any earthly inkling that he had a lady back here. "Everybody at the table was talking about Tin Can Laura," the man up front said. "She don't wear no stockings, Harris. And for a girl

37

who's had as hard a life as she has, she sure has a pretty face."

From where Uley and Aaron stood, they heard every detail about the stockings. The two of them gazed at each other in silence. "I begin to understand the depth of your problem, Uley." For years she'd stood around listening to stories like this one without being able to protest.

He took a deep breath. The timing, from his perspective, was perfect. "You leave me no choice. I've got to blackmail you, Miss Uley Kirkland. I'll tell them all. I'll tell every single one of them that you've had them duped."

Uley grabbed the bars with both hands. "You wouldn't *do* such a thing."

He brought his nose level with hers. "I might. Because I'm desperate enough to do anything."

"I would never forgive you."

"Doesn't matter. I'm gonna be dead on Wednesday. Doesn't matter one bit how long you hold a grudge. I won't be around to enjoy it."

She saw he had her backed up into a corner. "You promised me. You're a liar."

"That isn't the worst of my sins, if you'll recall. But you're right. I'll confess —" he added the rest for emphasis "— ma'am."

"Hush up," she said, lowering her voice. "Somebody might hear you."

"Does that mean you'll do it?"

She took one long, deep sigh. "What if Mawherter won't let me in?"

"He will. Anybody in this town would trust you over me."

"You think so?"

"I do."

They stared at each other, the silence ticking away between them. The irony of it struck her again full force. She'd worked years proving herself a trustworthy male in this town, and she was the biggest liar of them all.

Aaron didn't let up. Desperation ruled him now. "Get *down* there, Uley. The stage leaves for St. Elmo in two hours."

She collected her wits. She had no choice but to do his bidding. With head held high, she sauntered out to the front office, where Harris and George Willis had their heads together, still discussing the pretty Tin Can Laura, the hurdy-gurdy girl who kept her money stashed in a tin can. Uley walked up Grand Avenue to the Grand Central to tell D. J. Mawherter exactly what she wanted.

The hotel proprietor didn't even hesitate before he handed her the key. "You tell

Harris Olney somebody's got to be responsible for that criminal's room," he hollered as she started up the stairs. "You tell Harris to bring that man down here to settle up before they hang him Wednesday. I can't get any gold out of a dead man."

She hurried up the steps to the second floor, thinking, If he dies, I'll be halfway responsible for it.

No, she argued with herself. Aaron Brown is responsible for it. One hundred percent totally responsible for his choices. *Just the way I'm responsible for mine.*

She found the room, unlocked the door and stepped inside. In a tiny room with pine walls and no plaster stood an iron bed, a rickety bureau that looked like someone who should have known better had tried to build it, and a washbasin. Mr. Aaron Brown's satchel waited in the corner. She heaved it up and began to unfasten it, feeling more and more uneasy and curious as his private items began to tumble out onto the quilt.

He owned a beautiful black suit and a bolo tie made of leather and elkhorn. He owned two stiff-as-a-board starched shirts and several pairs of woolen socks. And — oh, goodness — he possessed white drawers just like her pa's.

Purposefully she started digging in another area of the satchel.

She found what he'd sent her for, a box of blue stationery and a quill pen and a little bottle of ink, all tied up in a linen square. She pulled those items out and put everything else back in place. She folded his writing utensils into the cloth to carry them.

There.

That had been easy enough.

She was almost out the door by the time she saw his other belongings atop the bureau.

He owned a bottle of bay-rum aftershave. She pulled the cork and sniffed it. The scent, keen and exotic, pleased her. She found it difficult imagining anybody as dirty as Aaron Brown ever cleaning up and shaving and splashing on something that smelled this good.

He also owned a pocket watch and a Bible. She wondered, as she picked up the Bible and flipped it open, whether he was an Old Testament Christian or a New Testament one. Probably Old Testament, she decided. After all, that was where it said "An eye for an eye." He was in jail, waiting to hang. She figured he probably hadn't been listening in Sunday school when his

41

teacher had brought up the Ten Commandments.

Uley set the Bible down and picked up the watch. She guessed, just from handling the timepiece, that it wasn't worth much. Feeling only slightly guilty, she clicked it open. *To my beloved son Aaron,* the inscription read. *May your heart always know when it's time to come home.*

She arranged everything on the bureau just as it had been when she arrived, thinking of her own ma and missing her beyond measure. How wonderful it would be, she decided, to know you had a mother . . . someone to go home to . . . no matter how old you were. For a moment, thinking of Mr. Aaron Brown and the awful fate awaiting him, she felt sadness. Rather, she felt sadness for his *mother.* She imagined hanging was a tragic thing when it happened to the baby you'd once cradled in your arms.

She gathered the belongings Aaron had requested and closed the door behind her. She walked back down Grand Avenue. Now that she'd seen the suit and the bay rum and the watch, she felt as if she knew him somewhat better. She didn't stop to wonder at any of it. All her discoveries really proved was that attempted murderers read the Bible and smelled good and had mamas at home who loved them, too.

Aaron thought he'd go crazy waiting for Uley to get back to the jailhouse. He'd never heard anything so good as the sound of her soft voice in the front office. Harris and Uley came back to his cell together. "Here's your writing supplies," the marshal said, eyeing him. "You aren't going to use that quill pen for a getaway weapon, are you?"

"No, sir," Aaron answered with mock respect. "I'm gonna write a letter, Marshal. Do you have any problem with that?"

The marshal didn't answer that question. He changed the subject instead. "Mawherter says you've got to settle up down at the Grand Central. I'll take you up there next Tuesday so you can pay him."

"That's real kind."

It became increasingly clear the marshal wasn't of a mind to leave them, so Uley made the only comment she could think of. "You've got a nice suit, Mr. Brown. You want me to make sure the undertaker buries you in it?"

"Doesn't matter to me any," he told her, clearly wanting to be free of both of them so that he could begin his last correspondence. "Doesn't matter what clothes I'm wearing. I won't be around to see it."

Harris Olney waited until Uley left the jailhouse before he went storming back into Aaron's presence. "You'd better start thinking before you get innocents like Uley Kirkland involved in this," he growled.

"I have a letter to write," Aaron stated calmly. "Uley was the only person I could convince to go down to the Grand Central and get my things."

Harris scowled at his prisoner. "I know you're writing Elizabeth."

"I surely am."

"I knew it, Brown!" Harris said. "I'll be glad when Judge Murphy comes over Alpine Pass and I can stop looking at your dirty hide. What're you going to tell Beth?"

"The bad news. That I'm going on to eternity and I'm not taking you with me."

Harris stomped out, and Aaron could hear him in the office, slamming drawers and cussing until, finally, the room grew quiet. Aaron Brown stood behind the bars, waiting. He knew what was coming next.

Harris returned. "No need to involve that kid Kirkland in this anymore," he said. "I can post that letter for you on the after-

44

noon supply wagon."

Aaron stood there and laughed at him. "Sure you will. You'll post it right into the rubbish bin. Uley's going to do it. I'm going to make sure this letter stays safe from you."

"What kind of a hold do you have over Uley, anyway?" the marshal asked. "How are you getting that kid to take such good care of you?"

Aaron couldn't help grinning. He wouldn't breathe a word to Olney. He'd promised her, after all. "Guess Uley just feels responsible for what's going to happen to me come Wednesday morning." He sat down, pen in hand, and started scribbling, and Harris finally left him alone.

"My dearest, dearest Beth," Aaron wrote, beginning his letter. He didn't have much time, but even so, he paused for a moment. He found joy in finally placing his words upon paper. He rolled the pen between his fingers and then dipped it again into the ink. Ah, he thought. Indeed the pen *is* mightier than the sword.

He began to write again.

I hope this letter reaches you post-haste. It is difficult to write, little one. You see, your Aaron is bound for the promised land, and very soon. I fear that Harris Olney has won out over us at last.

I know your tearful advice was given in love; however, I could not heed your wise words. You know what I came here to do. I did not succeed. I did succeed in placing myself in a good deal of trouble. I was thwarted in my efforts to capture Olney by a do-gooder who jumped upon me when my six-shooter was pointed directly at Olney's back. (Yes, believe it, even out here in the lawless gold country, a few do-gooders have found their way.) The only law and order in this place is Harris Olney himself, and a faceless judge who is due to come back and convict me on Tuesday. My demise is scheduled for Wednesday.

I love you, dear heart. I write this so that you may have an answer to the questions you would have entertained when I did not return. Will there be a potluck supper next Wednesday night? Please have everyone at church pray for me that evening at services, even though I will already be gone.

Dear heart, break this gently to Mama.

Thank you for being such a precious and gentle spirit.

All my love,
Aaron

He stopped writing and gazed out the window at the sky. As the hours passed, he found it harder and harder to believe an angel of mercy would come to Tin Cup and snatch him out of his jail cell.

He turned away from the window.

He reread the letter, folded it and slipped it inside the fancy blue envelope he knew Elizabeth would recognize in the stack of mail just as soon as it came off the stage at Fort Collins.

With a flourish, he addressed it to her: Elizabeth Calderwood, Flying S Ranch, Fort Collins, Colorado.

Chapter Three

Uley was so mad right now, she wanted to spit in the dirt. All morning long she'd let her head grow bigger by the minute, thinking Aaron Brown was writing some important correspondence about his crime to the governor of Colorado — only to find out he had been wasting his time doing *this* instead.

The letter was addressed in the neatest handwriting she'd ever seen from a man, all perfectly drawn, without so much as one blot: Elizabeth Calderwood, Flying S Ranch, Fort Collins, Colorado.

She wanted to just spit in the dirt.

Uley decided Aaron Brown would go to his grave next week getting everything he could from her. Uley had heard the marshal offer, in as gentlemanly a way as possible, to post the letter so that Uley wouldn't be put out of any more time. But Mr. Aaron Brown would have none of it. He'd made her promise, right there in front of the marshal, that she would deliver it herself and wait to see it safely out of town.

So here she stood, mad enough to hurt something, watching for the supply wagon to head out over Alpine Pass.

Elizabeth Calderwood. Uley didn't know why it irked her so that he had taken up her whole day, said it was something important, then posted a letter that must be a gushing goodbye letter to some girl he'd been sparking back home. She thought about the aftershave and the handsome black suit and figured some girl would probably fall for him if she knew him all gussied up and smelling good. Too bad Miss Elizabeth Calderwood couldn't see him now, all stinking and mean down in that jail, and being held for murder. Uley bet seeing him like that would take the stars out of any woman's eyes.

"Yah!" Lester McClain hollered at the mules as he shook the reins and urged his freight team forward.

"Any snow up there?" somebody called to him as he pulled out of town, headed for the road that disappeared into the pine trees.

"Nope," Lester shouted back. "Those drifts at the top are almost gone. The pass is clear all the way to St. Elmo."

Uley watched as the horses tugged the wagon loaded with freight and passengers up Washington Avenue . . . toward the first bend in the road . . . up into the lush green stand of lodgepole pines that stood sentry at the edge of town.

There.

His ridiculous gush letter was gone and on its way.

Aaron Brown was none of her concern anymore.

But four days later, just after Lester McClain arrived back in across the 12,154-foot pass with a bag of incoming mail, the sky above Tin Cup turned gray as pewter and the wind started howling down through the gold hills like something alive. By three that afternoon, when snowflakes as big around as tea cozies started falling, everybody figured they were in for one of those late-spring storms that everybody talked about, the kind that caught everybody unawares, the kind of storm that killed things.

Up north, in the part of the valley called Taylor Park, a wide, sagebrush-covered expanse of grazing land, Jason Farley donned his Stetson and started out looking for the cows in his herd that had already dropped their calves. As the wind roared and the temperature dropped, he figured this was going to be the kind of night a new calf wouldn't survive.

Down south, Aaron Brown stood at the window in the Tin Cup town jail, looking out at the snowflakes, thinking this was the last snowfall he would ever see. *What part of this is Your purpose, Lord? What's the point of teaching me humility if I'm not going to be around to be humble?* And then for some reason, his mind traveled to Miss Uley Kirkland.

What would it be like, he wondered, to pretend you were a person of a different gender? Why, he wondered, would she do it? Perhaps she concealed some horrible disfigurement somewhere, although Aaron couldn't imagine where it might be. She looked perfect to him, at least when he overlooked the fact that she was wearing a man's work pants. She was small, but she was brave, as stout-hearted as anything else that survived in this harsh territory.

She had certainly bested him.

Aaron felt, just then, as if he'd come a far, far piece from home. Outside, it snowed harder.

Up on the gold hill, Dave McNalley stuck his head out of shaft eleven at the

Gold Cup. "It'll be cold tonight," he told the other miners. "The temperature's probably dropped thirty degrees since noon."

Uley's pa laid his tools down and glanced over at her. "We best get on down to the house."

"You're right, Sam," the foreman said. "You two have to travel farther than most of us. You best get out of here."

In the middle of the winter, when the temperature dropped twenty degrees during a storm, the snow flew dry and light, a dusting of talcum that shrouded everything. This storm came warm and wet and heavy. The snow pelted Uley and Sam's faces as they squinted against the wind, driving toward them with stinging chunks of ice that took Uley's breath away. They bundled up in blankets from the saddle packs. They hadn't seen fit to bring coats with them this late in the season. The horses, given their head, picked their way down the rocky path. Uley struggled to keep her eyes open. As they came out of the trees and headed across the wetland beside the creek, their progress turned treacherous.

The snow whipped sideways against them. They couldn't see the creek that meandered across their path as the horses plodded forward, the ground beneath their hooves thick with mud and ice.

When they spoke, the wind sucked their voices away.

Heads ducked, ears wrapped, they struggled on together, clutching their saddle horns in case one of the horses should stumble. The storm came from all directions at once, straight at them, from across, from above. As they entered town, Uley could barely make out the crude log buildings lining the street. The wind cut against them. The wet snow plastered itself to everything it touched. The horses floundered in drifts clear up to their cinch straps.

Upstairs, above Ongewach's Saloon on Washington Avenue, Santa Fe Moll gave her girls their nightly talking-to.

"Moll," Wishbone Mabel said, "look at it snowing outside. Nobody's going to come looking for entertainment tonight. Nobody's going to be able to *find* this place tonight."

"Won't do," Moll said, narrowing her eyebrows and shaking her head at all of them, "when miners start showing up and you're all sitting around like you ain't expecting anybody to be here because of the snow. There you are in calico, that will never do. You must look good, be clean, and smell sweet, just like true ladies. Now get going and get into them silk dresses!"

As they all groaned and moved in the direction of their rooms, Tin Can Laura scanned the place. "Where's Joe? I don't see him."

"He's probably downstairs in the kitchen, looking for scraps," Mabel answered. "He always goes down there this time of night."

Laura gathered her skirts and took the steps running. "Hey, Joe! Hey, kitty! Come on up here!"

Joe, who was due to have kittens just about any day, was the only living thing in the world Laura loved. A saloon patron had given her the calico cat for Christmas back when she'd been a Pitkin girl. Because of Joe, Laura stayed welcome wherever she wanted to go. The mama cat always proved an excellent mouser.

"Snow's coming heavier," Cook said as Laura got downstairs. "I'm betting people outside can't even see where they're going."

"One thing's for certain," Charles Ongewach commented. "No freight wagon will be coming in over Alpine Pass tomorrow. And wouldn't you know, McClain was supposed to bring over my new piano. I've been lookin' forward to it ever since that old miner Scheer danced on mine with his hobnailed boots."

"Judge Murphy won't make it in, either," Cook said. "Aaron Brown's hanging is going to have to wait."

Laura came up beside them. "Either of you seen Joe? It's almost time to open up, and I've got to lock her in my room."

"Sure have," Cook said. "She came down here meowing to get out before the storm started. I let her out the door and ain't seen her since."

Laura grabbed her shawl off a hook by the door and draped it across her shoulders. "I've got to find her."

Charles Ongewach donned his coat, too. "Here. Take a rope, Laura. Tie yourself to the building, or you won't find your way back. I'm right behind you."

Charles stayed close to the side of the building, feeling his way along the rough-hewn logs until he rounded the corner, calling for the cat at the top of his lungs. Laura started straight out across Washington Avenue, or what she thought was Washington Avenue, with the rope knotted around her waist. In the shelter of the sa-

55

loon, the gale had seemed overrated. But when Laura reached the street, the icy whorl hit her full in the face. The wind whipped around her, sucking away her breath. Snow pelted her face. Within moments, the shawl covering her head was weighted with ice that clung like molten glass.

Laura struggled on. "Kitty. Joe! Here, kitty."

As she reached the middle of the street, horses loomed up beside her. At the same time, she heard the doleful cry of a cat. "Joe!" She tried to rush forward, but the rope stopped her. She released the shawl and fumbled with the knot at her bodice. "Joe!"

The knot fell away.

She dropped the rope and rushed toward the sound.

Laura found Joe howling in the middle of the avenue, her stubby fur coated with thin ice. "Joe . . ." She scooped the frightened animal into her arms and turned toward Ongewach's.

The snow came stinging from every direction.

She couldn't see more than six inches in front of her face.

"Charles?" Her words died away in the

fierce bray of the wind. Joe struggled against her, clawing at her inside the shawl.

The rope couldn't be more than five steps in this direction.

She took the steps. But the rope wasn't there.

She turned once, remembering the horses that had just passed along the street. "Help," she screamed against the wind. "I cain't find my way."

Uley and Sam kept their horses moving flank to flank, the huge animals snorting over and over again as their nostrils filled with snow. Uley thought she heard someone calling but she couldn't be sure.

"Don't think we should stop," Sam leaned into his horse's neck for warmth. "No human would be out on this road. You must've heard an animal."

Uley hollered above the wind. "*We're* on this road."

"Guess you're right."

"Which way?"

"Don't disorient your horse," Sam said. "Rein him in and back him straight up beside me."

"Yes, sir."

Very slowly, the horses backed up, obeying the commands of their riders, until Sam felt a hand on his leg. The sound had grown louder now, a young girl crying. "I cain't find my way. Came out here to fetch this foolish cat."

She appeared behind and to the left of them, materializing like a vision in the swirling snow. "You one of those girls from Moll's place?" Sam hollered. But it didn't really matter who she was. They couldn't leave her out here to freeze.

She nodded.

"Come on up."

Sam reached a hand down for her and pulled her across his saddle. She sat sideways in front of him, her frozen skirt in icy folds against the horse's neck.

"You two taking me back? I've got to be dressed in silk and smelling nice in half an hour."

"We're not taking you back," Sam said. "The horses know where we are. I'm not doing anything to confuse them. You'll have to get back later."

"But I'll be missing a whole night's wages." She glowered at Uley across the front of the horse, still clutching the cat in her shawl.

She looked like a lost cat herself, scraggly and frozen, not the sort of girl Uley would ever have associated with if she had stayed in Ohio. She and her pa shouldn't talk to a hurdy-gurdy woman. *But Jesus would have spoken to a girl like her,* Uley thought, *wanting to show her how much He cared about her.*

Sam and Uley rode without speaking the rest of the way. When they finally tethered their mounts outside the little cabin on Willow Street, Uley thought coming home had never felt so good. They went inside, and Sam lit the lamps while Uley started a fire in the cookstove. "Here," Uley said while Sam went back outside to unsaddle the horses. "I'll heat you up some water, and you can get a bath in there. If you don't mind a pair of knickers and a fellow's shirt, I can get you some dry clothes, too." Looking at the girl, she decided they were just about the same size.

"I never wore a fella's clothes before. Don't know if I should."

"They'll be dry and warm." Uley shot her a little smile and filled the kettle. "That's all that matters, you know. What's your name?"

"Laura."

"You got a last name?"

"Nope. Just Laura."

Uley stopped short. She knew Laura. She knew every detail about her. She felt the horrible burning of a blush again as she asked the question. "You're Tin Can Laura, aren't you?"

"Yeah," the girl answered. "That's me." She studied Uley's red face, not without some discomfort of her own. "You're awful young to know about hurdy-gurdy girls."

"Everybody in Tin Cup knows about hurdy-gurdy girls."

"I figure so."

"You're awful young to *be* one." Uley thought, *Why, with all the stories I've heard about her, she's no more than a young girl like me.*

Joe clamored to be let out of the shawl. "You think it'd be okay if I let my cat out?"

"Sure."

The two of them sat on the floor together while the water in the kettle warmed, watching Joe stalk across the floor as if Laura had just put her through the most demeaning ordeal a cat could ever undergo.

"He's a nice cat," Uley said.

"A nice cat that's gonna have kittens any day."

They looked at each other and, for some reason, started laughing. "What a crazy thing," Uley said, almost giggling and giving herself away. "A cat named Joe who's gonna have babies."

"You want one of them?" Laura asked. "Moll wants me to sell 'em. She says I could get twenty-five bucks apiece for them, because everybody needs mousers."

Uley shook her head. "I'd love one. But I sure don't have money like that."

"I'd give you one. Since you and your pa picked me up and got me warm. I'd tell Moll it was a thank-you present. She'll make me give her half the money anyway. She always does."

Uley's eyes widened. "For the work you do?"

"Yeah."

The kettle was making tinny noises on the stove and Uley knew the water was ready to boil. She stood up to pour it into the deep tin tub in the corner.

"Are you Uley Kirkland?" Laura asked.

"Sure am."

"Thought that's who you were. I've heard all about you at Ongewach's, how you jumped on that man that was trying to kill the marshal last week."

"You have?"

"Yep. Everybody in town knows you. They all say it's amazing, because you're such a little thing, without so much as peach fuzz on your chin, jumping on a

61

murderer and getting him down."

"Is that so?"

"They say you're just about too good for your britches, never coming into Frenchy's or Ongewach's, always talking to them about committing their lives to Jesus and such."

"Your water's ready. Come get your bath."

"That Aaron Brown, he's one amazing fellow. He was up at Ongewach's the night before he tried to do the shooting, playing cards and all dressed up and smellin' good. I've got to tell you, it's too bad he done what he done. He was the best-looking, best-smelling man we've had in that place for the longest time."

It irked Uley, having everybody always talking about Aaron Brown. "Well, he's sure not smelling very good now."

"Nope. I bet not."

Uley hung up two quilts so that Laura could have some privacy. She grabbed some of her own things out of a drawer. "Put these on when you get done. That way you won't catch your death."

Laura's eyes met hers. "Thanks, Uley. I've never had anybody take care of me, not since I was little and my mama did it."

Uley turned away, feigning propriety.

She didn't want Laura to see her face just then. She didn't have a ma to take care of her, either. "Did your mama die?"

"Yeah," Laura answered as Uley heard her sinking into the warm tub. "She did. Did yours?"

"She died coming out here."

"This is real hard country for women-folk," Laura said. "That's why there ain't any real fine ladies in this town. This is real hard country for ladies."

Aaron Brown had never been so glad to see a wet spring snowstorm in all his days. It seemed like somebody up there was on his side after all. The snow fell and fell, and by the end of the second day, Olney came in and regretfully told him what he'd figured out already. It would be another week or two before the pass opened and the hanging judge came back into town.

That was sure fine news to Aaron.

Word of the storm and what had happened all over town filtered in, even into the jailhouse. Charles Ongewach had gotten frostbite on his nose trying to find one of Moll's girls in the blizzard. The mines had closed for two days. Jason Farley had never made it back to his cabin. Everybody figured he'd frozen to death looking for new calves. The county would send out a search party for his body as soon as the snow started to melt. Wasn't any sense doing it before then.

Uley stopped by to see Aaron once, eight days after the storm, toting a bucket of hot beef pies. "Thought I'd just come by to see you," she said after Olney let her in. She wasn't exactly sure why she'd come. She just kept thinking how Laura had talked about him looking good. She decided she'd just go back to make sure he hadn't gotten any ideas about sharing her secret with anyone. And she felt sorry for him, sitting in jail all cooped up and waiting for Judge Murphy to come. "I brought you some pasties."

The pasties smelled like heaven to Aaron. "Did you make these?"

"Yeah."

They stood and looked at each other through the bars. He smiled at her, showing his gratitude, and Uley decided she could forget how he'd blackmailed her so he could send that letter. He didn't look nearly as good as Laura made him out to be, but his eyes were just as blue as the sky on a June day. Uley looked at his eyes the longest time. She decided she liked them.

"What are you staring at now?" But he

was staring at her, too.

"You'd better eat those before they get cold."

He sat down and obliged her, hoping that, if she saw how eagerly he ate, she might come visit and bring food again. "Don't know why you did this," he said. "Nobody's ever brought me food in jail before."

"You ever been in jail before? Or is this your first time?" She guessed he wasn't a hardened criminal. Hardened criminals didn't carry watches from their mothers and bay rum and Bibles.

"Nope. Never until now." He decided to make conversation with her between chomps. "I've heard all sorts of stories in here this week."

"Yeah. That weather took everybody by surprise."

"It's too bad about Jason Farley."

"They're gonna bury him up on the Catholic hill. As soon as it thaws and they find his body, that is." The Tin Cup cemetery had three hills for burying — the Catholic hill, the Protestant hill and Boot Hill.

"You figure I could talk them into burying me on the Protestant hill?" he asked her. The question seemed to come from nowhere, but he'd been thinking about it all night long. "I used to go to church."

But Uley shook her head. "Nope. It'll be Boot Hill for you, Aaron Brown. Although they probably wish they could bury you on the Protestant hill. There's lots more room there. Boot Hill is running over."

He laid the remainder of the pasty on the cloth napkin. He wasn't too hungry anymore, come to think about it.

Uley realized she *was* staring at him. She lowered her gaze to the ground.

Her unconsciously ladylike action made him think of one other story he'd heard this week. "So you and your father rescued Tin Can Laura out in the snowstorm."

Uley raised her eyes to his again, and this time she was smiling. "She was out looking for her cat. Joe just had kittens yesterday. Laura's going to give me one. There's a gray one I'm going to name Storm. I've already been over there to pick it out."

Aaron couldn't help grinning. So that was where the rumors had come from. When he started laughing, it came out as a belly laugh, pure and simple. "Everybody in town's saying you're sweet on her, Uley. Everybody's saying that's why you finally set foot into Moll's place."

"What?" She gripped the bars, evidently not totally understanding what he was saying. When she finally figured it out, her face turned as pink as the roses he remembered from back home.

He liked it when she blushed. He hated to admit it, even to himself, that was why he'd told her the sordid story in the first place. He'd known what it would do. He'd known she would look all embarrassed and soft and vulnerable, despite her woolen pants and the funny little hat she wore to cover all that hair. He enjoyed exposing her femininity. He liked knowing a secret no one else did.

"Mr. Brown," she said, sounding every bit the schoolmarm. "You mustn't let them *say* that."

"I don't have any influence on what they *say*," he reminded her. "I'm locked up here in the jailhouse. I just *hear* everything."

"If you hear anything else like that," she said, "don't tell me about it. I don't want to know." She shoved the napkin inside the bucket she'd used to carry the pasties and she turned to depart.

He stood behind the bars, just grinning at her, just grinning at everything. Despite his bleak future, Aaron decided it felt good to have a true young lady to tease, something to occupy his time and amuse him, as he whiled away his last days.

Uley didn't know why she bothered being nice to Aaron Brown. The man was a scoundrel, a known criminal bent on having fun with his secret at her expense. A proper man didn't tell a proper woman such stories. But then, she thought, correcting herself, she wasn't exactly a proper woman. For one minute, and one minute only, she let herself picture Mr. Aaron Brown. She pictured his twinkling blue eyes as he'd asked her about Laura. She pictured the way his smile had turned up more on one side than on the other as he teased her. This was his appeal, certainly. He was the only person in Tin Cup, Colorado — besides her father — who treated her like what she really *was*. He was decidedly irksome. And handsome. But not decidedly handsome. Even so, she figured, he would clean up real nice for his funeral.

Just as Uley reached her bay gelding, a shout rose from out in the street. "Supply wagon's coming in! They've got the pass open!"

It seemed like everywhere Uley looked,

she saw people racing up Grand Avenue to meet the wagon. Here it came, winding its way down through the lodgepole pines, its wheels clattering over the rocks in the road. Nine days had gone by since the wagon had last brought supplies and mail from the outside world. Uley ran, too, wanting to see everything coming in from St. Elmo. As the team pulled to a halt in front of the town hall, she heard a murmur pass through the crowd. "Murphy's on that wagon. We'll have a trial tomorrow, for sure."

Judge Murphy. She'd forgotten all about Judge Murphy. Her stomach felt as if it had dipped down to her toes. Tomorrow would come Aaron Brown's trial. The next day would come his hanging.

Uley wondered if she should run back and tell him. But she halted where she stood. The muttering and swearing in the streets stopped. Instead, every man surrounding the wagon started whispering.

"Well, I'll be . . ."

"What on earth is *that?*"

"Don't believe it. Just plum don't believe it."

The first thing Uley saw coming out of the wagon was a skirt the same color as Aaron Brown's eyes, all fluffed out and as big around as a tepee. The next thing she saw was an extended arm, the hand covered by a delicate white-laced glove.

Every man in the street took his hat off. Every one, that is except Uley, of course.

"Well, I'll be," somebody whispered next to her. "I ain't seen a gal like that since I left Nebraska."

The woman alighted, holding her skirts just high enough to keep them from dragging in the slush. She looked just like a picture from Uley's one tattered, hidden copy of *Gordon's*, which her Aunt Delilah had mailed to her from Ohio. The woman's skin glowed as white and smooth as a porcelain pitcher. Her thick golden ringlets clenched together like a fistful of cattails and gathered in a blue bow high on the back of her head. As McClain lowered her bandbox to the ground, at least twenty men moved forward to help her.

What would it be like to wear a dress like that? Uley thought. It made her waist look so tiny, Uley didn't know how she could even take air into her lungs. Great folds of cloth hung in full loops against the small of her back.

"Hello," the woman said, in a light, melodic voice, tilting her head like a little bird at the group of men standing mesmerized

70

in the mud. She was so pretty she even took Uley's breath away. "My name is Elizabeth Calderwood. Could one of you gentlemen direct me to a lawyer's office? I've come to hire someone to defend Mr. Aaron Brown."

Chapter Four

So this was Elizabeth Calderwood — in the flesh! So this was the gal who'd gotten the blue, perfectly penned goodbye letter Mr. Aaron Brown had been so desperate to get out of Tin Cup!

Uley stood right smack in the middle of the road, one hand clenched around her horse's reins, watching the men of Tin Cup compete over the new arrival the way a hungry dog would over a bone. Charlie Hastings took it upon himself to step forward and direct Miss Calderwood up Washington Avenue toward the Pacific Hotel. There she went, her skirts dipping back and forth like a chiming school bell, her head held high, with all those yellow curls hanging down her back like bedsprings.

If Elizabeth Calderwood knew she was leading a parade up the street, she took no notice of it. Every man there, every single one of them, followed her.

Elizabeth Calderwood stepped into the

Pacific Hotel and, as the little front room filled with awestruck men, made her way to the desk. Pacific Hotel, the handcarved sign read. Frank Emerson, Proprietor. First-Class in Every Respect.

"I'd like to pay for a room for two weeks, Mr. Emerson," she said, in a voice so light and high she might have been singing.

She could have paid for a room for two years, so many men pulled gold pouches out of their pockets to help.

"No, but thank you, gentlemen." She waved them away, holding aloft one tiny gloved hand and acting as if she attracted this much attention each day of her life. "I'm perfectly able to pay my own expenses."

Five men volunteered to carry her one trunk up the stairs to the room Emerson assigned her. The remainder of the throng milled about in the tiny lobby, waiting for her to descend the stairs.

When she did, she flounced out into the street again. Everyone else clomped right along behind her. She marched past the sign reading J. C. Theobald, The Cobbler, and into the building marked Otto Violet, Attorney-at-Law and Notary Public, Tin Cup, Colorado. Twenty minutes later, she emerged. She opened the lace parasol she carried and twirled it high over her head, striding purposefully toward the Grand Central Hotel. Mawherter's eyes about popped out of his head when he saw what came prancing in through his front door. "Good day, sir," she said. "I'm here to pay off Mr. Brown's bill."

"The name's Mawherter. D. J. Mawherter. At — at your service, ma'am."

"I'd like to have Mr. Brown's belongings. May I send someone up to get them?"

"Yes, certainly." The way Mawherter leapt to assist her, you would have thought the Queen of England had entered his front lobby.

She deposited a fair amount of money on his ink blotter, and he swept it away. This time, seven men accompanied her to bring down Aaron Brown's one trunk and one satchel.

Elizabeth Calderwood certainly had no qualms about going through his personal things, Uley thought, remembering with renewed consternation the bay rum . . . the Bible . . . the unmentionables that she should never have caught a glimpse of.

Elizabeth directed the men toward the Pacific Hotel. "Place them in my room, please. I'm certain Mr. Brown will have need of these items later."

"You're staying at the Pacific?" Mawherter asked her, goggle-eyed. He sucked in his breath and raised himself to his full height. Uley couldn't help thinking he looked like a rooster about to flap his wings. "We cannot have a fine lady such as yourself staying anywhere else except right here. I'll gladly give you a discount. . . ."

Elizabeth smiled graciously. "I'm already quite comfortable at the Pacific, Mr. Mawherter."

Her business clearly settled, Elizabeth Calderwood turned and asked directions to the jailhouse.

Everybody answered at once.

"It's right over there. . . ."

"Go to the corner to the west. . . ."

"You'll find it where Water Avenue comes into Grand. . . ."

"Take your second left. . . ."

"I'd be glad to show you the way. . . ."

Surprisingly enough, Elizabeth Calderwood seemed to have a fine head atop her shoulders. She sorted through all their mumbling and ended up going exactly the right way.

"That gal's about the prettiest gal I've ever seen," Charlie Hastings whispered.

"Seeing a woman like that is enough to make you clean up every once in a while, isn't it?" Dave McNalley joined in.

Uley had never dreamed grown men could act this way. As Elizabeth Calderwood proceeded toward the jailhouse, she hung back, wondering what it would feel like to get so much attention. The attention she'd gotten after she'd jumped on Aaron Brown and sent him flying was one thing. This was more than mere respect. This was *awe.* She figured it would be nice to have men — a man — look at her that way. She figured it would be nice to walk with petticoats swishing against her ankles like stream water. She figured it would be nice to have her hair bounce free at the nape of her neck and have curls encircled with ribbons.

She wondered what it would feel like to peer into a store window at all the fineries that a genuine lady expected, and to admit to yourself and to everybody around you that you would enjoy *having* such things.

It had been bad enough thinking of Aaron Brown inside that jail, knowing he was fully aware of her secret. Now, here came Elizabeth Calderwood prancing into town, making her think of any number of feminine practices! As Uley left behind the gaggle of men proceeding along the streets, she wondered what it might feel like to love a man who was going to die by hanging. Uley didn't figure that was anything she'd ever have to know.

"Just look at you, Aaron Brown," Elizabeth said, her nose stuck between two iron bars, her hands reaching to a place on either side of his face. "I've never seen *anybody* who needed to see a bucket of bathwater so badly."

He grimaced. "It's true. If I'd known you were coming out here, I'd have put on my best Sunday-go-to-meeting clothes. Best not touch me with your gloves, Beth. I'll get them dirty."

"Who cares." She laughed and encased his grimy cheeks with all her fingers. "I've come two hundred and fifty miles in a supply wagon and you're worried about me getting my *gloves* dirty? I thought I might never see you alive again. Just let me keep looking at your face."

He sighed, a long, forlorn chuff of air. "Here I am, still waiting to hang. You've got at least one more day to look at my face all you want to."

"I might even have longer than that, Aaron. I've hired a lawyer for your defense." She saw his horrified expression and went right on talking. She wasn't

77

going to give him the chance to holler at her for spending all that money. "I've also taken care of your charges down at the Grand Central Hotel."

"*Please,* Beth, I'm perfectly capable of defending myself."

"*Of course* you are," she said emphatically, at last drawing her hands away from him. "That's why you wrote me a letter to explain why you were already dead."

He opened his mouth here, then clamped it shut again. She *did* offer a good argument.

"No," she said, seeing his response. "We aren't going to do it your way. You're worth so much more to me than that."

"I didn't want you coming here. That isn't the reason I wrote."

Tears gathered in her eyes. It was the first time in two weeks she'd let herself cry about this. She'd been afraid after she got his letter that she'd start bawling like a mama cow and she'd never be able to stop. "I never would have made it in time if not for that spring snowstorm."

"I figure," he said quietly, "that storm was the answer to a prayer for some folks."

"An answer to a great many of them. How on earth did you get a letter posted so quickly?"

Aaron smiled at her through the bars, once more thinking of Uley. "I found someone who would help me."

"So you said."

"A youngster. Uley." It was all he was going to say to her. He'd promised Uley never to reveal her secret. With all she'd done, she'd earned his vow. And by the solid ground under his feet, he would keep it with Beth, too. He heard someone coming toward them. "That'll be Olney," he told Beth.

He didn't have time to say anything else. The marshal himself came in and gripped Elizabeth's arm.

"Harris," she said.

Eyes on eyes. Cold on cold. Like steel locked up against steel.

"Beth," Olney said. "I tried to keep you from getting involved in this."

"Aren't you going to welcome me to Tin Cup, Harris?"

"Don't reckon I will. I'm not real glad to see you."

"Didn't figure you would be."

"Why did you let him follow me all the way out here? You're the one with the cool head on your shoulders."

"A man's got to do what a man's got to do, Harris. It isn't a woman's place to stand in the way." Remembering the matter at hand, Beth untied the strings of her reticule. "Now tell me the amount of his bail so we can get paid up."

Aaron stood behind her, looking at Olney over one of her delicate chintz-clad shoulders. Harris looked back and forth between the matching sets of eyes, both stubborn, both just as blue and clear as the water running down Willow Creek.

"You're a stubborn woman, Elizabeth."

"You *did* set bail, didn't you?"

"Of course I did," he said. "I just didn't figure on anybody being around to meet it."

"You'd best give me the figure, Harris."

He stuck out his palm. "I just raised it to five hundred dollars."

"All right, then," she said boldly, handing him the bills. "Here it is."

Aaron raked his fingers through his hair. "You shouldn't be walking around with that much money. Anyone might have robbed you." Fully half the people around here were no-good or bandits, come here to Tin Cup to chase the elusive promise of gold. They'd just as soon get money jumping someone in the streets as digging holes in the mountains.

Elizabeth laughed at him. "There are

thirty men out in front of the jailhouse waiting to escort me to my next destination. I don't suppose it would be safe for any one of them to 'jump on me,' Aaron. There would be twenty-nine others waiting to bring the one to justice. Now, Harris, I suggest you bring the key and unlock Aaron so that we may be on our way."

Olney grudgingly obliged. "If it was up to me," he grumbled, "I wouldn't be letting you out, Brown."

Elizabeth held out one gloved palm. "I'd like a receipt for my bail money, Harris."

"We don't have anything as fancy as *receipts*."

"I would like a guarantee on my money. When Aaron shows up for his trial, I want every cent of it back."

"Women! We don't have any paper." Elizabeth pulled two sheets of onionskin paper from her purse and handed them to Olney. The marshal hung the keys back on the peg, dipped his pen in the inkwell and began to scribble.

I, Aaron — *a blotch* — Brown, do solemnly swear to be at the Tin Cup Town Hall for the trial — *another blotch* — murdering Marshal Harris Olney by shooting him in the back.

"How can you write something about me murdering you? You're standing right in front of me wording the thing."

"Well, I've got to make you sign *something* now that I've turned you loose. Got to make sure you'll come back for the trial."

"Here." Aaron reached for a second sheet of paper. "I'll write it."

"You go right ahead." Harris dipped the pen and handed it to him.

I, Aaron Brown, do solemnly swear to appear at the Tin Cup Town Hall on the scheduled date at the scheduled hour to attend a trial in the court of law . . .

"Confound it." Harris spat a wad of tobacco into the brass spittoon in the corner. "That's enough already. Sign your name to it and be done."

"Very well." Aaron brandished the pen.

"Don't forget about my receipt," Elizabeth reminded the marshal, handing him another sheet of paper.

"I do hereby — *blotch* — acknowledge receipt of $500 for the bail of Aaron Brown. The money — *blotch* — be re-

82

turned to Elizabeth Calderwood when Aaron Brown arrives to attend his trial. Signed on this day, April 25th, in the — *blotch* — year of 1882. Marshal Harris Olney."

"Thank you, Marshal," Elizabeth said, retrieving it victoriously and waving it so that the ink would dry. "We'll see you on the day of the trial."

"The trial is two days from now, Beth. We'll expect Aaron there at nine on Thursday morning. I figure the hanging will be Friday."

"We'll see, Harris. We'll see."

"Beth." Aaron touched her delicate, straight back with one of his grimy hands. "We'd best be leaving."

Together, they marched out into the street where Elizabeth's thirty-some-odd admirers were still waiting with profound patience.

"Show's over, gentlemen." Aaron kept his hand on the buttons at her waist. "The lady's with me."

"She won't be with you very long, Brown," Lesser Levy shouted. "Better enjoy the lady's company until Friday. After that, it'll be somebody else's turn."

"Ignore them," Aaron whispered to

her, pulling her closer.

"I have been."

"Wish Olney had given me my gun back."

"I can certainly see why he didn't."

"Where do you have us?"

"I've moved you to the Pacific Hotel. Thought it might be quieter over there."

"I'm surprised Frank Emerson would let me stay there, being suspected of murder and all."

"He doesn't know you'll be there, Aaron. I booked my room first. The way everyone acted when I came into town, I figured it would be a fair trade for Mr. Emerson. Figured they'd do anything to house a lady. If he gives me a fight when you book your room, I'll just tell him I'd just as soon stay down at the Grand Central."

Aaron had to smile at her. So Elizabeth wasn't above concocting a bit of blackmail on her own.

They walked up the street toward Otto Violet's law office, their heads together as they whispered, the hem of Beth's sky-blue skirt flipping in the breeze, Aaron's hand planted firmly against the small of her back, his fingers splayed against the fabric.

Uley rode behind them, astraddle one of

the Gold Cup's mules. She stopped Old Croppy dead in the middle of Washington Avenue. She felt something horrible down deep in her stomach, a grinding . . . like she hadn't had enough to eat . . . like her belly wanted to consume itself. It wasn't bad enough watching everyone following Elizabeth Calderwood all over Tin Cup. Now that Aaron Brown was out of jail, she'd have to watch the two of them sashaying along the streets, so happy to be together they might as well be at a barn dance instead of planning a defense at a trial.

Well, she'd just pretend she didn't care. She didn't care that Elizabeth Calderwood was the prettiest thing on two legs. She didn't care that Aaron Brown walked along with his hand on Elizabeth Calderwood's back as if he owned the whole town.

The problem was, she'd enjoyed having Aaron Brown all to herself, locked up behind bars, where she could talk to him.

Uley figured she was jealous. Only problem was, she couldn't figure out exactly what she was jealous about.

She'd come to town to buy supplies for Carl Hord and Captain Hall up at the Gold Cup. They wouldn't take kindly to her being gone this long. She knew she had to start up Old Croppy and ride him right by those two lovebirds on the street.

She kicked the mule once, and he bolted forward. She sat as straight as a new nail on his back, her knees locked around his bloated stomach, her hat pulled low over eyes that didn't look anywhere except straight down her nose.

The old mule walked right past Elizabeth and Aaron, his hooves sinking into the mud from the melted snow. Uley adjusted the seat of her britches in the saddle, knowing full well that she was covered with mud and mine dust. Would Aaron Brown stop her? Would he offer a kind word? Assuredly not. But still, for some absurd reason, her heart pounded as hard as a miner's hammer.

Old Croppy threw his head back, exposed most of his green teeth and brayed.

She'd give anything if Hall and Hord hadn't asked her to come back into town just now.

Just as she expected, Aaron Brown gave her no sign of recognition. She stopped the mule in front of Campbell, Stahl & Company and climbed off. She didn't have to worry about looping the reins over the hitching rail. There wasn't much of anything that would make Old Croppy move.

She knew he'd be standing in exactly the same position, right where she left him, when she came out of the supply store.

Out of the corner of one eye, she saw Elizabeth Calderwood and Aaron Brown strolling toward her. She didn't dare glance that way. She kept her eyes straight ahead, shooting in exactly the same direction as her hat brim.

Men!

She decided right then it was easier to just *be* one than it was to try to figure one out.

The first thing Aaron wanted to do when he saw Uley riding by on that mule was holler at her and run to her out in the street. But he couldn't very well say the things he wanted to say with Beth standing at his side. He'd made Uley Kirkland a promise, after all.

He didn't like keeping secrets.

He made a vow, right then and there, that he'd go after Uley just as soon as he got time to himself. He needed to offer his thanks when they were alone and bars didn't separate them. She'd posted the letter that had brought Elizabeth to his aid. He wanted her to know he didn't take lightly the things she'd been willing to do.

Doesn't matter whether I blackmailed her or not, he thought.

All the while Beth chattered to him, outlining the plans for his defense, Aaron kept his eyes on Uley, watching as she swung one leg over that dilapidated excuse for a mule and tramped into Campbell, Stahl & Company. Now that he knew that a young woman was hidden beneath those nubby breeches and that shapeless sweater and all that mud, he could easily see her womanly features. Uley wasn't all blustery and big around the middle like the fellows in this camp. When he watched her walk away, she looked all small and round and full of punch — like a fawn that leapt out of nowhere, turned its tail and bounded off into the forest. A gal, no doubt about it.

Every soul walking along the street tipped a hat and spoke to Elizabeth.

"Hello, ma'am."

"Good afternoon, ma'am."

"Nice to see you gracin' this town, ma'am."

"Welcome to Tin Cup, ma'am."

"At your service, ma'am."

No one paid any attention to Uley, whatsoever.

It made for slow going. At this rate, they'd be lucky if they walked two blocks before Otto Violet's office closed at sun-down. Aaron wondered how much of a turmoil Uley would create if she stepped out wearing skirts one morning? Skirts . . . on top of the silhouette he'd seen as she'd alighted from the pack mule.

It was quite a thing for a gentleman to ponder — if you could call somebody on trial for murder a *gentleman.* Aaron decided right then and there that he'd like to see Uley Kirkland wearing yellow muslin. Yes, yellow it would be. The color would look just perfect with that red-honey hair of hers.

Hair he'd only really seen once.

Hair he'd been dreaming of, he realized.

Before he and Elizabeth were able to move even a few yards up the street, here came Uley again, tramping out of the supply store, her miner's boots covered with dirt, her arms full of trowels and buckets and little orange boxes of square-headed nails. She started shoving things into the leather packs on the mule's back, shifting the weight around, pausing once or twice to eye the load and make sure it wasn't listing to one side.

She took up the rope and began working on the diamond hitch, working the hemp around and across and over so that the leather pouches wouldn't slip sideways. She got up almost underneath that animal and started tying knots. When she did, she glanced up, and before he could look away, she caught him staring at her, as unable to draw his eyes away from hers as a moth was unable to draw its wings from molasses.

Goodness, he should say something. But what?

Hey, Uley. You're doing a fine job of packing that mule.

Nope. He could do nothing with Elizabeth still beside him. Elizabeth, who was nodding her head every which way, as if she were a queen acknowledging her subjects.

He placed his hand on Beth's elbow and did the only thing he knew to do. He met Uley's gaze again. He grinned. And he winked at her.

Aaron wasn't used to winking at women. Just as soon as he did it, he felt himself go red in the face.

She sure didn't wink back. She glared out at him from between the mule's legs, her gray-green eyes pinpointing him. She looked like a wolverine that was just about to attack.

He figured he'd been crazy to picture her

in a dress. With Elizabeth beside him, there *did* seem to be a big difference between a lady in a dress and a mud-covered young girl who didn't want anyone to see who she really was.

Father, came the prayer from his heart. *You look upon hearts and not on the outsides. Would that You didn't know the hatred for Olney that's in my heart. Even in the middle of my punishment for it, I cannot make it go away.*

Chapter Five

"I don't care what I told you earlier, Miss Calderwood." Otto Violet stared across the desk at both of them, little round spectacles perched precariously on a monstrous nose that looked as if it might pitch them off at any second. He pointed to the dusty red book on his desk. "I cannot find any defense in my law records for you, Mr. Brown. You have committed an actionable offense, and I believe you should be punished for it."

"But I've given you a retainer," Elizabeth reminded him.

"That you have," he said. "So now I'm giving it back." He slid the money she'd given him just this morning across the desk at her. "I won't defend Mr. Brown. You went after our town marshal, sir. That is a case of public hanging, to be certain." He thumped the book for good measure and sent whorls of dust into the air. "I've been thinking of it all day. I don't like to lose cases. It mars my reputation. Therefore, I will not take this case at all."

"But you promised." Beth hadn't touched the money on his desk.

"I don't want you to worry yourself with this any longer. Come on." Aaron squeezed her shoulders. "We've other lawyers in this town to choose from. I'd rather argue on my own behalf than trust someone with my life who doesn't trust me."

She gathered the money into her reticule, and together they returned to the street. But Violet's refusal to represent them had been a blow to her. "There are only two others to choose from." She dabbed at her eyes with a perfectly folded linen handkerchief. "And of the three, Otto Violet is the best."

"I wonder," Aaron said speculatively, "if Harris Olney is passing his own money around in this town."

For all intents and purposes, Aaron might have been a different man when he and Elizabeth marched into Seth Wood's esteemed law office an hour later. He'd had his first bath in three weeks. He'd shaved, too. And he'd splashed himself with bay rum and had put on his very best Sunday suit. He hoped the physical improvements would make him look more defendable.

He held the door open for Beth as the

bell tinkled sharply to announce their arrival. And, strange as it might seem, Seth Wood was sitting at his desk looking as if he'd been waiting for their arrival.

"Ain't no use you two coming in here," he said brusquely. "I ain't gonna represent you, neither."

"You all been meeting and discussing my case?" Aaron growled. "Seems like everybody's decided not to get involved with this at once."

"We've decided we won't be crazy, that's all."

"Has Harris Olney been sniffing around offering to pay you money if you'll turn me down?"

"That's no business of yours, Brown. You know that."

"I know what's fair," Aaron said. "I'm entitled to a fair trial with a jury of my peers. Doesn't look like I'm gonna get that." He pointed a finger right between Seth Wood's eyes. "My blood will be on your hands, Wood."

"Nope," the lawyer said stiffly. "You've brought the blood on yourself."

By the end of their meeting with Wood, Aaron was as mad as a bear. "Beth, there's no use you traipsing around all day at my side. You're going to wear yourself out and not be any good to anybody tomorrow."

"I thought I could help."

"Well, I don't see that your presence is doing anybody any good." He didn't mean to be unkind to her. It was just that he was as frustrated as he'd ever been in his life. And he figured that, at this rate, he wouldn't have a life very long.

How he hated to see Olney win.

"Aaron."

"I'm takin' you back to the Pacific Hotel. "You've helped me by coming, Beth. If nothing else, you got me free to walk the streets for two last days before I go on to glory. At this point, I'm appreciating every extra minute I get." He had only one more chance at a lawyer. He wasn't placing too much hope in that one, either. He figured Harris had made a point to get to all of them before he did.

He delivered Beth to the hotel and saw her safely to her room. Then he went to visit John Kincaid, the third and last lawyer to set up business in Tin Cup.

"Now look," he said to Kincaid when he stomped in the door and saw the man sitting with feet crossed atop his desk, just waiting for him to walk in like all the others. "I don't like this cat-and-mouse game."

95

"Neither do I," Kincaid said, swinging his boots to the floor.

"I guess I just went and got my hopes up," Aaron went on. "Last week, I thought I was hanging for sure. This week, I start to see possibilities. Next thing I know, those possibilities are slipping away. I'm not a trapped animal, Kincaid. I don't take kindly to being pounced on and played with."

Kincaid rose slowly and went to stare out the front window of his office. "Never was too fond of Harris Olney myself."

"You're saying you're not gonna take his money to tell me no."

"I'm saying I'll decide the merits of taking your case on my own, Mr. Brown. Whoever represents you Thursday is going to have a tough go of it. Everyone's hungry for your hanging. And everyone's hungry for a hero. Unfortunately, you gave them one when you got tromped on by Uley Kirkland."

"Are you saying everybody wants to hang me just for *Uley's* sake?"

"It would seem a proper show of respect for what that kid did."

"I suppose I'm in trouble."

"You tell me something," Kincaid said. "You tell me if you were planning on pulling that trigger."

"Would it make any difference if I told you that I wasn't?"

"It might make a lot of difference. It might make a lot of difference in how I look at you."

"Okay, I wasn't."

"You telling the truth?"

Aaron was at the point of growling again. "I generally tell the truth, Kincaid."

"So why were you holding a gun on the marshal's back, Brown?"

"Because I didn't want the marshal to shoot me first."

"You'd be willing to tell me the whole story?"

Aaron hesitated for an instant, thinking of Elizabeth and all the things he wasn't certain he should say. But he had no other choice now. His plan had backfired on him. And Elizabeth had already proven how much she was willing to risk by making the treacherous journey across the Continental Divide.

"I'd be willing to tell you the whole story."

"I don't like Olney's money, either," John Kincaid admitted now. "Though I find his gold dust a whole lot more tasteful than I find *him*. Looks like I won't be bending to bribes." John Kincaid pulled out a red law book that looked exactly like the ones Otto Violet and Seth Wood had been thumping earlier. "Let's get down to business. We've got thirty-six hours to come up with a way to keep you from swinging high."

Just as Uley was clearing the cobalt-blue tin plates from the table that night, a timid rap came at the front door.

Samuel rose from the table and opened it. There stood Tin Can Laura in the dark, all dressed in red silk, with a huge matching plume on her head and enough kohl on her eyes that Uley almost didn't recognize her.

"Hello." She cast her eyes toward the smooth-swept dirt floor. "Gotta get back to Santa Fe Moll's. But Storm here's been tellin' me he wanted to come to his new place and move in. What with spring coming and all the moles coming out, you'll be needin' him to do his duties purty soon. Knew you wouldn't wanta be seen with me in the broad daylight, so I figured I'd better do this tonight."

Uley's heart lifted when she saw her new friend.

"Laura. Get in here," she said. "Have a piece of huckleberry pie. I was just fixing to cut it open." It suddenly seemed so important to her, treating Laura to sweets, making her feel welcome, letting her know that this was a place she could visit.

"Nope. Can't do it. Moll will have my hide when she finds out I left the parlor. But Storm's been caterwaulin' something awful. He don't like being locked up in my room anymore. It bothers the customers, having a cat howling next door."

"Here." Uley took Storm out of Laura's skirt and pitched him unceremoniously on the bed. Then she grabbed her coat. "If you're so set on not staying, then I'll walk you back."

"There's no need of it."

"Doesn't matter. I'll do it anyway."

"I heard," Laura said as they marched along through the slush, "that there's a real lady in town."

"Yep. She came in on the supply wagon today."

"Everybody over at Ongewach's is talking about her. They say she's got eyes like cornflowers and hair like sunbeams and a waist no bigger around than a willow tree."

"That's what they say, all right. Everybody's talking about her everywhere you go."

"Wish somebody would talk about me

like that," Laura said longingly.

Uley sighed. It was a deep, hollow sigh that reached down to her very soul.

The Gold Cup Mine, owned by Captain Hall and Carl Hord of the Bald Mountain Mining Company, was the first of the fifty-six mines in the valley to call off operations on Thursday. All the miners wanted to be at the Tin Cup Town Hall, supporting Uley Kirkland as the kid testified against the man who'd tried to murder the marshal.

Hord announced the Gold Cup's schedule at 9:20 on Wednesday morning. An hour later, others were announcing the plan, as well. The Spotted Tail would be closed. The Little Fred would be closed. So would the Ontario, the Jimmy Mack and the Anna Parallel.

"Can't believe the Bullion King won't be open tomorrow," Sam said as they all worked underground on Wednesday trying to get things ready so that they could leave for two days. "Doc Gillette doesn't even like to come out of his mine when somebody's *dying*. Remember when Pete Wiley caught his beard on fire? He had to wait four hours before Doc Gillette would come up out of the Bullion King and treat his burns."

"Well," Charlie Sparks said, "that just goes to show you how thankful everyone in this town is to Uley. This is one important trial around here."

"Three cheers for Uley!" someone else joined in. "Hip-hip-hooray!"

Uley kept her eye on the timber, pegging it into the corner of the rocks with hammer blows so fierce they made the granite shiver. "I don't like being the entertainment for the rest of this town. I'd just as soon I didn't have to go down there tomorrow." That was the understatement of the year. "Wish somebody else could go down there and testify in my place."

"There isn't anyone else can tell the jury what you saw, Uley," her pa said.

She went after the pegs even harder. "I know that."

On Wednesday afternoon, just when Uley thought all the hoopla was about to die down, Marshal Harris Olney himself came up shaft eleven wagging a lantern out in front of him. "Uley?" he shouted so loud that loose rocks fell off the ledges above them. "Is Uley Kirkland back here?"

Back here? Back here? Back here? The sound echoed all the way up the shaft.

"I'm standing right beneath your nose, Marshal. If you holler much louder than that, you're going to make the whole shaft cave in."

"I need you to come outside with me, Uley. You and me, we need to have a talk."

"I don't see as we have anything to talk about."

"Oh, but we do." Olney wrapped his arm around her shoulder and propelled Uley forward. "You saved my life, remember? I'm here to offer you compensation for all your trouble."

"And what might that compensation be?"

"I'll tell you when we reach daylight, son," he said.

Then, at the mouth of shaft eleven, Olney began to lay out his plan.

"I know you are just as eager to do away with that foul murderer as I am, Uley. I know you have eyewitness testimony against Aaron Brown. I'm here to encourage you not to falter in any of it. I have a hefty reward waiting for you in my office for the day Aaron Brown is hanged."

"I don't need a reward, Marshal," she said, feeling an odd twinge of guilt when she thought how Aaron's hanging would absolve *her* of a problem, too. "I'll just be glad to know that justice has been done."

It was seven o'clock that night, and Uley

was finishing up her father's washing in the tub beside the warm wood stove, when there came a sharp knock at the cabin door. Uley straightened, leaving one last flannel shirt in the water to soak, and poked all the tendrils of hair up beneath her hat.

Sam opened the door and stuck his head out into the darkness. "Hello?"

Aaron stood on the rickety porch, his Stetson brim crumpled in his fists. "I'd like to see Uley, if I may."

Samuel cocked his head, not quite knowing if he should let the man in or coax him off the porch with his shotgun. "Why on earth would you want to see Uley on the eve of your trial?"

"If you don't mind, sir. It's a matter of great importance. I need some private time with her, sir."

When Aaron said "her," Samuel's eyes grew as big around as the twelve-and-a-half-bit pieces everybody used for exchange down at Frenchy's.

"Yes," Aaron said, still wringing his hat. "I know about Uley. Didn't mean to find out, sir, I can assure you."

Uley stood right behind Sam in the doorway.

Clouds hid the moon and the lacy formations of stars that hung over Tin Cup when the night stayed clear. It was as dark outside as a cast-iron kettle.

"Please, Uley," Aaron said. "Come on out. Just for a minute."

Uley stepped around her father awkwardly, knowing that he, too, was uncertain how to deal with this. Her entire life, she'd never had a gentleman caller.

Which was understandable, seeing as how everybody in this town thought she was one herself.

"Pa," Uley said finally, saving them all. "No one knows what's going to happen tomorrow. If Aaron Brown wants to say something to me, this might very well be his last chance to say it."

Sam looked up at the empty night sky, as if he were expecting to find an answer there.

"It won't take too long," Aaron said, jumping on the opportunity. "She's right. It might be something I'll never get another chance to say."

Uley was uncertain as to how she felt about standing out on a dark stoop with a man who'd pulled a gun on the marshal. But she'd already proven once that she could handle Aaron Brown if he gave her trouble.

Sam looked at her.

She looked at Sam.

Sam turned back to the man on the porch. "I warn you, I'll be waitin' right inside this door, with my shotgun cocked and loaded."

"Yes, sir," Aaron said. "That was what I was expectin'."

Uley tromped out onto the boards and pulled the door closed behind her.

When the door shut, they couldn't even see each other, it was so black.

Aaron knew right where she was standing. He could hear her breathing.

Uley knew right where he was standing. She could smell his bay rum.

"Well, I must say," she told him finally. "You smell a mite nicer than you did the last time I caught a whiff of you."

"It's amazing what a wash tub will do for a man."

So what did Elizabeth Calderwood think when she saw you in need of a bath in that jailhouse?

She sure couldn't say it like that. She thought about it and decided she'd find out the same information a different way.

"Well," she said, "I'm surprised you were able to leave Elizabeth Calderwood long enough to come out here."

"Elizabeth's fine without me," he said. "She's safely inside her room at the Pacific Hotel. There are so many men on the lookout for her, she can't make a move without having a good dozen of them following down the street after her. They're looking after her like bees protect their queen."

"So I've noticed." Through the window, Uley could see her father lifting his gun off the rack and wiping down the barrel. "You'd best get on with what you came to say," she said. "It doesn't look like he's going to give you much time."

At precisely that moment, the moon moved out from behind a cloud and Uley saw his face.

"You make a habit," she asked out of the blue, "of winking at every girl you see beneath a mule?"

He looked straight up at the night sky and guffawed. "If one time makes a habit —" he was struggling to get the words out, he was so amused "— then I guess I'll tell you I'm guilty. I've just never seen a girl beneath a mule, Uley. What was I supposed to do? Come over and bend down there with you and look up at the underside of that animal's belly and say, 'Lovely weather, Miss Kirkland'?"

"Well, I don't know." She didn't know why she'd expected him to acknowledge her on the street. She'd just figured he would, that was all. He'd come marching right toward her with Elizabeth Calderwood at his side and acted as if Uley wasn't even there . . . that is, until she'd caught him just watching her for no reason at all.

And then he'd winked.

Winked.

The way Harris Olney winked when he passed Santa Fe Moll on the street.

"I was protecting our secret, Uley," he said. "I didn't know what else to do."

"Well," she said, crossing her arms, "I don't think that was a very good way of protecting it."

He stopped fiddling with his hat. He decided just to put it back on his head and go back to the hotel. "Forget it, Uley," he told her. "I wasn't winking at you, anyway. I was winking at the mule."

Alex Parent rang the Tin Cup town bell in the belfry of the town hall at precisely nine on Thursday morning.

Cher-*bong.* Cher-*bong.* Of course, there wasn't any reason to ring it. Some two hundred men were already jostling for position inside.

Miners and ranchers had been arriving from all over Taylor Park since just after seven. Another wagonload of men had just gotten in over Cumberland Pass from Pitkin. Judge Murphy had sent for them to come. He figured there wasn't anybody in the town of Tin Cup unbiased enough to give Mr. Brown a fair trial. Those Pitkin miners were the closest thing he was likely to find to a jury in Gunnison County.

The bell echoed off Gold Hill over to Siegel Mountain and American Mountain and back again. Cher-*bong.* Cher-*bong.* Cher-*bong.*

Those who hadn't been able to find seats were jammed inside the back foyer, standing on tiptoe and boot heels. The men around Uley were all craning their necks to see Elizabeth. Elizabeth Calderwood hadn't been in town forty-eight hours and the news of her arrival had already traveled as far as Pitkin and St. Elmo. That was almost faster than a good horse could run.

Judge J. M. Murphy sat behind the bench, a massive table of lodgepole planks made by the Beckley brothers, the only two men in town who took the time away from mining to build furniture, houses and coffins. Murphy banged his cup on the wood and did his best to call everyone to

108

order. "Let the record show that I call to order this court on April 27, 1882, the trial of Gunnison County, Colorado, and Marshal Harris John Olney versus defendant Mr. Aaron Talephas Brown."

Uley about fell out of her tumbledown pine chair. *Talephas.* Next time he talked to her about winking at mules, she was going to call him Talephas. That ought to put him in his place.

That is, if he lived long enough.

Murphy continued with his speech. "Seth Wood will represent Gunnison County and Marshal Harris Olney in this matter. John Kincaid will represent the accused."

Commotion broke out in the room.

Murphy pounded the table with the cup again, making little C-shaped dents in the pine planks. "Quiet! Or we won't go on! Seth," he hollered over the din, "come on up here and start your case."

Seth Wood approached the bench and whispered to Murphy while the talking died down. As soon as everyone could hear him, he started calling witnesses.

Carl Hansen came forward, put his hand on the Bible and was sworn in. He sat down beside Murphy and told all about how he'd been on his way to Frenchy's when somebody hollered, "Uley's got a man down over there!" He told how he'd run to help Uley and had found the accused — here he pointed at Aaron Talephas Brown — lying beneath Uley in the dirt.

"Thank you, Mr. Hansen," Seth Wood said. "Next witness, John West."

West walked to the front and told the same tale.

During the morning hours, Seth called at least a dozen men to the bench. Each one of those dozen men told the judge and jury the exact same story. At about eleven-thirty, Seth Wood stepped up beside Judge Murphy and looked right at Uley.

Everybody knew it was time for the lawyer to call his key witness.

"Uley Kirkland. Will you approach the bench, please?"

She hadn't figured on being this nervous. She felt like a marionette as she went to stand beside Seth Wood, a marionette with someone waiting to drop the strings.

Judge Murphy held out the biggest, blackest Bible Uley had ever seen. "Repeat after me," he said somberly. "I, your name . . ."

"I, Uley Kirkland . . ."

"Do solemnly swear . . ."

"Do solemnly swear . . ."

"To tell the truth, the whole truth and nothing but the truth . . ."

Uley figured everyone in the room saw her swallow. This was one time in her life when being a gal stood her in good stead. She didn't have a protruding Adam's apple bobbing up and down. To get her out of this mess, she uttered a silent prayer. *I promise I'll do my best to get it right, God.*

Out loud she said, "To tell the truth, the whole truth and nothing but the truth . . ."

"So help me God."

"So help me God."

From the front of the room, she could see everyone in town. She could see her father on the third row, sitting with his hands clenched between his knees. She could see Elizabeth Calderwood with her hair all done up in a bun and her neck as long and graceful as a trumpeter swan's. She could see Harris Olney just below her, his marshal's star gleaming. And she could see Aaron Brown.

Aaron Brown. Today, when it seemed the whole world was against him, she felt some regret that she hadn't been kinder to him last night. Then again, she found she was afraid to meet his eyes. Just suppose he winked at her again — here in the courtroom! It would totally unnerve her. Here. Where she needed to be quick-thinking and smart.

No, she'd look anywhere except at Aaron Brown. She trained her eyes on the windowsill beyond his left shoulder.

"Now, Uley," Seth Wood said, "tell us about the night in question. Tell us where you were and what you were doing."

Uley proceeded to speak in great detail about the renaming of Tin Cup and the ensuing invitations to Frenchy's. "I decided to go home instead. I was on my way when I greeted Harris Olney and kept walking," she said, in a clear, steady voice.

"What did you see as you walked down the street?"

"I saw a man standing there in the darkness."

"What made you think something might be amiss, Uley?"

"I saw the glint of steel in his hand. I realized he had a gun."

"The gun was drawn?"

"Yes, sir."

"What makes you think this man was after Marshal Harris Olney?" Seth Wood asked.

"I'd just passed the marshal. I'd just spoken with him."

"What did you do then?"

"I was frightened," Uley admitted. "I knew I couldn't call for help. I figured he'd turn that gun on me."

"What next?"

"I ran at him and jumped on him."

"Will you repeat that, please?"

"I ran at him and jumped on him."

The crowd roared.

"Hang Aaron Brown!" someone shouted.

"Uley caught him red-handed!" someone else bellowed.

"String him up!"

"Order in this court!" Murphy hollered. "We will not proceed until we have order!"

"Hang him!"

"Get a new rope! Tie it to that cottonwood tree. . . ."

For some reason, during the clamor, Uley felt Aaron looking at her. She glanced up from the windowsill — just a glance, just once — and there he was, watching her, his sad blue eyes telling a mysterious story all their own, something she didn't understand.

Uley didn't know what happened in her heart just then. She felt something wrench inside her and try to break free. A bit of sorrow, perhaps, because she'd had such a part in bringing him here.

Murphy was so angry now, he rose and started flapping his black-robed arms up and down like a bat. "The next man who speaks out of turn in my court of law is going to get thrown out. Understand?"

Uley supposed she felt compassion for Aaron Brown. She wished, for some absurd reason, that she could do something, anything, to make this part easier for him. But then, she decided, remembering the pasties she'd baked and the letter she'd posted, perhaps she already had.

The noise level fell a bit.

"Do you understand?" Murphy was still flapping.

The din subsided to a murmur.

The judge stared everyone down until the place was so quiet you could hear the flies buzzing.

"There you go, Seth," he said finally. "You may continue."

Seth came toward Uley and walked all the way around her chair. "You said you ran at him and jumped on him? You *overpowered* him?"

"I believe so, Mr. Wood."

"A little thing like you? Would you say that this man was so intent on stalking Marshal Olney that you totally surprised him?"

"Yes, sir. I believe he was. Surprised, that is."

"What happened after you overcame the man, Uley? Did he fight with you? Did you wrestle? Did you pin him to the ground?"

Oh, my goodness, here it came. She'd been so busy thinking about the accused that she'd forgotten to steel herself for this part. She'd known all along it would be coming.

The truth . . . the whole truth . . . nothing but the truth . . .

"We wrestled," she said. "He tried to fight me off, but I was too tough for him. I got his arms pinned up behind his head. He tried to roll and pitch me off . . ."

Father, forgive me for this.

"Yes?"

"But he couldn't do it. He rolled back the other way and threw his knee up in the air, trying to come up with enough balance to get his arms free."

"Yes?"

"We wrestled some more. I almost had the gun out of his hand, but he jerked it back."

"Did you get a good look at this man, Uley?"

"Yes, I did."

"Do you see him in the court today?"

"I do."

"Where is that man sitting?"

She pointed straight at Aaron. "He's sitting right there."

The uproar started again, but one narrow-eyebrow glare from Judge Murphy cut it off. "Did you exchange words with this man while you were wrestling, Uley?" Seth asked. "Did he say anything to you?"

For the life of her, she couldn't quite remember what he'd said.

All she could really come up with in her mind was that one moment, that one terrible instant, when he'd taken one look at her head without that hat and said, "You're just a *girl.*"

She sure couldn't tell the judge and jury he'd said *that.* Never in her life had she thought she'd be in a predicament like this one.

Never in her life had she thought she'd have to measure her words when she'd sworn on a Bible.

She smiled at Judge J. M. Murphy. She turned back and smiled at Seth Wood. "I'm sorry," she said, her voice as strong as she could make it. "I don't quite remember."

But in truth, she did. He'd said "You're a lady!"

"Something about Harris Olney, not

getting to go after him."

That's the way with hiding things, isn't it, Lord? You start out one small place and a secret starts growing and it never ends.

Chapter Six

Seth Wood dismissed Uley from the stand. Just as she rose from the chair, John Kincaid shouted, "I would like to cross-examine this witness."

Seth Wood seemed surprised. Then a shrewd smile appeared upon his face. He looked as if he were so certain of the outcome he could afford to be charitable. "Certainly, Kincaid." He made a gesture with one hand, as if to allow Kincaid through a door. "Be my guest."

John Kincaid stepped up and smiled at Uley.

Uley smiled back.

"I only have two questions to ask you, Uley," he said kindly.

"Okay."

"They aren't difficult questions."

"Okay."

"Your answers could be very important in the decision of this case."

Uley could feel her hands shaking in her lap. She had absolutely no idea what he was going to come out with. "I understand that." Her voice began trembling for the first time. She felt it, and heard it, wavering.

"The night you saw Aaron Brown in the street, the night you jumped on him and held him there until you got help, you saw a gun in his hand, correct?"

"Yes. That is correct."

"I ask you, Uley," Kincaid said pointedly, "if at any time during your altercation with Mr. Brown you actually saw him level the gun and take aim at Marshal Harris Olney?"

"I . . ." She had to think about this one. "I don't know."

"Think about it. You can remember what you saw that night, can't you?"

"Yes, I can."

"There is no hurry. We'll all wait for your answer. Did you see Aaron Brown aim the gun at Harris Olney?"

"I . . ." She glanced around the room. She'd never seen so many people staring at her. Made it hard to think, with those eyes all trained in her direction.

First she looked at Aaron. He was gripping his chair with both hands, as if he were afraid it might buck up and pitch him off. Elizabeth Calderwood appeared quite pale. Uley's father looked as confused as she felt. Then she found Harris Olney. The marshal was grinning slightly, with one jaw pouched out by his chaw of tobacco. As she met his gaze, his grin broadened. Then he nodded at her. Just a slight nod, indiscernible to everyone around him. He lowered his face and hunkered his eyebrows at her as if to say, Come on, Uley. Say yes and let's have it over with.

He wanted her to lie!

He had absolutely no idea what she had seen.

What was worse, he had absolutely no idea that she'd struggled with telling the complete truth already!

She raised her chin and told John Kincaid, "I'm ready to answer the question."

"Are you? You remember the details?"

"Yes, I do."

"Okay," Kincaid said calmly. "I'll repeat the question for the jury. Uley, did you see Aaron Brown aim his six-shooter at Marshal Harris Olney?"

She took a deep breath and plunged on as best she could.

She shook her head. "No." She watched while Harris Olney pummeled the arm of his chair and spewed tobacco all over the

120

shirts of the fellows sitting in front of him. "I never saw Aaron Brown aim his gun at the marshal."

Judge Murphy called for a dinner break because he knew he couldn't get the ruckus under control any other way. Uley took her bucket with her and found a solitary place in the willows that lined the creek. She'd just started gnawing on a sourdough biscuit when she heard something else coming through the willows toward her. Figuring it for a moose, she started shoving her dinner back into the handkerchief at the bottom of the bucket.

Just as she was about to jump up and move on, she saw the top of a brown Stetson parting the branches of the willows.

"Uley?" Aaron Brown said. "Who're you trying to hide from? Where did you go in here?"

She'd shoved almost the entire biscuit in her mouth, and she couldn't speak. "Ova . . . ere . . ." *Over here,* she was trying to say.

She heard him stop then begin to back away with great care.

She couldn't speak because her mouth was full. He must think he'd come upon some kind of animal or something. She plunged through the willows after him, trying to call to him. She was going to choke on this biscuit before she got it down.

He started running faster.

She started running faster.

He was pounding through the willows about as fast as he could go.

She took some pleasure in the fact that she was able to stay right behind him.

Of course, she couldn't have done it if she'd had skirts on.

At last she got the biscuit down. "Aaron," she shouted. "It's —"

He stopped the second he heard her. He stopped and turned around.

She plowed right into him, smashing into his chest with all the force of the moose he'd thought she was.

At the impact, Aaron wrapped his arms around Uley and stumbled backward into a clump of rosehips. She fell right on top of him.

"Good grief, Uley," he said, just lying there looking up at her. His Stetson had come off and was hanging atop one of the protruding rosehip branches. "You're awful good at knocking me head over heels."

"I was trying to answer you." She was staring right down at his face. "I heard you calling, and I'd just taken this big bite of biscuit, and . . ." She cast about, searching for her pail. It lay upside down, too, its contents scattered on the ground. "See, there it is. What's left of my dinner."

"I only meant to talk to you. I didn't mean to cause such a misunderstanding," he said, a slight grin on his face that made him look totally endearing. "But I thought you were a moose —" he began to chuckle "— and you were after me."

"I was calling you." It had suddenly felt imperative to talk to him. *I didn't see you aim the gun. You only had it out, at the ready.*

"You sounded," he said, "like a bull moose bugling."

She couldn't help herself. After the seriousness of the morning, it felt like heaven to giggle. Aaron Brown knew exactly what she was, that she was a gal. She felt perfectly comfortable being herself in front of him. "I'd just taken a bite of my biscuit, Mr. Brown. I tried to swallow it, but it wouldn't do my bidding." Her giggles turned to outright laughter. "So I ran . . . through the willows . . . after you, but . . . you were running. . . ."

"Uley," he said, giving in to laughter, too. "You must be lighter on your feet. I honestly thought you were a big, *hulking* animal."

"What a horrible thing to say about a lady, Mr. Brown."

"Isn't it? If I'd known, I'd have stopped sooner."

"But I'm glad you didn't —" she was clinging to her sides, and it felt glorious "— because laughter is such fun, Mr. Brown. I don't often do it."

He did his best to look askance at her. "I should hope not. Not in this fashion, anyway. I think I would have fared better with the moose."

"I think not," she said, still enjoying herself. "I think you're much better off that *I* caught you instead."

"Oh really?" He sobered somewhat. And she thought she knew what he must be thinking. *The same way that I'm better off because you caught me the other day, as well?* He was gazing up at her with his azure eyes in an odd way.

For some curious reason, as their laughter dwindled, Uley became aware of the length of him in the grass. She matched him span for span, limb for limb. Beside her arm, she saw his arm. His face

124

was so near to hers, she could see the beginnings of his whiskers.

"You've gotten mud on your face," he told her, somewhat somberly.

"Have I?"

"Yes. Right . . . there." He reached with one hand and touched her cheek. "You want me to scrub it off?"

For one instant, she actually wished he would. She wouldn't admit that, though. Not to him. "No need for that." She rubbed at her face with the back of her hand. The spot where he'd touched her skin seemed to burn.

It was time to stand and move away from him, but she didn't want to. When she'd been this close to him before, they'd both been taken so by surprise that it had been entirely different. This time, it was as if the laughter had tempered them.

Her breeches leg lay beside his breeches leg. Even though she wore a man's clothing, she felt every bit the woman inside. The feeling was not unpleasant. In fact, she rather liked the warm curl that had begun inside her.

"Uley . . ." Aaron said quietly, gazing up into her eyes as if he were gazing into the sky. Uley's heart beat a rhythm like the pounding of Ute drums.

125

He grasped her upper arm. "This is the craziest thing."

"Is it?" This was a man who had black-mailed her, who had threatened to reveal her darkest secret. She'd forgive him almost anything if he'd just keep looking at her like that. Then, perhaps there were things he could forgive *her* of, as well. "Is it? I don't know. I've never . . ." She didn't know exactly how to finish.

"You haven't what?"

But she had no right to be considering these feelings, she knew. Not with him squiring a sweetheart around Tin Cup.

"I do not feel free to voice it," she said. "You are saying this is a crazy thing. It certainly is, having you walking around free after what you've been accused of!"

He grabbed his hat from the bushes and swatted it back and forth against his knee to get rid of the brambles. "How is it that every time I try to talk to you, you get me off the subject? I came to your cabin last night and you got me talking about the underside of a mule. I came to find you today and you get me running through the willows. Will you just stand still and be quiet and let me say what I've been trying to say to you all along?"

"Well," she said, taking one step toward

him and knotting her fists, "I had no idea you had something important to say."

"Well, I do."

"You could have fooled me."

"I've got lots of important things to say."

"Well, then, *say* them."

"Okay. I will."

"Okay."

He just stared at her for a moment.

She stared right back.

He put his hat on his head. Then he took it off again.

He clenched it in both hands. "I risked coming to your house last night and you got me all mad and bothered. I risked coming to your house because I wanted to thank you."

"What for?" she asked suspiciously.

"Lots of things. But you make it awful hard for a man to get a word in edgewise."

"I guess I didn't expect thanks from you. Not since I'm the one who sprung on you and landed you in jail in the first place."

"But you visited me there."

"Because I was afraid you'd tell somebody what you knew."

"You brought me my writing supplies."

"Because you blackmailed me into doing it."

"You posted the letter for me."

"Because I thought it was going to be something important. I thought it was going to be a letter confessing your crime to the governor of Colorado."

"You made me pasties."

"I did. I made you pasties. I'll accept a thank-you for that."

"Thank you, Uley, for the pasties."

"You're welcome, Aaron Brown."

"You were most thoughtful in your answers today. You described exactly what you saw."

"It was my Christian duty to tell the truth." The guilt returned to niggle at her. She had lied by not repeating what he'd said when he'd recognized her for a girl. *Oh, Father, I'm trying so hard but, in my power, nothing turns out right.*

That was the gist of it right there. She'd given him hope by telling the jury about him not aiming that gun. She hadn't realized until that very moment how much he'd been depending on her. And he knew she'd been living a charade for years. Like everyone else, he had no reason to trust her. Every good thing she'd ever done for him had come because he'd held something over her.

"I hadn't thought of that until he asked

128

it. I never *did* see you aim the gun. I just saw you draw it."

"We were all counting on you remembering exactly what you saw."

"You never did aim the gun."

"No."

"Were you going to?"

"I don't know, Uley. It would've depended on what happened." He was just staring at her now, taking in every impish detail of her face, recalling their laughter and the way he'd felt when he found himself stretched out beside her in the marsh grass.

As he stared at her now, he had one thing on his mind, and one thing only.

"I've got to ask you a question," he said.

"Go ahead. People have been asking me questions all morning."

"I could be dying, Uley. They might hang me tomorrow."

"I know that."

"This could be a dying man's last request. This might be my last chance to do a little living on this earth before I go on to glory."

"That's what I thought about that letter, too. You keep making requests. I have yet to see the last one."

"This is different," he said. "This is between you and me."

"Is it?" The way he looked at her made her feel as if she had a feathery bird flying around in her middle.

"You know that night when you saw me? The night you saw the gun?"

"I'm not likely to forget it. Not as long as I live."

"Your hat fell off . . ."

"I remember it, Mr. Brown."

"Your hair . . ."

She knew what he wanted then, knew it as surely as if an angel had whispered it in her ear. Her chest constricted. "My hair?"

"Would you take off your hat?" he whispered to her. "Let me see your hair?"

The bird-like thing fluttered hard in her belly. But she did his bidding, pulling the funny little woven cap off her head and letting stray ribbons of her hair fall down around her cheeks.

Aaron just stood there staring at it. Her hair was so red, it blazed in the sunlight.

She stood there before him, allowing him to look, feeling more demure and feminine than she'd ever felt in her life.

"How long is it?" he asked.

"Down past my shoulder blades."

"Uley . . . it's awfully pretty." He wanted to touch it. He wanted to reach right out with one of his hands and see what it felt like in his fingers.

"Is it? I don't often get to see the color of it in daylight. I brush it at night, after we've blown out the lanterns."

He took one step toward her.

One step.

"It's about the prettiest hair I've ever seen." Gingerly, ever so gingerly, Aaron reached out with one hand. He ran the back of one long finger down a tendril that fell soft against her cheek. It curled slightly . . . and lay against his flesh soft like petals of larkspur. He wrapped his finger into it, laying the tip of his forefinger against the blush-pink of her cheek. "There," he whispered as he gazed at her skin.

He pulled his hand down and met her gaze head on. "Best get out of these willows now," he said abruptly. "Somebody might come lookin' for me, I've been away so long."

Then, before she could say anything more, he was gone.

John Kincaid kept the courtroom busy that afternoon rehashing old evidence. He called every single one of the men who had testified that morning, asking if any of them, in turn, had seen Aaron Brown aim his gun at Harris Olney. Not a one of them had seen anything.

The testimony continued for hours, and by four-thirty in the afternoon it was clear that the trial would go on another day. There'd be no hanging until Saturday morning now. And, despite all the talk, nobody really had any idea which way the jury would go.

Uley walked home that night with her father. She was so hungry she could scarcely stand. She didn't often miss the noon meal and her stomach had been rumbling for hours. But something else kept rumbling deep down inside her, too, something filled with questions and wonder and maybe a little pain.

She couldn't forget the way Aaron Talephas Brown had gazed at her in the willows.

She couldn't forget how it had felt to laugh a little with him in the green-smelling grass.

Why, oh, why had he asked to see her hair again?

Why, oh, why had he taken it where it lay against her cheek and brushed it once with the backs of his fingers?

As she sat thinking of it that night, brushing her hair out in the darkness yet again, she found herself so preoccupied that she didn't even count the brush strokes. Try as she might, she couldn't understand the small hurt within her heart, the anticipation and remembrance, so deep and fierce they left her breathless.

Oh, Father. She wanted to trust this man who looked at her in such a puzzling way.

She figured she didn't dare.

Her instincts usually served her well. Tonight they were defying her. The more she thought about him, the madder about things she got.

He'd pulled a gun even though he hadn't really aimed it at the marshal.

He'd blackmailed her into doing his bidding while he was locked behind bars.

He'd traipsed after her into the willows and had made her feel odd and wonderful things, when Elizabeth Calderwood, who was obviously sweet on him, had come all this way from Fort Collins just to offer her assistance.

He surely hadn't meant to follow her into the wilds and make her begin comparing herself with Elizabeth Calderwood.

Perhaps . . . perhaps . . . it was herself she couldn't trust.

That thought made Uley madder than ever.

She hoped they'd hang him fast. Uley didn't often think of how she missed her mother any longer. The past years had dulled the features of her face in Uley's memory. But, just now, the presence of her mother came back to her . . . the feeling of safety . . . warmth . . . sheltering love. . . .

It came to her as if she were peering into her own childhood through the eyes of another. The crinoline skirts. The delicate scent of lavender water. The precious voice saying, "I am sorry you have hurts, Julia. . . ." Because that was what she had always said, and Julia was who Uley had once been. "But learn from them, little one. Do not pump water from the well until you have the handle firmly in hand."

As Uley recollected it, the well handle had wrenched away from her of its own volition, smacking her in the left side of the nose and leaving a horrid green bruise that she'd worn for the better part of a week.

Until you have the handle firmly in hand.

Uley felt as if nothing in her life were firmly in hand at the moment.

Oh, Father. I don't even know what to ask for. If he's a guilty man, surely You'd want justice wrought. But, underneath, it seems he has a caring soul.

It took Uley the longest time to fall

134

asleep that night. She kept picturing her mother and pretending that her mother could explain the odd, uncertain ways of men to her. And, as she did finally drift off, she dreamed of a handsome man and blue eyes with as much fire in them as gold nuggets. A man who had touched her hair with one callused but gentle hand.

Santa Fe Moll opened the door of Ongewach's and frowned at Uley. "We ain't open this time of the mornin', boy. The girls work late."

"I'm not here for that, Moll," Uley said. "I just need to talk to Laura."

"Just need to talk, huh?" Moll fisted her green silk robe tighter around her arms and winked. "Maybe you wanna talk to me."

"No, ma'am. I need to talk to my friend only."

When Moll smiled, Uley could see remnants of tobacco leaves stuck all over her teeth. It was everything she could do not to step back three paces. "You know I don't allow my girls to give out their favors for free. You expect me to believe you'd only be *talking?* Everybody in town knows you're in love with that gal. If I let you up there, I expect to have my half of the money from Laura by lunchtime. Better yet, come back tonight. That's when things'll be in full swing around here."

"My pa won't let me come at night. I just need to ask her a question."

Indeed, Uley would never come around this place when business was going on. All the way over here, she'd been considering what it meant to come to such a place as this. But she wouldn't let fear or a sense of convention keep her from what needed to be done.

"Nope."

"Please."

"No, sir."

"Laura's my friend."

"And she's my upstairs girl."

"A gal's allowed to have friends, isn't she?"

"Any friends Tin Can Laura has cost two dollars an hour. And half of that goes to me."

"Seems like Laura's locked up just as tight as Aaron Brown was for hanging a man."

"There's different kinds of jails," Moll said, pulling a wad of tobacco out of a pouch and stuffing it into her cheek. "You oughta know that by now, boy."

Yes, Uley knew it. Oh, how well she knew it.

As Moll talked on and on about her profits, Uley noticed one bare foot descend the log steps. Two bare feet. Next came the hand-stitched, uneven hem of a flannel nightgown.

Laura tiptoed up behind Santa Fe Moll.

"I feed that gal. I give her a warm place to sleep and clothes to keep her dressed. Not just any clothes. *Pretty* things. Dresses the likes of which you could only find in Denver. I ain't lettin' anybody play around with what belongs to me. I've already lost money because of you. She could have sold that cat for at least twenty-five dollars. That would have given me twelve-fifty. But I'm figurin' I'll get it all back from you some other way. That is, seein' as how you're standing on my doorstep."

"Would you tell her I came looking for her?"

"Oh, no, boy. You come back tonight and wait your turn in line. You'll git plenty of time with her, same as everybody else."

"I just need to talk."

"Talkin'll be two dollars an hour, same as everything else."

Things sure did stay difficult, Uley decided as she watched Laura sneak back up the stairs again. There wasn't anything else she could do. She backed out of the doorway and away from Moll's tobacco-tainted breath.

"We'll see you this evening, son," the older woman said victoriously.

"No," Uley said. "You won't."

"Hey, Uley," came a voice from an upstairs window. "Don't turn around. I'm up here."

"I wouldn't think of turning around," Uley said. "She might charge me two dollars for it."

"I'll be down at the livery stable in an hour. Charles Ongewach is gonna pick up Moll's new carriage. I told him I'd go along and drive his wagon back. Can you come over there?"

"I'll miss part of the trial," Uley said. "And it doesn't sound like a very private place to talk."

"It will be. You wait."

"I've got to ask you something important."

"I'll answer you best as I can."

"I've got to *tell* you something important, too. More important than you can guess."

"I'll see you at the livery stable, Uley."

As it turned out, that morning was as good a time as any to leave the trial. John Kincaid practically went down every row, calling on every man in town who had the slightest interest in the case — and that was everybody — asking each one if he'd seen the defendant, Aaron Talephas Brown, actually *aiming* his gun at the marshal. Aaron sat at the front of the room beside the potbellied stove, his boot heels planted on the floor, one hand spread spiderlike on each knee, his eyes focused just above the heads of his accusers. Uley saw him scan the room just once, his eyes casting out over the crowd. His eyes paused when they came to her.

He stared right at her.

He didn't bother to hide it.

He sought her out in the room the way someone might seek out his best friend.

Oh, Father. If he's going to be hanged, help me know how to pray for this soul I've seen. And if You've got some other version of justice to be done, help that to come about, too.

There he sat, on trial for his life, and he was smiling at her. Smiling in a way that made her remember yesterday . . . her laughter, his chuckling, the new spring grass that had smelled dank and sweet as he crushed blades of it beneath his back.

She didn't hear anything else going on in the room.

She didn't hear the man just to her left shout, "Just because he didn't take time to aim, that don't mean he wasn't out to do a shooting."

She knew she needed to steal away and meet Laura. When she stood, she felt Aaron still watching her back, his eyes blazing into her back like two hot branding irons. She stepped over outstretched legs and scuffed boots, blindly trying to find her way to the door. She ran outside and up the street toward the stable. When she found Laura waiting beside the bright red wheels of a new carriage, she was still feeling the effects of Aaron's eyes locked upon her.

Chapter Seven

"Hey. I been waitin' for you the longest time," Laura said, raising one laced boot and placing it daintily on a spoke of the wheel.

"It wasn't too easy leaving that trial."

"How's it goin'? They gonna hang that man today?"

"Nobody knows what they'll decide. There's a lot of talking going on. Could even be next week before they do it." As she said it, a new and worrisome fear crept up inside Uley. Just suppose she started to care? Just suppose she started to care whether they hanged Aaron or not?

Uley trailed Laura to the far side of the livery stable. Laura swung high atop an old horse Uley knew belonged to Moll. "Come on," she said. "Follow me up. Charles and Hansen Smith are arguing price in there."

"He won't miss you if you leave?"

"Moll told him not to pay what they'd agreed on. She wants it for fifty dollars less. A hagglin' man forgets everything but what he's after. He'll be here all day. I ain't worried." Laura moved her small foot out of the stirrup so that Uley could swing up onto the horse. "Come on."

Uley obliged, noting with some satisfaction that Laura didn't think it necessary to ride sidesaddle. Uley swung up right behind her and wrapped arms around her friend's tiny, belted waist.

"Giddyap, Horace," Laura hollered, whacking the horse with her boot heels and making him bolt forward. They took off up the deserted street toward the north end of town. When they passed Jack Strater's cabin on the right, Laura turned Horace left, toward Willow Creek. "You ever been to the lily pond?" she called back over her shoulder.

"Nope. Never have been. Didn't know there was one."

"This is my peaceful place. Just wait 'til you see it."

The pond was a small, bean-shaped pool that reflected the clouds in the sky above it like a looking glass. Its edges were scalloped with brilliant green pads and floating yellow buds that would soon unfurl into flower.

"Isn't this the purtiest place?" Laura

asked as she slipped off the horse.

"Oh, it is," Uley agreed, flinging one leg over Horace and dismounting. It was a magical, hidden place, laced with the heavy fragrance of the coming blossoms.

Laura dropped Horace's reins, and the horse immediately clattered toward the water, lowering his head to snort and drink. Uley's friend seemed a different person as she raised her skirts and tiptoed through the mud to the water's edge. "I wait all year for the lilies to bloom," she told Uley. "This land belongs to Jack Strater. I don't get Christmas presents or birthday presents from Moll. The lilies are mine . . . least they are in my head, anyway. They come ready about the same time each spring."

"Strater doesn't mind you being down here?"

"Don't figure he knows. Don't figure anybody knows, except for the moose, and an elk or two. You're the first one I've brought down here, Uley. See —" she pointed to the mud "— there's been a moose down here waterin' since I was here yesterday afternoon."

"Thank you for sharing your place with me."

"You're welcome."

Horace moved away from the water, switching his tail at the early-spring flies and pulling up clumps of grass with his yellow teeth.

"What was it you wanted to ask me about, Uley?"

"I've got to tell you something first, Laura. And it isn't an easy thing to tell."

"Tellin' things is never easy." Laura swept up her skirts once more and ventured closer to the pads. Uley figured she was searching for a flower that was closer to blooming than the others. "I found that out a long time ago."

"This one is harder than most."

Laura sat down in the mud and pulled her boots off. "Hang on. I found a flower I want."

"Are you going to wade out?"

"I always do. You want a flower, Uley?"

"No. I suppose not." It would never do to be seen admiring flowers. But then she remembered what she'd come to do. It didn't matter. It didn't matter at all. "Yeah. Bring me one. I'd like to have one, too."

Laura wadded her skirts up to her knees and plunged in. "Ah!" she hollered. "This pond's fresh from the spring run-off. Feels like it should still be ice up on the mountain. My feet're already numb." She

144

splashed her way over to the pad she'd picked and snapped two buds off with one hand. She carried them back high atop her head, the hem of her skirt trailing behind her in the pool. "Here you go." She sat in the grass beneath a huge lodgepole pine and handed it up to Uley. Uley plopped down beside her. "Look at my toes." She leaned out over her knees and perused them. "They're purple. If I'd have been in there any longer, I'd have frozen them plum off."

"Willow Creek's cold like that this time of year, too," Uley commented. "Doc Gillette had to treat all of the placer miners last year for rheumatism in their hands."

Laura tucked her lily behind one ear. "Know what I like to pretend the most when I come down here? I like to pretend I'm a grand lady. Like that Miss Elizabeth Calderwood. Goin' out to a fancy barn dance with my beau on my arm. See?" She jumped up again and started to twirl around like a child playing in the wind. "It don't seem so farfetched when I've got a flower in my hair."

"I don't think it is farfetched," Uley said quietly. She knew the time for the telling was upon her.

"You're just saying that, you know. Just because you're my friend. And —" she blushed mightily "— because you might be sweet on me."

"No, Laura. That isn't it at all." Then she went on timidly. "I can say that . . . because I'm not who you think I am."

"What does that mean?"

"I've got the same dreams as you. I know that may sound funny, Laura, but it's true."

"How can you say it's true?" she asked innocently, still half smiling. "How can you know about the dreams and hopes of a girl?"

"Because —" Uley purposefully poked the lily stem up into the weave of her hat "— I am one."

Laura jumped up from the ground as quickly as if she'd just found herself seated beside a brown bear. "Don't you tell me that. Don't you sit there and expect me to believe that!"

Uley jumped up, too. "I expect you to believe it. You're the only one I can tell. The only other person who knows is my pa."

"I know I just met you," Laura said, "but I've known who you are for nigh on three years. Now you're tellin' me you're somebody *different?*"

"No. I'm not different. I'm just me. Who I have always been."

Laura took a step back and narrowed her eyes at Uley. "You can't be a gal."

"The clothes disguise it. Come on. Wrap your arms around my waist. Just the way I held on to you while we were riding Horace. You'll know it."

Skeptically Tin Can Laura reached one palm and touched the side seam on Uley's sweater. She followed with the second palm.

Laura gripped the sweater with both hands and squeezed. Her hands inched in . . . and in . . . and in. At last, they found Uley's shape beneath the shirt. She didn't have a tiny waist by any means, but it definitely tucked in at the right place, then splayed out again where a feminine body would curve into hips. "Uley? I would never have known."

"I told you."

"Did your mama give birth to a girl child and name it Uley?"

"No. But that's what you have to call me. It's what everybody thinks. Wouldn't do to change that now."

"You're a gal."

"I am."

"But why are you keeping it a secret?"

Uley told Laura the story of her mother dying on the way here, before they'd even made it west of Ohio, and her aunt Delilah, who'd offered to keep her so that her father could come to Tin Cup to follow his dream.

"My father never *will* get rich. He worked his own claim when we first got here, but he never found anything. That dream was theirs, Laura. It belonged to both of them. My mama, too. She's the one who had to die for it. I sure wasn't going to stay back there with Aunt Delilah. I wanted to come and do my share of the work. When we got closer, and Pa found out what kind of camp Tin Cup was, this was the only way he'd let me come. So I did it." She couldn't help the pang of conscience for the deception she'd made. She'd never known how wrong this would feel. "I didn't know how confused I'd feel about things sometimes."

As she spoke, Laura's gray eyes grew round and full of sparkle. By the time Uley had finished the tale, Laura's grin spread all the way from one dimple to the other. "That means you really *are* my friend."

"Of course I really am your friend. That's what I've been trying to tell you."

"But I thought you were sweet on me.

And that's why . . . why you wanted to be with me." Laura was starting to stumble over her words. Maybe it wasn't right to discuss these things with a real girl. A real *lady*. "Because you were a boy."

Uley smiled. She sat back down and flopped flat on the ground. "You cannot imagine how good it feels to have finally told somebody."

"That day you rescued me from the storm. Your pa knew what I was. He let me come with you anyway."

"Yes, he did."

"You helped me. I would have frozen stiff out there."

"I think so, too."

"You —" Laura couldn't quit staring at the girl sprawled out in the shade. "You jumped on Aaron Brown and knocked him flat in the dirt. You saved the marshal."

Uley sat up again and wrapped her arms around her knees. "I've done many things that aren't . . . natural. . . ."

"Uley. You are a regular lady. You shouldn't be goin' around with me."

"You are my friend," Uley said kindly. "That's what matters. Not what you do. I'm a timberman in the Gold Cup Mine, you know."

"But you saved my life."

"And you gave me a kitten for it. And now, Laura, you may very well save my life, too."

"What do you mean?"

"I have questions to ask you."

"About what."

"About men."

"Uley, you should know all about men. For three years, I've thought you *were* one."

"I don't know about men in this certain way."

"Oh."

"I have no one else to ask. Mama is gone. You're the only one who can help me."

Laura plopped down beside her. "I've never had anyone ask me for help before."

"I need to know things, and I need to know them quickly."

"What? I'll answer you."

"When you start caring for a man, does it make you feel different? Or special? Or wise? Or happy? Or sad? Is it wonderful? Or is it detestable?"

"Goodness, Uley. Slow down. I can't answer all those questions at once."

"Try. Try to tell me. . . ."

"What man? Surely no one. They all think you're a fellow yourself."

"Oh, Laura. Just tell it."

"If you cared about someone as you say," Laura said, "you would know the answers."

"Not necessarily. Laura, I'm afraid."

"Ain't nothin' to be afraid about, Uley. You'll see when the time comes. Fellows are generally all the same —" Laura picked up a rock and started scratching lines in the dirt "— except when one thing happens."

"What one thing?"

"When you fall in love with one of 'em. That makes everything turn topsy-turvy, it does."

"Do you know about it?" Uley asked. "Have you ever fallen in love with one of them, Laura?"

The scratches in the dirt grew deeper. "Once. It was a long time ago. Back in Pitkin, before I moved over the pass."

"Do you mind talking about it?"

"Never talked about it before now. Nobody's ever asked me about such things."

Uley waited.

"Every time he came around, I felt something different. Something awful and wonderful and so strong I couldn't sleep most nights. When a man you love kisses you, Uley, you feel like everything inside of you is so warm you're gonna melt right there where you're standing, just like those

151

lit candles melt at Ongewach's, in the vestibule."

When the afternoon session of the trial began, John Kincaid said: "Judge Murphy, I call the next witness for the defense to come forward — Elizabeth Calderwood."

Elizabeth Calderwood? Uley pondered. What could she know about the night Aaron stepped out of the darkness?

Elizabeth stood and smoothed down her skirts, stepping carefully between the pine chairs and up onto the platform. So many men were packed around her that there was scarcely room for her skirts. Whispers shot through the crowd once more. Today Elizabeth wore a creamy muslin lined with ribbons as soft a shade as butter. The ribbons flounced prettily as she placed herself beside Murphy and laid one daintily gloved hand atop the massive Bible.

"I, Elizabeth Calderwood, do solemnly swear . . ."

It seemed to Uley that every man in the room took one step forward, crowding closer to her, exactly the way they'd crowd through the door of the assay office to examine the day's intake of ore. "Now, Miss Calderwood," Kincaid said, "may we proceed?"

"It is *Mrs.* Calderwood, sir," Elizabeth said. "I have been married once."

"Yes. Very well. *Mrs.* Calderwood. Will you tell us what you know of the relationship between Aaron Brown and Harris Olney?"

"Yes." Elizabeth twisted the lace-edged handkerchief she held in both hands. "Harris and Aaron have known each other a long time — since they were boys." Elizabeth spoke in a light alto voice, smiling at Aaron. "They used to play together in the churchyard. I used to watch them. I used to beg them to let me play, too, except they wouldn't. I was a girl, you see, and they'd both decided I was too scrawny to be much good at climbing trees or fishing for cutthroats in the streams."

"So Harris Olney and Aaron Brown are lifetime friends, Mrs. Calderwood?"

"No. They've known each other a lifetime. I wouldn't call them friends." She shook her head at the attorney, tossing her curls about her shoulders. "Not now."

"What occurred, Mrs. Calderwood, to change all that?"

"A piece of land," Elizabeth said, "and a French soldier's grave."

"Tell me more."

"We owned a cattle ranch on the Cache

la Poudre River, just north of Fort Collins. The French soldiers, when they were in Colorado sixty years ago, buried all their black powder on the banks of the river. Some say the soldiers found gold in the Poudre. Some believe —" here she glanced pointedly at Harris Olney "— they buried the gold for fear their commanding officer would make them turn it over to the government."

"Yes?"

"Atop a knoll, about a mile from our house on the ranch, is one indentation in the ground, three feet across and six feet long, and marked with a stone. We believed, my husband and I, that the place was the simple grave of a young soldier. Harris saw the indentation and thought differently. He tried to convince my husband, Fred, to dig up the hole and find out what was beneath it. But Fred wasn't one to disturb a final resting place. He told Harris to leave well enough alone."

Otto Violet, the attorney representing the state of Colorado, rose from his seat and began stalking back and forth in front of the podium. "What does this long tale have to do with Aaron Brown and Harris Olney, Miss Calderwood? Could you get to the point, *please?*"

Elizabeth frowned. "It is *Mrs.* Calder-wood. I believe I've already mentioned that once. And I am getting to the point, Mr. Violet. It isn't easily shortened."

"Please —" he rolled his eyes and poked out his protruding belly "— do leave out the extraneous details, Mrs. Calderwood."

"We heard the dogs baying the next night, Mr. Violet. My husband grabbed his six-shooter and climbed atop the knoll. There he found Harris Olney digging into the indentation. Fred ordered him off."

"Continue," Kincaid said, obviously stepping in front of the pacing Violet to assert his authority.

Uley watched as Elizabeth's eyes began to fill with tears. She dabbed at them with one corner of the hanky. "It is difficult to continue, Mr. Kincaid. Two days later, my husband mysteriously disappeared. Many of the fort's residents saw a band of Utes roving across the valley. Harris volunteered to follow the tribe and spy on them, saying he believed they might have taken Fred captive. At the time, I didn't understand how such a thing could be possible. The Utes were a friendly people. Fred greeted them often when they came past Fort Collins." Her voice broke here, and she couldn't go on.

"Come on," Violet hollered. "We haven't got all day for this. I want to hang this low-life tomorrow morning at sunrise."

The tirade clearly shored Elizabeth up. She lifted her chin and spoke, her eyes locked on Harris Olney's as if he were the only man sitting in the room. "Three days later, he returned with my husband's body. Harris said the Utes had killed Fred and left him on a post near their campsite. But I think he killed Fred —" there was a sudden uproar in the courtroom, and Judge Murphy was helpless to stop it "— while they journeyed together toward home."

"What are you saying, Beth?" Olney jumped from his seat. "I was the one who stepped in and helped you after Fred died. I was the one . . ."

"You are the one who went back up on that knoll and dug up a man's grave. I figure you would have stayed around digging forever if Aaron hadn't come riding into town two days later, shouting about what he'd witnessed out in the wilderness."

"I had to know about that grave. A man has natural curiosities."

"This man —" Elizabeth said, pointing at Harris "— has natural greed. He killed my husband for a chance at gold, then carried his body into Fort Collins like a mourning friend."

Murphy thwacked his tin cup on the podium over and over again. "Order! Order!" Still Elizabeth and Harris squared off, shouting at one another over the din of the crowd.

"Listen to me!" Harris shouted. "How can you say such things? I was in love with you, Beth! This has nothing to do with Fred."

Uley felt her heart plummet. This was torture of the worst kind, virtually unbearable. Was every man in the *world* in love with Elizabeth Calderwood? First Aaron, then a dead husband named Fred, and now even Harris Olney?

"Order!" Murphy shouted, still banging the cup. "Order! Now! Or we won't go on at all." He began bellowing out names like an angry schoolmarm. "Wilson! You're out of here. Toby! Right behind him. Charley Johnson! You, too. You can stay out in the street until you're calm enough to be quiet and sit down." He waited, stern-faced and solemn, while the men did his bidding. Then, at last, he turned to Elizabeth. "I fail to see what any of this has to do with Aaron Brown and the fact that he pulled a gun on our marshal."

"You see —" Elizabeth cast her eyes downward, meeting the inquisitive gazes of the spectators "— Aaron was afraid Harris would come to some harm at the hands of the Utes. He followed Harris up Poudre Canyon. He was just about to go in and help rescue both of them when he saw Harris and my husband leaving the Ute camp alive."

Nobody spoke for a good long while. Elizabeth sat in the chair, her hands clasped together, obviously fighting for composure. "So there you have it," she went on shakily. "Harris didn't know he had anything to fear until the hour Aaron rode back into town and confronted him with what he'd seen. Within the hour, Harris disappeared from Fort Collins. It took Aaron almost a year to find this man holed up here in Tin Cup, acting as if he liked upholding the law instead of breaking it."

Harris pounded upon the chair in front of him. "You don't know what you're talking about, Beth! A woman's mouth . . ."

"I tried to convince Aaron not to come. Every man I've ever loved has been lost. I can tell you, sir, that Aaron never intended to murder Harris Olney. His only plan was to bring Harris back to Fort Collins to receive his just reward, in a courtroom just like this one."

"You're certain of that?"

"Yes, sir. I am. Aaron spoke of it at length to me and my mother, though we discouraged him in his endeavors. You could send for the pastor of our Baptist church, sir. We prayed about it constantly after Aaron left home, that some blessing would come along and stand in the way of what might become a bloody altercation. I believe that prayer was answered, though I see that God answers us in improbable ways. I never asked God to land my brother in jail and on trial for murder."

It took precious seconds for Elizabeth's words to reach the thoughts in Uley's head.

I never asked God to land my brother in jail and on trial for murder.

My brother . . .

A wild thrum of expectation began to spread through Uley's vitals. Her brother? Aaron Brown was Mrs. Elizabeth Calderwood's *brother?*

A tiny seed of hope began to grow within her, and with it came a totally unexpected outburst of joy.

Who cared whether Aaron Brown had tried to do away with Harris Olney?

She'd deal with that the next hour . . . the next day. . . .

For now, she only remembered the way Aaron Brown had examined her hair with one leather-tanned finger, the way he'd sprawled beside her in the grass, the way he'd examined her face as if his eyes could delve deep into her spirit.

She felt a woman for the first time in her life.

She felt an aching for the first time in her life . . . an anticipation.

Elizabeth was his sister. A sister, one he might set out to love, protect and honor all his life in deference to the family name! Elizabeth, dainty, particular Elizabeth, with eyes like cornflowers and hair the color of midday sunshine, didn't belong to Aaron at all except by blood relation.

"So you see," Elizabeth continued on the stand, her countenance regained, unaware of the turmoil and expectation her words launched in Uley Kirkland's heart, "you cannot fault Aaron for what has happened here. He was only doing what he believed right . . . to protect and vindicate his sister by searching out the man who has taken a terrible toll from my own life."

Harris wasn't taking things lying down. "You have no right to make accusations like that one, Beth. You don't know what's in my heart. You never —"

Aaron was on his feet in an instant. The two men on either side of him jumped up to restrain him. "She was a married woman, Harris. Whatever your motivation was, you had no right to be bothering her. You put Beth in question. If you'd loved her truly, you never would have done that. Then, when her husband turned up dead —"

"Stop it," Elizabeth told them both. "I won't have it from either of you. This isn't the —"

"Mr. Kincaid," Judge Murphy said from the bench, "kindly dismiss Mrs. Calderwood and call the defendant forward. I have questions to ask the man myself."

"Yes, sir," John Kincaid said, extending one hand to Elizabeth's and helping her down. "I call the defendant, Mr. Aaron Talephas Brown, to the stand."

Aaron shook free of the two men who continued to hold him and walked forward with determined steps. He seemed a different man from the one Uley had peered at through the bars at the jailhouse. He wore the black suit she'd examined in his room down at the Grand Central Hotel, with a white linen shirt and the bolo tie —

two black leather thongs gathered together by a dollar-sized circle of horn. Looped into his pocket she could see the gold chain leading to the watch inscribed by his mother.

He'd cleaned up nicely.

And determination did him justice, she thought, as he strode past her toward the witness stand, pausing — it was just a hint of a pause, really — beside her leg. Without even looking down, he seemed to know she was there.

He strode on forward, his wide shoulders stretching the fabric of the coat, his dark hair cut in a straight line across the back of his neck to barely brush the stiff line of his collar. He lifted his Stetson off his head with one hand and held it there, while he put his other hand — a hand Uley remembered well, with fingers that were slim, and brown as honey oak — upon the Bible.

"I, Aaron Talephas Brown, do solemnly swear to tell the truth, the whole truth . . ." He turned sideways as he spoke. A crease in his hair from the seam in the Stetson circled his head like a halo. Uley could see he'd been to the barber. At the end of each sideburn, skin the same texture and color as a finely rubbed saddlebag gave way to a half inch of white where sun hadn't recently touched his face.

He positioned himself in the chair, his polished black boots set with heels and toes aligned, and for some reason — some unknown, wonderful reason — his eyes found hers.

"I have a great many questions, Mr. Brown," Judge J. M. Murphy stated, leaning so far forward on his hands to get a good look at the defendant that his elbows made him resemble an overgrown grasshopper. "Do you agree with the story your sister, Mrs. Elizabeth Calderwood, just gave witness to on this stand?"

"I do, Your Honor."

"You came to Tin Cup in order to subdue Harris Olney and carry him back with you to a trial in Larimer County?"

"I did, Your Honor."

"Why, then, did you have your gun drawn on him? Did you suppose you'd be more persuasive that way?"

"I wouldn't have approached Harris Olney in any other fashion, Your Honor. Harris is the marshal. I knew he'd be carrying a sidearm."

"Did you stop to think," Murphy asked, "what it would look like when you pulled that gun?"

"He was after me," Harris shouted, outraged. "He's always been after me."

"Sit down, Olney." Murphy scowled down his nose at the marshal. "I'm the judge in this county, not you. I'll thank you to remember that, or I'll throw you into the street, too." He turned back to the man on the stand. "Is there anybody you can think of, anybody at all, who saw what happened in that Ute camp? These men —" he nodded to indicate the jury "— need to hear the story from an impartial witness before they can make an honest decision."

"Yes. Old Dawson Hayes. He spends most his time trapping up and down the canyon, and he's known to follow the Utes because they know the best places to find varmints."

"Where can we find this Mr. Hayes?" Murphy asked.

"Probably out trading pelts with the Utes," Harris hollered. "That Hayes is the craziest old man in Colorado. You can't tell me you want to rest this case on —"

"Out!" Murphy shouted. "Out! Didn't I tell you to shut up and be quiet? I can't run a trial in here with everybody jumping in like corn jumping in a fry pan! Out."

Harris jammed his hat on and headed for the door. "What is a trial for if you can't get loud and express your mind about somebody?"

"You've expressed your mind just fine," Murphy said. "It's Aaron Brown's turn. Now out with you."

Harris stalked into the front foyer and stomped down the new wooden steps outside.

Murphy waited until the top of Harris's head passed by the last window. Then he sighed resignedly and leaned back in his seat. "Don't see how we can go much further with this trial, Brown. We've got a pretty young lady here who says she's your sister. Other than that, it's his word against yours. And Olney's word carries some weight here in Gunnison County."

"I'm aware of that," Aaron told him.

"You got any way to get word to Dawson Hayes? Could you send a message and get him here?"

"I don't know, Murphy. I don't rightly know."

"Confound it." Murphy rose and gazed down at the rows of miners below him. "A man's got to have the wisdom of Solomon to do this job. Anybody here want to offer up an opinion?"

"Yeah," somebody shouted. "I'd like to hear what Dawson Hayes has to say."

"Me too," somebody else chimed in.

Uley looked from one side to another. Everybody around her seemed to agree. Her spirit felt as if it were sprouting wings, starting to soar. Everything good seemed to be showering down in one day. First, Elizabeth. Now, perhaps, a reprieve in Aaron's trial. "Me too," she hollered, raising one knotted fist into the air. "I want to hear what Hayes would tell us!"

"That's it, then," Murphy bellowed, rapping the wood one last time with his cup. "Your decision is also mine." He clasped his hands behind his lower spine and began to pace back and forth. "We'll give Dawson Hayes three weeks, Brown. That's all."

Three weeks, Uley thought. Only three weeks? It would take Hayes almost that long just to get here.

"If this fellow arrives in Tin Cup willing to tell his side of the story, we'll listen to it."

"That'll give me a fighting chance," Aaron said.

Murphy hurried to finish before the ruckus began all over again. "If that man doesn't show his face in this town by three p.m. on the seventeenth of May, we'll call this jury back together and get these men to make a decision based on what they know. I'm not waiting all summer to resolve this problem. In three weeks, it'll all be over — one way or another."

The confusion began in earnest. The men bellowed and slapped each other in greeting. In one corner of the town hall, a good fist-slugging fight was beginning to heat up.

Aaron rose, shook Murphy's hand with a firm grasp and began to make his way toward the door. Elizabeth elbowed her way through the crowd to follow him. All around Uley, men were fishing money out of their pockets and making wagers.

"Two dollars says he'll hang."

"Three bits says that man Hayes'll never show his face this side of the Divide."

"I'll take you up on that. Three bits says Hayes'll come but Brown'll hang anyway. Olney ain't gonna let any man get away with what he's tryin' to do."

"Four dollars says the man stands a chance. He's gotten this far, after all."

"Nope. I'll go the round with you. Four dollars says it's a hanging jury. We'll be watching Brown swing from a cottonwood tree May the eighteenth."

Uley pushed her way past all of them, sickening at the thought that Aaron

Brown's life had been reduced to an object of entertainment and speculation. If there had been a preacher in this town, the men wouldn't have been wagering in the streets. In her heart of hearts, she had to admit Aaron might be telling the truth. After she'd detained him, pitched him down and sat upon him, he very well might have killed her — if he'd been intent on gunning Olney down.

Perhaps, perhaps, he hadn't been.

It seemed as if Uley's life had irrevocably rushed ahead of her, in one day — no, in four short hours.

Laura knew Uley had been born a female.

Uley knew Elizabeth and Aaron had been born brother and sister.

And Aaron had three weeks, to prove to her — to everyone — that he wasn't guilty of the charge against him.

Three weeks.

Twenty-one days.

Which wasn't very long at all.

Chapter Eight

When Uley knocked on the upstairs door at Frank Emerson's Pacific Hotel and Elizabeth Calderwood opened it, Uley never once stopped to think that Elizabeth might consider it odd that she didn't sweep off her woven cap and extend her a hearty greeting. Her mind had traveled well past such things. Her heart was clattering inside her rib cage the way a smithy's hammer clangs against iron.

"I've come to see Aaron. Is he here?"

"Yes, of course." Elizabeth frowned. "He's composing a letter at the moment. Who should I say is — ?"

"I'm Uley. Uley Kirkland." As an afterthought, Uley stuck one hand out to Aaron's sister. "Nice to meet you, ma'am. Glad to have you in Tin Cup."

Elizabeth cast one more glance her way. "Come in, please. I'll summon my brother."

Uley followed Elizabeth past a sturdy bed built entirely of lodgepole logs and draped with a yellow quilt. Elizabeth opened the heavy pine door leading to the adjoining room and stepped inside. There sat Aaron, perched on a stool and laboring at a desk that must have been of his own making — two barrels stood on end, with a wooden plank stretching between them. He was working laboriously at his letter, dipping his pen into the inkwell, then letting it remain there while he stared at the same blue stationery Uley had once gone to fetch from the Grand Central. His head slumped toward the page, his fingers jutting up through his hair.

As Uley watched from behind Elizabeth, the right words seemed to come all in a bunch. Aaron grabbed the pen from the well and began scratching them out, writing several sentences before he sank the pen back into the well and stuck his fingers back into his clove-coloured hair to begin the process again.

"Some young man's here to see you, brother," Elizabeth told him.

He raised his head. "Don't know who'd want to see me."

"Uley Kirkland."

"Uley?" His neck straightened, and he rose from the stool. The pen and well wobbled dangerously in his haste, but not enough to splatter the desktop. "She — He — Where?"

"Here, Aaron." Uley stepped out from behind Elizabeth and moved toward him. "I just wanted to . . . I don't know . . . thought perhaps . . ." She wasn't at liberty to speak to him frankly while Elizabeth was there with them. A sudden thought saved her. "Perhaps you wanted me to post that letter when the supply wagon goes out tomorrow at noon."

"This time I am capable of posting my own letter," he said, moving forward and casting his eyes down at her. "I am not locked in the jailhouse anymore."

"Thank goodness."

"You think that's appropriate? That Murphy let me have time like this? To find Hayes?"

"Maybe. Yes. I'm wondering, thinking I shouldn't have been the one to stop all of it that night. I don't know." She had a great many things to say, but now that she was here she didn't know how to say them.

Aaron had many things to say, as well. "You are questioning my guilt?"

"Indeed I am, Aaron Brown," she said, ever so softly.

His Stetson lay brim side up on the washstand beside him. He picked it up with one hand and settled it atop his head, then turned to his sister. "Elizabeth, will you excuse us for an hour this evening? Uley and I have matters to discuss. I believe we'll go for a carriage ride."

"A *carriage* ride?" Elizabeth asked, clearly astonished. "With this young fellow?"

"Yes," Aaron said. "Will you come, Uley?"

Uley peered up at Aaron to see his eyes sparkling with mirth beneath the brim of his hat. Elizabeth probably thought her brother had gone mad during his long, tedious days waiting for justice. "It isn't necessary, Mr. Brown," Uley said. But she wanted to say instead, *I'd love to take a carriage ride, Aaron. A carriage ride would be my pleasure.* But she couldn't. Elizabeth Calderwood certainly wouldn't expect a young fellow to say that.

It was as if Aaron read every thought in her eyes. "I hoped you'd agree. Good evening, Elizabeth."

"Aaron."

"I won't be gone long."

"Is it safe for you to be roaming the streets? Suppose a lynch mob decided to take matters into their own hands? And what about Harris Olney?"

"You think Olney would go after me and jeopardize his chance to go scot-free? He's too smart for that. Besides —" He turned to Uley again and winked. *Winked,* for the second time since she'd known him. "Besides, Uley isn't going to let anybody get away with anything. The people in this town know that. They wouldn't try anything with Uley along."

Elizabeth looked skeptically at the small figure standing beside her brother, a figure whose face had turned decidedly pink. "Very well," she said. "I learned years ago that it does no good to warn you of things."

"You're right. It doesn't."

Uley followed him down the carpeted steps at the Pacific Hotel, tromping with her boots in exactly the same cadence as the man two steps ahead of her. How long will I descend stairs this way? she wondered for some absurd reason. She wished she could do it somewhat differently, gliding downward with toes pointed beneath ruffled skirts, sliding one gloved hand along the fancy mahogany banister until she reached the ground.

What might Aaron say if he turned to see her coming toward him in such a manner?

She knew she was getting what she deserved after all. She lived entangled by a snare of her own design. She had taken matters into her own hands without a thought to the honesty of her ways, without a thought to what the implications might be. *Oh, Father. Are You teaching me this? Was I listening to You when I chose this, or was I listening to an answer of my own making?*

She didn't speak to him again until they reached Washington Avenue. "Uley isn't going to let anybody get away with anything?" she said, mimicking him. "The people in this town wouldn't try anything with Uley along?"

"Well —" he shrugged and grinned mightily "— I had to tell her something, didn't I?"

"You make me sound as if *I'm* the marshal of this town."

"You very well should be. You're the one who brought me in, after all. Let's go this way —" he pointed "— to the livery stable."

"I wondered where you'd find a carriage," she said. "Don't have many carriages around Tin Cup, Colorado."

He glanced down at her fondly. "A gal like you deserves a ride in a carriage, Uley.

174

I saw one over here the other day, one with shiny red wheels and a cushioned velvet seat the likes of which I haven't seen since the last time I left home. I've the money to pay for it."

"It isn't there. Santa Fe Moll bought it this morning."

She didn't understand why he looked so disappointed. "And just how do you know that?"

"I met Laura over there. Charles Ongewach did the bargaining, and Laura rode the extra horse. We did some talking about things . . ."

"What things?"

About how a woman feels when a man looks at me the way you do. Because I had to know. Because of how I feel when you come around me. "Just things."

"Things gals talk about?"

"I suppose."

They'd almost arrived at the stable. Aaron laid one hand on her arm in the darkness. Uley felt all her hairs rise on end as his fingers sent a shock coursing through her like the water in Willow Creek running downstream over rocks. Each time Aaron grazed his fingers against her skin, she felt as if his touch might sweep her away. "Laura knows, then."

"I told her today." The look he saw in her eyes spoke of many things, among them joy at having shared it, given it over at last to the confidence of a friend.

"I'm not the only one who knows anymore." He knew it was selfish, but he'd enjoyed being her only confidant. In some inexplicable way, the knowledge had tied her to him. Now he felt as if, in telling Laura, she were pulling free.

"Look," she said, tugging at his sleeve. "There's our carriage."

In front of the livery stable stood a dilapidated supply wagon, its splintering sideboards weathered to a dun gray.

"That isn't the vehicle I had in mind." Aaron guided her past the wide double gates and the sign reading H. H. Smith & Co. fronting Washington Avenue. Around the corner on Walnut Street, they both could see the firelight flickering through the uneven glass panes of Hansen Smith's cabin, throwing oblique golden shapes onto the ground outside. Aaron knocked on the door.

Smith answered it, squinting out into the darkness. "What's going on out here?"

"I'm here to hire that carriage you had parked out in front this morning."

"Can't do that," Smith said. "Sold that

176

carriage to Santa Fe Moll and Charles Ongewach."

"I'll have another one, then."

"Don't have another. Took me seven months to order that one and get it in over the Continental Divide."

"Do you have anything that would be worthy of —" He stopped. He'd been about to say, "Worthy of a lady." He certainly couldn't expound on that subject when it was Uley riding by his side. "Worthy of a ride through the trees this evening?"

"Only thing I've got is that wagon out front. Did you see it?"

"I did."

"For the right price, I'll come out and hitch up the mules."

"Don't want mules. I want horses. The finest ones you've got."

"You planning on doing something spectacular, Brown? Mules'll pull that wagon just fine."

Aaron sighed and reached toward his pocket. He kept forgetting he wasn't on the Eastern Slope. On the eastern side of the Rockies, a gentleman would never take a lady out for a jaunt behind two mules. He'd better get used to this, he decided. He was guaranteed only three more weeks of life. And every one of those last days would be spent here in Tin Cup, minding the gold camp, spending time with Uley and fuming over what Harris Olney had tried to do to his sister. "Are mules my only choice?"

"Won't have horses until next month, when I buy what's left of Jason Farley's estate. He had three horses over there I'm sore in need of."

"I'll have the mules."

"You two come on in by the fire while I go open up the barn," Smith said. "Won't take long." He passed Uley in the yard and smacked her on the back. "You getting lucky, boy. Ongewach and I figured you were alone with Tin Can Laura almost three hours today. If Moll finds out, she'll charge you."

He hurried on.

Aaron stepped in beside the fire and grinned at Uley as the fire glimmered against her face. "Your friendship with Laura doesn't come easy, does it?"

"No," she said, shaking her head. "It doesn't." She stared into the crackling flames a moment before she went on. *I'm afraid, Father. Is this something of my own making too, or that You're calling me for?* "I don't suppose it would come any easier if they knew I was a gal, either. Maybe it would be even worse."

Hansen Smith came back five minutes later and informed them that he'd harnessed the mules.

"We'll be back in an hour," Aaron told him.

"I'll be in bed by then," Hansen Smith instructed them. "Just tie the lead mule to the rail when you get back."

After Hansen Smith's fire, the darkness seemed to close in around them as Aaron easily lifted Uley to her spot in the wagon. She scooted across the seat to reach for the reins and felt splinters pierce her underside.

"Don't scoot," she warned Aaron. "You'll be sittin' on a seatful of splinters, just like I am."

After he climbed up, he reached behind them and pulled out two wool blankets. One he folded and set on the seat beside her. "There you go, ma'am," he said, teasing her. "No more discomfort for you. Here's the velvet cushion I promised." The second blanket he draped about her shoulders.

The breeze had dropped at dusk, but a dry chill always crept in at night this close to the timberline. The clear-star cold of evening came as a vast difference from the fireside in Hansen Smith's cabin. "Yah!" Aaron bellowed as he flipped the reins. "Get on now, mules. . . ."

The wagon lurched forward and, unaware, Uley placed one small hand upon Aaron's knee for balance. The harnesses rattled and the hooves clattered against the stones in the street.

Without speaking, Aaron turned the team toward the north, heading downstream with the creek. They heard it dancing along beside them for a while, dashing over rocks and doubling back to bubble against its banks. For a time they wound among the trees, the great, spindly lodgepoles jutting against the starlit sky. The sharp tang of pine mixed with the fertile loamy scent of spring, and the air was redolent with the smell of things just beginning to grow.

Uley suddenly realized where she'd laid her hand.

She pulled it back swiftly and placed it beside her on the ancient seat, atop the blanket.

At her movement, Aaron looked across at her. When she began to redden, he quickly looked ahead.

Uley stared straight on, pretending not to notice. Oh, but she did . . . she did.

From their left in the darkness came the croaking sounds of frogs echoing back and forth. It was early yet for such a seasonal proclamation. Uley grinned. "They're like us, aren't they?"

"Who is like us?"

"The frogs."

Aaron slapped the reins once more, and the mules picked up their pace. "I don't know that I like being compared to something that has grown from a pollywog."

"I mean they can't wait for things. They've found puddles already, and they're croaking as if they've found a marsh when all they've found is a muddy spot in the meadow grasses."

"Ah," he said. "But when the puddle dries, the frog will find another home."

"Crazy frogs," Uley commented. "They think they've got one thing when they've got something altogether different."

"Reminds me of you," Aaron said, very quietly.

They fell silent again.

Sorry was the man, Aaron thought, who took a lady for a jaunt behind mules. No one could know how disappointed he was at not having been able to hire the carriage. He'd been wishing to take Uley for a ride ever since he'd seen the fancy contraption parked out in front of the livery early this morning. This was another of the things he'd grow used to, he supposed, spending weeks in a forsaken mining camp, a place where the town's madam drove a vehicle so extravagant it took seven months to bring it in over the Divide.

He'd had great plans. With the carriage, he'd wanted to make Uley feel . . . what? Like the lady he thought she wanted to be? Like the young woman he couldn't help but see in her?

They rode on in silence, two stiff forms silhouetted against the stars, shoulder to shoulder, inches apart, faces turned toward the lane. Their hands — oh, how conscious Aaron was of their hands. His hands gripped the reins, while her hands gripped the blanket around her shoulders. His hands drenched the leather with sweat, while hers trembled from the chill.

Aaron thought of her tiny hand grasping his knee. He thought of the way her fingers had curled against his leg, depending on him for balance. Remembrance of her touch sent an agitated sensation skittering across his skin.

As Uley sat beside him now, she found herself fully aware of Aaron, certain that this moment would come back each time she smelled the sage or perused the stars or sat atop a wagon.

It was she who spoke at last. "I hadn't meant to interrupt your letter-writing. I know you haven't any time to waste getting your message off to Dawson Hayes."

"I needed time away to think, Uley. The words weren't coming. And Elizabeth kept peering over my shoulder like a headmistress waiting to rap my knuckles with a ruler."

"You think he'll come?"

"I think I'll be lucky if the letter ever reaches him."

They'd broken through the trees now, and ahead of them, as a V of land opened up into a wide-spread valley, lay the sage flats and the ranch that had been Jason Farley's. The surrounding hills crested in a loaf-shaped butte to their right, from which rose the massive, ghostly crags of the Saguache Mountains. A nighthawk whistled through the air as he dove toward the field to scoop up an evening-hatch fly.

"What does Saguache mean?" Aaron asked, still feeling the newcomer. "It's Ute, isn't it?"

She nodded. "It means *Blue Earth.* I've always thought it the perfect name for them. Don't you?"

He reined the mules to a stop, and they sat awhile, each silently surveying the majesty of the summit which rose high above them, glowing silver in the moonlight. "I do."

As Uley gazed up at the snow-encrusted line of peaks that formed the Continental Divide, Aaron couldn't help but study the profile of her face, its lines — which he saw now as delicate and ladylike — etched velvet-soft in the moon's glow. Suppose . . . just suppose . . . I were to reach across and kiss her, he pondered. What then? For both of us?

As if she'd sensed his thought, she turned from the mountains to face him. Even as he saw his wishes reflected in her eyes, he knew he dared not succumb to them. He had no right to devastate her so. In three weeks, he might very well be a dead man.

He slapped the mules with the reins.

Uley glanced away, but not before he saw her anticipation turn to disappointment in her eyes.

I'm sorry, he wanted to say. *I can't make you care for me, Uley. I've asked too much of you already.*

She watched without speaking as he directed the team into a wide arc in the road and headed them back toward Tin Cup.

She's not the type to take a kiss lightly, Brown, so you'd better make very sure you're willing to involve her heart in this before you do.

As the wagon rattled back to town they both sat rigid as planks, inventing their own private stories to explain away the thing that had just happened between them.

After she sent me sprawling in the dirt and turned me in to the marshal, Aaron thought, she wouldn't be happy if I tried to kiss her. No matter if I began to care for her, I'm a common criminal who'll probably hang.

After he had to *make* me bring his stationery and post his letter, Uley thought, he wouldn't want to kiss me. *Oh, Father. No matter if I care for him, no matter if I'm a gal, after what I've done, I'll never be a proper lady in his sight or in the sight of this town.*

Ahead of them, the store fronts along Washington Avenue appeared against the trees. Only a few were dark at this late hour. The others were saloons, open all night tonight, because the miners had just been paid. Lantern light radiated from storefront after storefront. As Aaron and Uley wheeled past Frenchy's Place, the

swinging front gate gave way, and out top-
pled a drunken miner, his stein of beer still
held high, despite the tangled condition of
his legs.

"A toast," the man shouted into the
streets. "A toast to our proud marshal! He
is gonna hang that yellow-bellied —" he
weaved to the left "— gun-totin' —" he
weaved to the right "— good-for-nothin' —"
his left leg went right, and his right leg
went left "— skunk." The man's hairy, bul-
bous body went down, face first. The stein
shattered. Beer hit the dirt, making nickel-
sized circles in the dust.

As a second inebriated miner left
Frenchy's, the swinging doors flapped
open long enough to illuminate Aaron's
profile. His jaw was set rock-hard. "Better
be getting you home, Uley. I've got a letter
to write tonight."

"I hope it gets to Dawson Hayes,
Aaron," she said. "I really do."

The wagon and the mules clattered on
through town, past the town hall, where, in
three weeks' time, Aaron's fate would be
decided. He didn't even cast a glance in its
direction. "Elizabeth and I'll be moving tomorrow morning," he said. "We can't afford two rooms in the Pacific Hotel for the
next three weeks."

"I don't know why not," Uley commented. "Everybody in town was willing to give Elizabeth a discount."

Aaron laughed. It was a sharp, harsh sound that didn't ring true. "Yeah, but they're chargin' me double."

She looked at him in shock. "They'd do that?" But then it dawned on her. The men of Tin Cup were exercising the same skewed judgment against Aaron that she was so afraid of herself.

"Yeah," he said. "Elizabeth and I are moving into Aunt Kate Fischer's boardinghouse tomorrow noon."

At his mention of his sister, Uley remembered the reason she'd paid a call upon Aaron Brown in the first place. "Aaron." This time she placed her hand upon his arm.

He looked down at it, and then — wonder of wonders — he covered it with his own. "Don't remove it this time," he told her gently, as a pink the colour of an August primrose tinted her cheeks. "Thank you for your company, Uley. I've enjoyed our ride."

"Me too," she said. "And I wanted to tell you, I thought . . ." She didn't know how to say it. She found it difficult to speak with his hand upon hers. Their fingers seemed to fit together with such perfection, his broad strong knuckles lying directly over hers.

"What?"

"I —" she took a deep breath and plunged in "— haven't trusted you completely."

"Oh," he said, grinning, glad that was all it was. "Is that why you turned me in and got me locked up?"

"No." She shook her head, and he could imagine all her hair waving around her shoulders. "After that. I've thought . . ."

She hesitated again.

"What have you thought, Uley?"

"That you . . ."

"That I what?"

At last she said it, as fast as she could. "That you were being untrue to Elizabeth because of the way you went looking at me sometimes."

He threw his head back and laughed right up at the stars. Then he took off his hat and grinned at her. "Nope. I wasn't being untrue to Elizabeth. She's my sister."

"I found that out today. It's the first I've known of it. It surprised me, I can sure tell you."

"I'll bet it did."

"That's why I came tonight." It was her

turn to gaze straight up at the stars. "I just wanted, wanted . . ." She trailed off.

He completed the sentence for her. "To tell me why you keep backing away."

"Yes."

The wagon halted in front of the Kirklands' cabin. She sat gazing at him, the anticipation in her eyes palpable, waiting for the assurances he might pass on to her now. But he gave her none. He couldn't. All he could think of as he sat there in the dark beside her was the cottonwood tree where the three forks of Willow Creek met, with the hemp rope slung over one of its strongest branches, waiting, just waiting.

It wasn't fair of him to make Uley start caring about him now that his life might have a heart-wrenching end to it. Chances were Dawson Hayes wouldn't even see the letter he still had to compose until it was almost autumn. Aaron knew he'd be long gone by then, buried up with the rest of the crowd on the knoll marked Boot Hill.

"Best go in now, Uley," he told her, knowing he was disappointing her now, knowing he had no other choice. "It's getting late. And I've still got that letter to write."

Harris Olney slept at his desk in the jailhouse, his boots propped up higher than his head, his arms jutting akimbo from his shoulders, his hands cradling his neck. His snores came in short, insistent bursts, fierce enough to rattle the weekly *Tin Cup Banner* that lay spread open on his chest.

The snoring stopped suddenly, and the marshal's feet hit the floor as he moved to a sitting position. "That's it," he bellowed, "that's it."

"What's it?" Ben Pearsall was whittling on a chunk of pine, dropping the shavings into the fire. "You been dreaming about bears, Olney? You sure did sound like one."

"Bears? Not at all, Pearsall. I've been dreaming about how to get rid of Aaron Brown once and for all. This is so easy, I don't know why I didn't think of it yesterday."

"What's easy?"

Olney got up from the old oak chair and rummaged through his things on the shelf. "Where's my inkwell? Where's some paper? I can write my *own* letter." He found the paper he sought, dipped the pen and began printing laboriously. Pearsall watched as he saw a vivid blue stain start to soak through the paper.

Harris wadded up the paper, pitched it

into the corner and began again. He worked so hard at it, he held his tongue pinched between his teeth. Finally, he finished. "There. What do you think of this?" He held it up so Old Pearsall could read it.

Ben Pearsall leaned forward and squinted.

Dear Dawson Hayes
Here — *blotch* — is sum money. No need to come to Tin Cup. We — *blotch* — do not need you.

Pearsall went back to his whittling. "You didn't sign your name. Cain't send a letter without signing your name."

"That's just it," Harris said, grinning. "That's just what I'm going to do. It's a letter from me. But Hayes won't know that." Olney shoved the pen away and pulled his six-shooter from its holster. He began to polish it with a piece of hide. "He'll think that letter is from Brown himself."

"I don't like it, Harris," Pearsall said. "I don't like it at all. It makes me think sometimes, seeing you acting like you've got something to hide."

Harris's eyes met Ben Pearsall's over the upturned barrel of the gun. "I'm the law in this town, Ben. You questioning the law?"

"Naw," Ben said, backing down nonchalantly, but figuring he'd gotten his point across. "I guess I wouldn't be doing anything like that."

Harris laid the gun down and stomped to the door. "Hey!" he hollered out the door. "Anybody trustworthy around here who wants to make good money?"

Several men in the street stepped forward to volunteer.

"I just need one fellow," Olney said, placing the letter in the hands of the first one who approached him. "I'm looking for a messenger to get over to Buena Vista."

Chapter Nine

The day Charles Ongewach's new piano came in over the pass, the saloon owner set up a flyer in his front window, inviting everyone in Tin Cup for a celebration. It had been eight months since old man Scheer had climbed up on Ongewach's upright grand while wearing his hob-nailed boots. Scheer had paid eight months' worth of gold dust to buy the establishment a new one.

Pastor Benjamin Creede, the circuit preacher who rode into town on a bay mare one day with saddlebags full of Bibles, read the flyer in the window and immediately removed it. "How can you invite the entire community to an event that takes place in an establishment of ill repute?" he asked Ongewach that morning when the saloon owner happened to poke his head outside to check on the weather. "If you want to have a community event, you ought to have it at the town hall."

"You don't understand," Ongewach said

in the same tone of voice as if he were telling someone that the floor needed mopping. "Nobody in this town has problems attending a function in this place. Everybody comes here every day anyway."

"That is exactly why I'm here," Pastor Creede said. "To evangelize this wild country."

"If we needed somebody to do that, we would have hired a preacher ourselves."

"I figure you've got one or two law-abiding citizens who wouldn't be willing to attend a shindig at your place. Besides, I heard a rumor that there might be a hanging up in this part of Gunnison County. Wouldn't do for a man to be God-forsaken at such a time, to meet his Maker without making his peace."

Although Ongewach curled his lip at the idea, a new flyer went up advertising the piano delivery party in the Tin Cup town hall the next day. The party was moved. And the piano, all gleaming and polished like a Sunday shoe, was moved again by wagon and stood in the town-hall corner when Uley and Sam arrived soon after supper. Its wood glowed with the maroon patina of hand-rubbed cherry. Its stool sported a brass plaque on one side that read St. Louis, J. Watsabaugh. Its music rack was encircled by elaborately carved pea vines and flowers.

❧ Bunting hung in scallops from the ceiling, and lanterns flickered behind glass chimneys. Uley found herself hard-pressed to picture this as the same room where the town had been named Tin Cup or where the charges had been read against Aaron or where the circuit-riding preacher, Pastor Creede, had endeavored to set up worship services on Sunday. Samuel and Uley had attended, along with two others whom Uley recognized from a neighboring mine. Now, as everyone from ten miles around seemed to be arriving, she heard someone calling, "Uley! Over here!"

She found Laura waving frantically from where she stood beside the woodstove among a group of Moll's other "upstairs girls." She had never seen Laura gussied up before. If Uley hadn't recognized her voice and seen her waving, Uley might never have recognized her friend.

Laura wore a vermilion dress covered with velvet and bows. A thick feather boa fell across Laura's creamy, white shoulders. Laura's eyes seemed huge and round and dark. She'd painted them with kohl, Uley supposed. Her lips were stained a brilliant crimson, the color of a plump, ripe strawberry. She looked like a porcelain doll someone had decorated with an artist's brush, a bit unreal.

Uley made for the woodstove but her father grabbed her arm. "You mustn't do that, Uley." It had been a long time since she'd seen him so reproachful. "Here we are within sight of the whole town. Ongewach got a fit of conscience when that pastor talked to him about the party, decided he'd invite the whole town over here, including the hurdy-gurdy girls. It wouldn't do, you walking over there to talk with the whole town watching. Those girls are dressed for work."

"But it's just Laura."

"I know that. And I know you fancy yourself her friend. Goodness knows, that girl needs one. But people are talking and I don't like that the talk includes you."

"Let them talk. It's just a bunch of old coot miners anyway."

"I have certain responsibilities," her pa said. "Many I have neglected with you. Your mother would never forgive me for letting you live as roughly as I have."

The weight of frustration leveled in her chest. She couldn't help being angry at her father, being angry at all of them for their conventions and their antiquated rules.

Even living out here in the barren wilderness, they thought they knew how things should be!

"You don't know what goes on between men and women, Uley."

"Well, I'd sure like to find out." Her anger took its final form against her father and against the responsibilities he'd let her take but, still, imposing rules on her these years. She conveniently forgot the fact that this charade had all been her notion in the first place.

She spun away from her pa just in time to see the double doors swing open. "Hey," a big Swede hollered from the porch. "It's the fellow who tried to shoot the marshal, and he's got the *lady* with him."

Sure enough, here came Aaron, with Elizabeth on his arm. He doffed his Stetson in the familiar one-handed way that made Uley's heart pound. Instantly half the men in the room began to line up beside Elizabeth.

"There's no use being angry at me," her father said, still following their prior course of conversation. "We both knew it would come to this some day. I know you've befriended Laura. But you mustn't be seen with her here."

Uley saw Aaron glancing around the

room. Breath caught in her throat. *He's looking for me.*

Their eyes met. Then, once he'd found her, he never glanced in her direction again. Instead, he headed to the opposite corner of the room while the other men gathered around his sister yet kept as much distance from *him* as they could.

A cry went up. "Where's the piano music?"

"Yeah. What good does that fancy piano do sitting in the corner if there isn't anybody tickling the ivories?"

"To my new piano and my old friends." Charles Ongewach held up a hand in a mock salute. "We only got one problem I can think of. Nobody in Tin Cup knows how to play the thing."

Uley sensed Aaron by her side before she saw him. She looked straight up and met his dark eyes. "It's going to be a long evening," he remarked blandly. "All these miners and only one lady to go around."

"If we had a piano player," she said slowly, her eyes never leaving his face, "I guess we could sing or something. If we were singing, you wouldn't have the time to worry about that horde of men following Elizabeth."

"Elizabeth wasn't the lady I had in mind."

She colored.

"I love it when you do that."

"What?"

"When you blush the color of an Irish tea rose."

That left Uley quite beyond words.

"Your eyes look as green as a good fishing pond."

"Blushing is the one thing that's often threatened to give me away, Aaron Brown."

"So what were you mad about when I walked in here? I found you in the crowd and you looked like a snarling mountain lion waiting to spring on something." She'd looked ruffled and mad and beautiful, only he wouldn't tell her that.

"Laura's my friend. Pa knows that. And he wouldn't let me go." She pointed toward the girls in bright-colored dresses beside the woodstove. The tarnished doves, Laura among them, were waving at fellows in the crowd and giggling among themselves.

"Don't blame him. I wouldn't have let you join that group, either."

"I don't like it anymore," she said. "I don't like everybody judging everyone else by their appearances or by the choices they've made. They're doing it to you, too, Aaron, or else you wouldn't have had to move out of the Pacific Hotel."

"Aunt Kate's been kind," he said. "She's letting me do chores around the place to help earn our keep. And you've been kind, too. But appearances are important, too, not in the way you mean, but because we choose how we want people to see us."

"I don't understand."

"I chose to come to Tin Cup after Olney. You chose to come to Tin Cup with your father. Laura chose the way she makes a living."

"Yes, but when the time comes to do it differently, people won't let us back up and start all over."

"There's only one person who lets us do that," Aaron said. "Jesus Christ. Who loved us as we were and died so that we might be made new."

Uley's heart caught in her throat. So the Bible she had found among his belongings *had* meant something. He loved the Lord as she loved the Lord. If they shared faith, they might be able to get through this together.

"We make choices. We live with them, Uley."

"Or die with them," she said very quietly, wishing she did not have to speak those words.

"Yes."

As conversations rose around them, there might as well have been nobody else standing in the room besides Uley Kirkland and Aaron Brown.

"Life is never fair, is it?" she asked.

"No." He looked like he wanted to slip his hand over hers again, only he didn't dare. "It isn't."

The chorus about the piano rose around them. "There's got to be *somebody* in this room who can play the piano."

"Craziest thing I've ever heard, old man Scheer spending his life's *earnings* on a piano and Ongewach's gone and thrown a fancy party for it and nobody's here who can make it *play?*"

Lesser Levy pulled a leather pouch from his pocket, flipped it in the air and caught it again. "Here's a pouch of gold dust for anybody who can make that thing play a *song.*"

Jasper Warde started toward the pouch.

"Not *you,* Jasper. I want somebody who can play with two hands."

The sound in the room skittered away to silence. One miner looked at another. No one moved. No one stepped forward. No one uttered a word. Not a one of them knew the difference between a middle C and a B flat.

"What? There ain't *nobody?*"

Levy looked just about ready to tuck the pouch inside his shirt when a diminutive voice spoke from beside the woodstove.

"I can. I can play it for you."

All eyes turned in her direction. All eyes stared with disbelief at the assembly of questionable women, where one had stepped forward as if she had some right to be a regular member of this community.

"Who? Who said that?"

"I know the songs. You let me play, everybody'll be singing clear until sunrise."

All eyes traveled up the satin skirt covered with ruffles, the velvet fabric and the satin bows as gaudy and bright as the carriage Moll had purchased and decorated. Everyone looked to the pretty little mouth painted the color of a ripe strawberry, and the eyes rimmed with dark kohl.

"I've been playin' since I was little." Laura's chin was set as high as if she'd been the governor's daughter or the queen in some far-off land. "Ain't nobody knows it, though." She laughed. "Until *now,* I guess."

The mutterings swept through the crowd like a breeze swept through the aspen leaves.

"Ought not to let *her* get anywhere close to the piano."

"Ongewach shouldn't have invited women like *them* to this party anyway."

"Shut up, Warde. It's not like you don't frequent Moll's establishment once a week. Always willing to point a finger."

"Come on down here, girl." Lesser Levy motioned her to step forward. Santa Fe Moll stepped right beside her.

"Not *you*," Levy growled at Moll. "This here's Tin Can Laura's night. *She's* the one who's going to save this party. And if I hear you took away half of her pay for this, I'll come over there and rob you myself, just the way you've been robbing these girls."

Moll stepped back.

"That's the way. This pouch of gold belongs to Tin Can Laura."

As Laura stepped through the crowd, the men cleared a path for her to the shiny new piano. She pulled the stool out and made herself comfortable upon it, wiggling back and forth once or twice and adjusting her skirts to make certain her feet were situated as they should be. She laid her fingers upon the keys and, for one full moment, looked at them as if she liked remembering them there.

Finally, satisfied, she glanced over her shoulder at the room full of men and grinned. "Just learned this one last year." Her fingers darted over the keys without her even having to look at them. Out came the first strains of "Where the Columbines Grow."

No one moved. No one sang. Everybody stood frozen, listening to Laura play.

Uley tugged at Aaron's sleeve. "See? It's just what we were talking about." There she sat, the young girl Uley had befriended, the soiled dove, playing as if she were a fine miss performing in some parlor.

When Laura finished that song, she moved right along to "I'll Take You Home Again, Kathleen." All around her, the miners began stomping in rhythm and joined in with the song.

Uley refused to listen to Aaron and her pa. She couldn't keep herself any longer from standing beside her friend.

"How do you *do* this?" Uley asked, astounded. "Where did you learn to play like this?"

"I just hear somebody singing a song

and I can play it. All I've got to do is listen and there it comes. Been doing it ever since I was five. What do you think?"

"I think you are amazing."

"Thank you."

"Did you figure *these* out by yourself?" Uley could barely see Laura's fingers, they were moving so fast.

"Nope. Not all of them. Somebody taught me once."

"Who?"

"Somebody I have no right to talk about anymore."

"Who?"

"Nobody."

"Laura, tell me."

"Just a fellow I knew once."

All at once Uley understood it. "The one you spoke about when we were at the lily pond?"

"The very one."

"Who was he? Did he play in a saloon?"

"No. He didn't. *No.*" And this time, as Laura answered her, Uley was the only one who noticed her skip a few measures with her left hand so she could scrub away at her nose. Goodness, but it looked like Laura was ready to cry. Her nose had turned as rosy as a crab apple. "He was the minister who rode in over in Pitkin, trying to start a church."

"Laura?"

"I don't want to talk about it, Uley. He was like you are, you know? Always telling me I was worth something."

Uley touched Laura's shoulder in front of God and everyone else who might be watching. "Seems to me that there's a few of us you need to start listening to."

"Telling him goodbye was the worst thing I've ever had to do. I had to, though. There wasn't any other way."

"It that why you left Pitkin and came to Moll's place?"

"Of course it is. All I've got left of him is this piano playing. Most of what I can play is church hymns. Guess I'll start on those in a little while, too, if everybody here keeps singing along."

When Laura struck up the tune to "Little Brown Jug," her fingers raced along at the same robust tempo as a horse's canter. When Aaron stepped close to Uley and chimed in with everyone else in his deep baritone voice, the room spun around her and the music filled her head, and all she could comprehend at that moment was the rainbow array of everyone around her. She felt a span of warmth across her shoulders and realized that Aaron had wrapped his arm across her back. All the world seemed to reel around Uley.

This is what happiness is, isn't it, Lord? Oh, Father. I don't want it to ever end.

"Uley?" Aaron whispered. And in the way he uttered her name, he asked scores of questions that she couldn't answer.

"I don't know what to do," she whispered back. "I don't know how . . ."

"Neither do I."

"I want everything to change. I want nothing to change."

"They may well hang me in sixteen days. It isn't fair to you if I've made you care for me. I've tried so hard not to."

"Everyone in this room thinks I'm something I'm not," she said. "I don't know how to be anything else."

"I think," he said, very quietly, "you could be anything you wanted to be."

Oh, Father. It's what I've been telling Laura. So easy to say the words to someone I love. So difficult to believe them for myself.

On the piano, Laura began a rendition of "The Little Eau Pleine." In that precise instant, Dave McNally clomped right up to the piano and deposited a rusty tin can on the polished cherrywood beside her wrists.

"Here you go, Tin Can Laura. This is what you've forgotten, I think." His laughter was mean, loud enough to get everyone's attention. "Can't have you performing without your tin can, can we? Best leave it right here."

Laura's hands froze on the keys.

"Aw, shut up, Dave." Levy yanked his gun out of his holster. "Couldn't you have left your sour mood outside?"

But Uley could see the damage was already done. Laura started the song where she'd left off. But as she played the gentle ballad, her arms began to shake. Tears pooled in her eyes. She missed a note. Uley saw a tear roll down her nose and drop onto the ivory.

"Confound it, Laura." Ongewach rushed forward with his hankie. "Stop your crying." He didn't hand the handkerchief to her. Instead he dried off the piano keys. "You'll mess up the finish on my cherrywood."

In frustration, Laura let the song dwindle into silence. She stared at her fingers for a full ten seconds before she pounded the keys with all ten of them at once and made such a racket it made everyone jump. She picked up the tin can and chucked it as hard as she could into the crowd. It glanced off Peter Sturge's head and then bounced off one of the plate-glass windows. She squared her shoulders, gave an unnatural smile and, holding her head high, headed for the front door. She shoved it open with both hands and marched straight out into the night.

At Laura's exit, the entire room — remarkably — remained silent.

Uley gripped Aaron's arm. It was amazing how close she felt to him, after standing beside him and singing, participating in the evening's gaiety. "I've got to go after her."

"You should. She'll be in need of you about now."

Uley shot him one glance, one glance only, that told him everything he needed to know. His support at that moment meant everything to her.

She elbowed her way past the miners who had gathered around the piano now that they'd heard it play. She wove her way toward the huge mahogany door. She sidestepped her way past Charlie Hastings and Hollis Andersen. Just as she reached the lantern-lined vestibule, she found herself nose to nose with her father.

"I'm going after her, Pa."

"I had a strange premonition you

would be headed that way."

"I've got to. I know you don't approve. I'm sorry."

"Don't figure there's any use trying to stop you."

"There isn't."

Her father stepped out of her way and sighed. It was a heavy sigh, a sound that carried the weight of the past years in it, the weight of everything he'd tried to do without Sarah, bringing up a child in this forsaken place all on his own.

"You're growing up, Uley," he said softly. "It isn't easy for me to let you go."

They stood this way, toe to toe, face-to-face, for one long moment, silent, loving and respecting each other, sizing each other up.

"I had best go find my friend," she said at last.

"I won't stop you, Uley."

He stepped back a pace so she could pass.

Uley stood in the street, peering first up one side of the avenue and then down the other. The dirt thoroughfare appeared deserted.

"Laura?" she called.

No answer.

"Laura? It's me."

The only sound Uley could hear was the sparkling dance of Willow Creek purling against its banks beside the meadow. She waited a long time, listening, before she started in the other direction.

"Uley," came the timid voice behind her. "I'm here. Wait up, would you?"

"I'm sorry." Uley spun toward the voice. "I'm so sorry for what happened in there."

Laura stepped into the moonlight from the shadows that fell from the Tin Cup post office. When she raised her eyes to her friend, the moonlight struck her face, making it look like it glowed from within. Tears sparkled on her cheeks.

"That was awful in there."

"Makes you never want to step out and do anything, doesn't it?"

Uley sat on the edge of the boardwalk.

Laura sat beside her.

"I deserved what I got in there, I figure. I'm being stupid, crying this way."

"You cry," Uley said. "When you're hurting, it's good to cry. And it seems like there's nothing these men around here know how to do except hurt people."

"I didn't think anybody would take exception to me playing music at a community gathering. Don't they know I'm just like them inside? It had nothing to do with that pouch of gold. That's not why I was playing. I was playing because of something inside my heart." She held the pouch in her palm where they both could see it. "I just wanted to do something special for everybody. Something different."

"You did something special, Laura. Don't you ever question that."

Laura gazed at Uley through two eyes ringed with smudges of kohl. "You think so?"

"Of course. Everybody was having the time of their lives in there before McNally had to get obnoxious. Your eyes are all messed up. Reminds me of a coon." Uley reached with the tip of one finger and wiped off a smudge. "Here."

"It's supposed to make me look pretty."

"It did at first in a funny sort of way. But I like your face better the way God made it. Without anything to cover it up. You don't look like *you* with Moll's kohl and dye all over everything."

"Funny thing," Laura said. "I don't feel like me, either."

Uley rocked back and surveyed her work. "That's much better."

"I wish I could go downstairs at Ongewach's and play the piano every night. But Moll would never agree to it."

"You have a right to make a living any way you want to, Laura. Moll doesn't own you."

"It's different than you think. I owe her something. She's been good to me, Uley."

"Not as good as someone else might have been."

"She took me in when I might have starved to death otherwise."

"She's added gold dust to her larder because of it."

"Every man in this town knows what I am. I could never be seen as anyone else."

"You never know until you try," Uley said.

"These miners see you one way, they'll always see you that way. And it ain't just in Tin Cup, neither. It's all over the state of Colorado."

Father, haven't I also said those words?

"That's just how people are."

Is that why You've brought me to this place, making me hurt, so I can help someone who's hurting worse than me?

"Well, you don't have to be how people think you have to be. The Father doesn't look at you the same way people do."

"I don't know about that."

"Laura, the preacher in Pitkin who taught you how to play hymns — did he tell you how asking Jesus into your heart could make all things new again?"

"Yes," she said. "I never could have been good enough."

"Don't you understand about the Lord, Laura? There isn't anyone who could have been good enough. That's why He gave His life for us.

"You don't have to know," Uley said. And as she spoke she might as well have been speaking to herself, too. "You just *ask* Him. You invite Him to take over all your struggles and to help you let go, and then you watch to see what He'll do."

Oh, Father. I believe that with my head. It is my heart that falters.

"That's what you think, isn't it, Uley? But that's not so easy to do."

"How can you be so sure?"

"Look at Aaron Brown," Laura said. "There's a question about him bein' innocent now. But these folks around here ain't gonna give him the benefit of the doubt in any case. They stand firm on their idea that every man in Gunnison County is guilty until proven innocent. Ain't supposed to be that way, but it is. They see things as they see 'em."

214

"Mr. Brown," Uley said very carefully, "may go free."

"And he may not."

Laura wasn't staring straight into the night anymore. She'd tilted her head and was scrutinizing Uley's expression, one ear propped atop a knee.

"You'd best get used to that idea, Uley. Else you're gonna have a bad heartache later. I figure I know the name of the fellow you were talkin' about down by the lily pond the other day."

"I sure don't know what you're talking about."

"I reckon you're starting to care for Aaron Brown."

"Now, why would I go and do a fool thing like that?"

"Don't know. Guess it's a question you'll have to ask yourself."

Uley propped her chin on her knees, too. "I'm not asking myself questions right now."

"No," Laura said. "You're just answering them for other people."

Uley was silent.

"These miners found out you'd been fooling 'em all this time, saying you were a fellow when you are a gal, they'd probably run you out of town on the next supply wagon."

"You're probably right."

"Me, they look at me and know what *I'm* worth. Just plunk the money in the can and walk away. And Mr. Brown, they won't rest easy until his dead body's swinging from that cottonwood by the three forks of Willow Creek."

"Don't say that."

"I'm scared for all of us."

"Laura."

"Uley, will you help me do that Jesus thing that preacher was talking about? Will you help me pray and get Him to take charge of my life the way you say He will? So these things won't turn out the way I think they're going to happen?"

And so, Uley took her hands, much the way her own mother had taken Uley's hands when she'd been a little girl, and helped her pray to ask Jesus to make His place of love and salvation deep in Laura's heart. She hugged Laura hard and long. Then she peered up into the stars, looking for answers in the millions of them that glittered in the sky above. How she wished that, just this once, she could see into all eternity. But maybe . . . maybe . . . it was better that she couldn't. "Now, it's over now. You're wrong to be afraid."

"I ain't wrong. You know I ain't."

And so they sat together, Laura with both knees snuggled up close to her, Uley with her back against a cottonwood trunk one knee drawn up, the other foot set squarely in the dirt.

Well, maybe she'd helped Laura find her new answer. And they'd found each other. Maybe that was a beginning to what the Father had in mind.

Chapter Ten

"I've been thinking," Aaron said to his sister as he hauled water upstairs for Aunt Kate at the boardinghouse, "about staying forever in Tin Cup."

"You will be staying forever," Elizabeth answered without missing a breath, "if Dawson Hayes won't come for your trial." She hated talking about it, but it had to be faced. "You'll spend an eternity here beneath the dirt up on Boot Hill."

"I won't spend an eternity up there no matter what happens," he said. "I'll be in heaven, without a care in the world. Angels will be strumming their harps, and the streets will be lined with what everybody's digging in the dirt for here."

"Angel songs," Elizabeth said pensively. "Do you think they could ever be as beautiful as the song of the meadowlark and the robin?"

"I don't know," he commented offhandedly. "I may soon see." He set the pail down on the pine washstand and watched as the water sloshed against the sides. "Now Kate'll have water for all her folks."

"So . . . what do you mean about staying in Tin Cup?"

Aaron faced his sister. "I mean that I like it here."

"You'd leave Fort Collins?"

"It's different than the Eastern Slope. Full of life. Full of promise and brawn. Full of gold. It appeals to me."

"Oh, no," she said with a sigh. "Don't tell me you've gone and picked up the gold fever, too."

"No. It just seems like Tin Cup is sitting on the edge of the new frontier, Beth. My guess is that ladies'll start coming here soon. It would be a fine place to open up a business. Another livery stable. We could offer choice horses and well-built wag-ons —" he grinned "— and carriages."

"Who ever heard of a *carriage* in Tin Cup?"

"We could bring in the best Studebaker carriages money could buy. You might just be surprised, Beth," he told her.

She *was* surprised . . . by the eagerness she saw in her brother's eyes, and the hope. She hadn't seen him so happy and so full of dreams since before he'd left to pursue Harris Olney to Tin Cup. What could it

219

be, she pondered, that was making him dream of a future when he was facing a trial in eleven days that might very well send him to his death?

"I mean, if a miracle happened and Dawson Hayes came and I wasn't found guilty and I settled somewhere new —" he dumped the pail into a barrel and made ready to make his fifth trip to Willow Creek "— it might as well be here."

Laura and Uley's best place to meet was the lily pond. Now that Uley knew where it was, she wandered down there often in the afternoons after the mines had closed, usually carrying a pail containing warm corn bread slathered with honey and molasses from C. A. Freeman's Miners' Service Depot.

"Maybe, for all our sakes," Uley said quietly to Laura one afternoon as she licked crumbs from her fingers, "I'm going to have to prove you're wrong about some things."

"I don't know what you mean," Laura told her.

"You figure nobody around here will give you a respectable job. I figure somebody will. D. J. Mawherter ran an ad in the *Tin Cup Banner*. He's looking for a clerk."

"It won't happen. He'll take one look at me and turn his nose up in the air like he smells something sour."

"You don't know until you try."

"I know what Moll will do if she finds out. She'll have my hide on a fence post. Plus she'll charge you two dollars an hour just for squirin' me around town."

"Are you afraid, Laura? That's what it is, isn't it?"

"You don't have to be, Uley. But I do."

Even so, Uley fought to convince Laura she wasn't giving the miners around town an equitable chance. And she realized she was fighting to convince herself, too. It was, she supposed as she lay in bed thinking of it, a venture she needed to take on for herself, as well. *Father, we're supposed to do things we know are Your will, even though we're afraid of them, aren't we?* What happened to Laura now would directly affect the choices Uley knew she must make, too . . . choices about what she wanted . . . who she wanted to become . . . and how she was going to get there.

Uley lay contemplating her situation for two nights, sometimes dozing fitfully in and out for a few hours, sometimes propped up with pillows in the old

221

wrought-iron bed trying to read her Bible. Finally she let the scriptures drop and looked around the room, seeking comfort in familiar things. Her hair was down for the night, falling softly about her shoulders. Storm sprang onto the bed and nosed around her with his whiskers. *We've got to do this,* she thought as she fingered the kitten's striped fur. *We'll be sorry our whole lives if we don't try now.* As if in answer, Storm made two entire turns and then dropped heavily against the bend of her hip.

"We'll do it tomorrow, then," Uley whispered to the kitten, still scratching and sending fur flying up from her fingers in little puffs. "I'll speak to Laura through the window on my way to the Gold Cup tomorrow morning. We'll talk to Mawherter in the afternoon."

If people thought it strange the next day when Tin Can Laura, a tarnished hurdy-gurdy girl, strolled into the Grand Central Hotel in broad daylight with Uley Kirkland, the young fellow who'd brought justice to the town, nobody stopped them to say a word. Uley thought Laura looked exemplary, all dressed in her best yellow calico, with her hair pulled up at her nape with a tortoiseshell clasp she'd borrowed from Wishbone Mabel.

"Hello, Mr. Mawherter," Uley said. "We're here about the job in the *Banner.* You found anybody for it yet?"

"Nope."

"Well, we were interested in the job."

"Say no more," D.J. bellowed, slapping Uley on the back. "You're hired. We'd love to have you. Mining is dirty work. I'll pay you just as much as you're making over at the Gold Cup. You've certainly proven that you're a conscientious, upstanding citizen of this town."

"No, sir. That isn't it at all," Uley managed to say. "Laura's looking to work for you."

Mawherter's eyes about burst out of his head.

"Laura's aiming to make a new start in life and she'd like to start it with you."

Mawherter didn't stop to think twice. "Sorry, young man." His eyes had gone as hard as the shale Uley chiseled out of the Gold Cup every day and sent up the shafts with the mules. "We don't have an opening here for the likes of *her.*" As he said it, he didn't even look at Laura. He just jammed one finger in the air in her general direction, all the while aiming his words at Uley.

"She'll do a fine job for you. She's a hard worker."

Mawherter grinned rather nastily. "That's what I hear. I hear she does a *fine* job at Santa Fe Moll's place. Let her stay there."

Uley had heard enough. "Come on, Laura. Let's go."

But Mawherter wasn't finished. He kept right on going. "You see this?" He jabbed the same crooked finger toward a framed advertisement on the wall. Grand Central Hotel — Tin Cup, it read. First-class in Every Respect. Situated in the Most Desirable Business Part of the City. Charges Reasonable.

"Don't see what that has to do with us," Uley said.

"You don't, do you?" Mawherter pulled a cheroot from the inside of his coat pocket, trimmed the end of it with a tiny pair of gold scissors and poked it between his teeth. As he talked, it dangled out of his mouth like a worm hanging out of a bird's beak. "I am advertising that this hotel is first-class in every respect," he said, the cheroot waggling, leaning far enough toward them both that it seemed as if he might jump right over the counter at them. "Number one, I'm not going to have a woman working here as a clerk. I need somebody responsible. And, number two, even if I was going to have a woman as a clerk, I wouldn't have Tin Can Laura. I cannot have a hurdy-gurdy girl standing here to greet my guests."

Uley had never been so angry. It was all she could do to keep from grabbing the odious cheroot from his teeth and poking it back at him. "Laura wouldn't *be* a hurdy-gurdy girl if you would employ her here."

"Nope, I will not do it."

"But she wants to *reform*."

"Let her *reform* in some other hotel besides mine." This time Mawherter allowed himself the luxury of peering right down his nose at Laura. "Once a soiled dove, always a soiled dove."

Uley gripped her friend's arm and made ready to go. "It is plain to see Mawherter does not possess a kind heart." With that, she yanked Laura toward the door.

"It doesn't have anything to do with my heart, Uley Kirkland," Mawherter called out to their backs. "My heart's in the same condition as everybody else's in this town. I'm just smarter than some. That is the only way I can run a business and make a —"

They didn't hear his last words. The door, thankfully, slammed shut behind them.

Laura clutched both of Uley's arms. "I cain't bear this, Uley. Don't make me do it anymore."

"He's only one of many, Laura. We have other possibilities."

"He said himself he's got a heart as good as anybody's in Tin Cup." Two tears balanced on her lower lids, ready to fall. "Nobody around here's gonna let me better myself. There'll just be too much talk for anybody to want to give it a test."

"We are not finished yet," Uley said, shoring up her own courage. It couldn't end like this. It couldn't be this way. But by fifteen minutes after five that evening Uley knew that it was. In thirty minutes' time, they presented themselves to two other business owners who'd advertised in the *Banner* for assistance. J. C. Theobald, Tin Cup's cobbler, who had announced in the newspaper he needed someone who "could polish shoes with neatness and dispatch," at least was kind.

After Mawherter's reaction, Laura had been certain Theobald would hurl shoes at them. Instead, he evaded the question, telling Laura gently he needed to hire someone who had much more experience with shoes than she had.

As they moved to leave the shop, he smiled at both of them sadly. "Wish I had something I could do to help you two," he said. "I cannot have a hurdy-gurdy girl from Moll's place polishing my boots. I'm bringing my wife out next fall. She would never understand."

Last, they tried C. A. Freeman's Miner's Service Depot, the largest dry goods store in Tin Cup. A sign on the front door read Miner's Underwear, Waterproof Goods, and Powder. Two hands were drawn on the sign, fingers pointing to call attention to the message Quick Sales and Light Profits.

Calvin Freeman was sweeping the floor beside the shelf of red wool union suits when the bell atop the door tinkled to announce their arrival. His reaction, when Uley questioned him, was much the same as Mawherter's.

"I need a gangly kid who can stand on a bucket and dust my shelves of canned goods," he said without preamble. "Don't need no dirty birds. Now get out of here before you offend some payin' customer."

Together, and full of remorse, they rode Uley's horse back down to the lily pond. The lily pond was such a respite for them, a place where they could stand together at the edge of the water and watch the stars twirl above them or could blow dandelion spores aloft, watching the thready white fronds lift into the air and, like their fantasies, travel in every direction. Today they did none of those things. Today they stood side by side, staring into the water as if they were gazing into something they didn't understand. The horse sucked at the water with its velvet muzzle, snorting greedily and sending the wavering image of their faces into ever-widening ripples.

"I'm sorry, Laura."

"I thought you said it'd be easier if I just let God take charge."

"Not easier." Uley touched her arm. "*Better.* There's a difference between those two."

The horse continued drinking.

"Nobody's gonna let me do it here, Uley," Laura said. "And, strangely enough, that makes me want to do it all the more."

"Well, maybe that's all the more reason for it then."

"If I want to get away from this stained life, I'm gonna have to leave Tin Cup. I just don't know where I could go."

But Uley knew. Uley knew where a fresh start could come. For both of them.

Aunt Delilah in Ohio.

Aunt Delilah would teach them both to be ladies. She had been writing Uley for months, begging her to come back East for just that reason.

Until now, the thought had made Uley feel entirely bereft. But with Laura along, the going would take on a whole new purpose.

"I do. I know of a place."

"Where? How could we do it?"

"Mama's sister in Ohio. Aunt Delilah begged me to stay with her years ago. Instead, I opted to come here with Pa. But maybe it's time to go back. Maybe it's time to reconsider, have a wise woman teach us how to both live proper Christian lives."

"You'd take me with you?"

"Of course I would. You're the main reason I'd really go, Laura. But I don't know how we'd travel." She spread her hands and studied them, hands with dirty nails and rough calluses, hands that might become a lady's hands. She imagined them just then with clean nails, soft, supple fingers as pink as the pads on the underside of Storm's paws. A woman's hands.

"Whatcha lookin' at your hands for?"

Uley hid them behind her back. "Just wishing, I suppose."

"When can we go?" Laura asked.

"It'll cost for two of us to travel so far on the Overland Trail. We'll have to put some money away." For Uley, the thought was an unexpected comfort. She still had days, weeks, to be with her father, to bring to a close her life in this place.

Poignant deliberations, all of them.

"We don't have to wait." Laura fished around beneath her skirts and pulled out a small leather pouch. "I took this down to the assayer's office just yesterday."

Uley stared at it. The pouch of gold from Lesser Levy. The gold Laura had earned playing Charles Ongewach's new upright grand piano.

"There's plenty in here to get us to Ohio and back again, Uley. We could go tomorrow if we wanted to."

"No."

Uley's soul felt as if it was pirouetting out of control, like the tornado she'd seen as she and her father came across Nebraska. They couldn't go now. Her thoughts, incredibly, were not of her father. They weren't of the Gold Cup. Her conscious thoughts were now where her unconscious ones had been all along.

Aaron Brown.

After she left, she'd never see Aaron

Brown again. She'd never stare at his dirty face behind bars again or hear him say, "It's about the prettiest hair I've ever seen." She'd never again feel her heart singing just to have him standing near.

"We can't go, Laura," she said, wild-eyed. "Not yet. I'll go. But don't ask for it now."

"Why not?"

Why not, indeed? What could she say? How could she explain it?

Because I care for a man who might hang in eleven days, that's why. Because I've done the unthinkable. I've given Aaron Brown my heart.

The thought of the eleven-day count saved her just then. How many nights had she lain in bed trying to forget the up-coming jury verdict? How many days had she chipped away at the granite with the broadax in the Gold Cup, taking to task the events that had brought a man to this point?

The trial. She couldn't leave because of the trial.

"They might need me to testify again, is all."

"They won't. The only person who gets to testify is Dawson Hayes. That is, if he shows up."

"Judge Murphy might want me to retell the story. Three weeks is a long time to remember every detail, especially if you aren't used to thinking about particulars."

"Uley, you don't sound like you want to go at all."

"It'll be hard to leave my Pa, Laura." *The rest of it I'll confront as it comes.*

"And what of Aaron Brown?" Laura asked.

"I don't know," Uley said.

"Until the trial, then." Laura was examining her friend's face, not fully understanding the turmoil she read in Uley's eyes. "I've been frightened Moll might come lookin' for this gold. But I'll keep it on my person for eleven more days." She tucked it high inside the bosom of the demure shirtwaist she'd begun to wear. "Now that I've become a new woman, there's not anybody who can get their hands on it here."

The main item on the menu today at Aunt Kate Fischer's Hotel and Boarding House was "possum." Nobody knew exactly what type of wild game it was. Certainly, no possums lived within two thousand miles of Tin Cup. But possum was the special dish Aunt Kate had learned to cook during her arduous journey from slavery to the North. Now, when she wanted to give her boarders a fine treat, she fed them her best. She fed it to them barbecued, usually, in a sauce that smelled of heavy molasses and brown sugar.

"Enjoy your lunch, Thomas Tonge?" Aaron asked as he swept up after the meal. Sweeping was one of the many chores he did for Aunt Kate in return for his and Beth's keep. So was scrubbing the pots in the back room. He'd donned a knee-length apron for that job.

"Yep," the huge Swede replied. "It vos good. Where does that meat come from? You know?"

"I do," Aaron said, still brandishing the broom. "A flock of those possums flew over just the day before yesterday." Actually, they'd been huge black-headed geese, their bellies glowing silver as they flapped across the sky in formation. "Kate went out with her shotgun and blasted five or six of them right out of the air." He couldn't help grinning. "Rare things around here, those possums."

"Und I got a ving, by golly," Thomas stated excitedly. "You tell Kate Fischer I'll be back for more lunch tomorrow."

"I'll do that, Tom," Aaron said, smiling.

233

Kate Fischer came rambling in just in time to hear the last exchange. "Aaron Brown!" she hollered. "You givin' away my secrets?"

"No, ma'am." Aaron didn't usually say "ma'am." But Kate Fischer commanded respect. "Just answering questions the best way I know how."

"That's good." She beamed at him. "You're doin' a fine job down here. Never seen the floor so clean. And the pots are shinin' like somebody's lookin' glass."

"I aim to make you glad you're putting me up, Aunt Kate. And Beth, too. We're both thankful."

"Any sign of Dawson Hayes?" she asked. "Any word at all?"

"Nope. Still no sign of him."

"There's a supply wagon due over the pass in fifteen minutes. He could be on this one."

"That's what I think every time the wagon comes in," Aaron said honestly. "I see it coming closer and I start counting the heads."

Kate went into the kitchen to begin preparations for supper. Aaron kept on sweeping, doing his best to keep from thinking of the rig that, even now, would be rattling down this side of Alpine Pass.

He pulled the watch from the fob in his breeches and snapped it open. For the millionth time, he read the engraved inscription from his mother.

May your heart always know when it's time to come home.

Just past 2:10 p.m. The supply wagon was probably all the way past Lake Tillie by now.

He snapped it shut and resolutely shoved it back into his pocket.

Suppose, just suppose, Dawson Hayes was on that wagon.

He kept right on sweeping, watching the dirt separate into silty black lines as the broom passed over the planking. The straw bristles raked the pine floor as the dust flew toward the door in a low cloud.

If Aunt Kate had heard the snapping of his timepiece cover, she didn't let on now. "You best get on down there, Aaron Brown," she called out of the kitchen. "Might be somebody on that wagon you need to meet."

Aaron didn't want to watch Lester McClain driving the supply wagon into town. He didn't want to stand on a felled log, craning his neck, trying to make out Dawson Hayes's rumpled gray hair and beaverskin cap.

Yet he knew he couldn't stand it if he didn't.

He propped the broom against the door jamb. His heart was clattering inside his ribs. "Thanks, Kate. I'll be back directly."

"No need to come back," she declared. "You've done enough work for one day."

"I'll bring the water in tonight."

"That'll do fine."

Aaron went out the door running. He didn't even stop to remove the apron. He sprinted toward the town hall, the soiled apron flapping.

Several residents were lounging nonchalantly on the wooden steps of the town hall. "Wagon in yet?" he asked.

Apparently they weren't as nonchalant as they appeared. They all answered at once. "Not yet."

"It should be roundin' the corner in two or three minutes."

"You think your witness'll be on it?"

Aaron was winded from the run. "I don't know. Could be any day now."

"Best be in the next week, or you won't be around to see it," Charlie Hastings commented.

"Yes," Aaron said, frowning slightly and shading his eyes, still seeing nothing coming around the corner. "It had better be in the next week."

At just that moment, a mule's bray came from the opposite direction. Aaron glanced up and felt his stomach pitch. Here came Uley riding Old Croppy down from the mine, looking every bit as if she were heading to Abbey & Company to pick up equipment for the Gold Cup. Only thing was, she wasn't looking toward the store. She reminded him of a blue heron, neck outstretched, chin raised. She looked for all the world as if she were craning to see the supply wagon herself.

At that precise moment, Aaron remembered he was wearing Aunt Kate's dirty apron. He fumbled with the tie at the base of his spine. He couldn't see what he was doing. The silly thing knotted in his fingers.

"Confounded thing," he muttered.

"Looks like you've been helpin' Aunt Kate cook up her possums," Hollis Andersen said from where he lazed on the steps.

"I've been helping her clean pots," he said. "It was the only way she'd let a man on trial stay in one of her rooms."

"That woman doesn't have much schooling," Hollis said, grinning, "but she *is* a smart one when it comes to practical things."

"I'm finding that out. I'm grateful to her, no matter how much work she's gotten out of me."

Uley had seen him, apron and all. He could see Old Croppy veering toward him. "Hello, Mr. Brown," she called out.

He decided her low, lilting voice was as pleasing as wild honey. She flopped the reins over the mule's head and jumped down beside him.

"What's this you're wearing?" She tugged at the hem of the unsightly apron, cocking her head at him like a sparrow.

"It's Kate Fischer's. I can't seem to get it off. I was in a hurry, and there's a knot back there, and I don't —"

She had already walked around him. "Ah, apron strings," she teased him. "I hear they've been the undoing of many a man."

"That," he told her, "and a late supply wagon."

She laid one hand on the back of his shoulder. "You waitin' for the wagon today, Aaron? You think he'll be on it?"

"I don't rightly know," Aaron said, wishing he could take her fingers in his and turn toward her. "He could be." Her fingers, against his shoulder blade, seemed to sear into his very bone.

"You haven't heard anything, then?"

"No," he answered sadly. "I don't figure I will. Hayes'll come if he gets my letter in time. He won't bother to send word. It wouldn't beat him here."

Why are you watching for the wagon, Uley, after I've done my level best to push you away?

The jangle of a wagon rig cut into the still afternoon.

"Wagon's comin' in," Hollis hollered, jumping from his step and dusting the brim of his hat against his leg.

The cry echoed up and down both sides of the street, seeming to come from everywhere at once.

"Wagon's coming in!"

"McClain's bringing his team in!"

"Look's like he's got passengers."

"Wagon's coming in!"

"We'd best get rid of this knot," Uley said softly from behind him. He felt her hand uncurl and slide to the base of his spine. "You won't want to be wearing this if Hayes arrives today."

While she worked on him, he rose to the toes of his boots and shaded his eyes against the glare.

He'd never seen a wagon move so slowly.

"Yah!" he heard McClain bellow to the

mules as he cracked a whip above their heads. "Get on along." The sound carried a good half mile. "We got passengers to unload."

Chapter Eleven

All the while the wagon bumped up Washington Avenue, Uley's fingers flew at the knot. Even the excitement of McClain pulling in couldn't rival the tumult she felt as she stood behind Aaron, unfastening his work-worn apron strings. Was this the way a wife would untie apron strings for her husband? Perhaps after he'd spent a grueling day as a smithy or a cooper or a shop clerk?

Uley felt, for this one moment, as if an untying such as this one could be some ultimate act of caring. She pretended, just then, that it was so. She found one end of the bleached canvas and followed it gingerly as it wove through two loops and then back again. She found the other end and pulled it out backward. It came, flapping. "What did you do to this thing, Aaron Brown?" she asked, not certain whether he could hear her voice quaking. Was it only her ears that noted the difference as she tried to speak? "I've not seen such a rat's nest since I tried to knit once."

She heard the lift in his own voice. "You tried to knit?"

"I wanted to make Pa a warm sweater for Christmas the first year we were in Tin Cup."

He laughed. "I can assure you I wasn't trying to do some fool thing like that. I only wanted to untie it quickly. I saw you and Old Croppy coming up the way. I didn't want you to see me unless I had on my fine suit."

"Ah . . ." She chuckled lightly as her fingers continued to work. "So that's why. And I only want you to see me in a dress that's pink, with so many petticoats under it I look like a chime in a church steeple." Aunt Delilah had sent her a copy of *Graham's* just last week. It wasn't the latest, but Uley had still read it cover to cover.

"Keep describing it," he said teasingly. "I can almost picture you."

She hadn't forgotten what they were both waiting for. "You see him on that wagon yet?"

Several of the men on the steps beside them had run on ahead to greet McClain. But not Aaron. He was purposely prolonging the waiting. If Dawson Hayes wasn't on today's wagon, he didn't want to know it. "I don't recognize anybody."

He stood stock-still, legs spread wide, gazing up the road, while she stood behind him, taking him in. The cotton shirt was pulled taut between his shoulder blades and wrinkled at the hip where his apron bunched it. His sleeves clung where his forearms twisted with muscle. The domestic garment from Kate Fischer's only served to emphasize his brawn and broadness. She guessed he'd been in such a hurry to get down here, he'd forgotten his Stetson. So many times when she saw him, the brim of it shadowed his eyes. Without it, he seemed strangely exposed, vulnerable.

Her hands paused. Vulnerability. Broad ruggedness. And this was Aaron Brown.

The moment forced her to acknowledge the flush that filled her every time she came into his presence, something she didn't entirely understand. She stood absorbing it, anticipating it, this sweet longing that rose from nothingness into burgeoning flame.

It was everything she could do to keep from laying her head against his back, drawing him near, turning her anticipation into action. But she had entirely no idea how a proper lady would respond to something like this. Would a proper young lady feel this at *all?* Laura had said so. But suppose Laura was wrong. Suppose this longing, this . . . this *desperation,* was something unprecedented.

The instant passed and was gone. She felt, rather than saw, Aaron tense. "Do you see who's in the supply wagon?" she asked, not really wanting to know the answer.

"Yes," he answered her quietly. "Dawson isn't with McClain. I should have figured as much."

Her spirited plummeted. "I'm sorry, Aaron. I'm so sorry."

"Me too." He sighed, sounding more lost than ever. "Ah, I didn't figure he'd make it in today, anyway. Everybody else started me expectin' it."

At long last, Uley freed him from the apron. "There you are," she said, throwing the strings wide. "You're unfastened."

"Thanks." He tugged the thing off and held it wadded in one hand, facing the wagon.

Neither of them knew what to say.

Neither of them wanted to leave.

"Well," he said finally, tucking the discarded apron up under one arm. "You have to take nails or something back up to the Gold Cup?"

"That and two spools of filament. I've got to strap the spools onto Old Croppy."

"I'll help," he said.

And so he did. Uley handed the rope to Aaron beneath the mule's glistening flank. He took it from her hand, masterfully crossing it back over beneath the packs, line over load. Instead of flipping it across Old Croppy's back to her, he held it out so that Uley could take it from him.

When she did, his hand released, then gripped again, trapping Uley's fingers lightly against the hemp.

She looked at her hand. She looked at him. She felt the warm pressure of his flesh against her own.

"Aaron?" she asked, mesmerized.

He said nothing. He just slid his hand up toward the pack, releasing her. She stood there for a moment as their gazes locked across the spindly mane of the mule.

Abruptly she broke the spell, bending to put more of the mule's barrel-shaped body between them.

She passed him the rope again. This time, as she did, he claimed her hand.

She pulled it away.

Wordlessly he worked the rope over Old Croppy's back again, waiting for her to extend her hand and take it.

She did, this time giving him pause by meeting his palm beneath the mule's body. In her eyes Aaron plainly saw the illicit turn her thoughts had taken as she stood with him at the roadside. She let her hand slide between his own, and their fingers slowly meshed together. There they knelt, with Old Croppy between them, bound together by their absorption in each other as certainly as the rope lashed Old Croppy's packs.

The mule brayed impatiently above them, and Aaron suddenly seemed to remember where they were. He squeezed her hand, freed her and cleared his throat. "Can I walk you up the hill, Uley? I'd like to know you've made it safely."

It was these small hints of gentlemanliness that endeared him to her totally. "Yes," she said, making ready to stand. "Oh, Aaron, please do."

He took Old Croppy's reins, and they started across Grand Avenue.

At last he found the courage to ask the question that had been plaguing him since he first saw her craning her neck in the direction of the wagon. "Why did you come, Uley? What did you have at stake in McClain's arrival this afternoon?"

How could she answer such a question?

My heart is at stake, Aaron. I wait for that wagon with my heart skipping just like I know you do.

Father, what should I say to him? "I watch for the wagon every day it comes in. That's all. There might be something important on it." *Or somebody. Like Dawson Hayes, who could save your life.*

They walked on, both of them silent, as the aspen leaves quivered above in the breeze, casting mottled sunlight upon the ground in startling green hues.

Could I truly make my life here? Aaron wondered. *If that jury lets me live and Uley agrees to stay by my side?*

Would I leave this? Would I give my life up to go to Ohio, to become somebody different? Uley asked herself. *Because I'd want to be somebody different for him.*

As Aaron walked, he faced the very real possibility that Dawson Hayes might not heed his letter. Until he'd stood by the town hall with Uley fiddling at his apron strings, he hadn't even considered the possibility that Hayes might not come. Now the full weight of that possibility struck him.

What could he do?

His own stubbornness had got himself involved in a situation that he couldn't get away from anymore than he could swim upstream.

The answer was simple. He couldn't. He could only ward it off for the few days remaining by remembering his dreams, by sharing them, by focusing upon the treasures life had given him and on what might be yet to come.

Aaron hesitated beside an aspen, snapped off a low-lying branch and ran it alongside his leg, the way a boy would run a stick along a picket fence. "Beth and I have been talking," he said.

"I'd have given anything for a sister to talk to," Uley commented.

"She is quite refined," he said, staring off into the sky. "A refined lady can be a prize for any man, whether she is his sister or his love."

"Yes. I'm sure that's so." He didn't see her face as she said it, so he couldn't see that his words had cut into her very soul.

"Beth and I will stay in Tin Cup if the jury finds me innocent. Beth has too many sad memories to face at home at the farm. And I've always wanted to try my hand at a livery. I plan to rent out the finest horses, carriages and drays. I believe I could give Smith some healthy competition."

He'd expected his words to please her.

But now, as he glanced sideways, he saw that her face had gone pallid.

"What is it, Uley? What's wrong?"

None of the things she wanted the two of them to share could come if he stayed in this place. She'd even entertained the notion of returning from Ohio to Fort Collins, twirling a parasol as she sauntered up beside him. "Hello," she'd say as she gave him a delicate curtsy in a dress just like the one she'd seen in *Graham's.* "Fancy meeting you here, Mr. Brown."

"Oh, Aaron . . ." she said bleakly. She couldn't say more. She wouldn't discourage a dream that might give him strength during these last heart-wrenching days.

"And if I get out of this alive," Aaron said, "I'm going to hire John Kincaid to prosecute Harris Olney. Beth has convinced me I was wrong to take matters into my own hands. But to me that always seemed the right way to accomplish things. I learned a long time ago not to rely on anybody else."

"Why is that?"

"When I was a boy, I had a pa who taught me such things. He taught me the only proper way to build a barn was to hammer in every peg myself. He was a stubborn man, my pa. He taught me the only way to make certain a cow had given all her milk was to keep my own hands squeezin' the udders. He thought the best way to hay a field was to go out with the thresher and cut it down himself."

"Sounds like he didn't trust other people much."

"He didn't. I found out when I was older that he'd had an older brother who'd stolen money once. My grandma kept their life savings in a tin canister on the warming shelf of the stove. His brother up and went to Texas, saying he was gonna make a living bringing longhorns up the Colorado Trail to Kansas. Three days later she found all the money gone. She never saw him again, and she never forgave him. I figure, from things Pa said, she never forgave my pa, either. She held him guilty just on the grounds they were brothers."

"What a horrible burden for a mother to place upon her son."

"I know that. He lived under it all his life. And he passed it down to me." Aaron stopped where he stood then, just gazing at Uley, not knowing whether he should tell her how much what she was doing meant to him. But if he didn't tell her, she'd never know. "A month ago, I wondered if I could trust you. Everything you'd ever done for me had come because I blackmailed you into it. You have seen me at my worst. You have viewed me as a murderer. Yet I don't believe you see that anymore."

"I don't."

"Why not?"

She hadn't admitted it to anyone, not even herself. "Because I believe you told Judge Murphy the truth, Aaron. I don't think you're guilty of the accusations brought against you."

"What makes you so sure?"

"A feeling I have. A . . . a . . . reassurance, I suppose."

"Why?"

"Because I know you."

They were nearing the mine. Anxious to postpone their parting, Uley stopped, dropping Old Croppy's lead rope, and bent to pick several candlelike stems of kingly purple larkspur. Their scent was strong, not quite pleasant but she still held the flowers against her nose, scarcely daring to look at Aaron.

"That's how it is," he said softly. "A man learns to trust when others trust him."

She raised her eyes to his. "Surely there has been someone else who believed in you. What about Beth?"

"Never in the same way. Never in a way that took the worst of me and turned it into the best of me, as you've done."

She had no answer for him. She was powerless to still the thundering of her heart.

"Tell me about you, Uley," he said gently. "Tell me about your life before you came to Tin Cup. Were you once a carefree little girl?"

Despite herself, she smiled. "Of course. Pa ran a dry goods shop in Wheeling, West Virginia. We had a willow tree in the backyard that made a perfect playhouse. I could slip inside the circle of its limbs with all my tea-party things, and Ma couldn't find me."

"You? Tea parties?" He eyed her mischievously, looking her up and down.

"I had grand parties. But that wasn't the only thing. We had a limestone cave back behind the house. A neighbor boy, Jarvis Henderson, was afraid to go in. He said his mama told him not to go in because the cave had a ghost. I had to prove to him that was just an old mama's trick to keep boys out of caves."

"How did you prove it?"

"I took him by the hand and led him all the way back. Mrs. Henderson about skinned me alive when she found out about it. She wouldn't let Jarvis play with me for a month afterward."

"Were you excited when your ma and pa decided to come out West?"

This time, she took longer in answering. "Pa had talked about gold for years. He kept hearing the stories and dreaming of them. Ma didn't want to come. He was making a good living at the store, and we were all comfortable. I heard them talking one night. He said, 'Sarah Kirkland, a man has to have something to look forward to. A man has to follow what's in his soul, or else he'll wither up and die like a bad crop of corn.' So we sold everything and started out."

"Even though she didn't want to?"

"I know you are a God-fearing man, Aaron Brown. You've spoken to me about the Lord. I found your Bible among your personal belongings that day you sent me to your room. You know what the Bible says about a woman following her husband. It would have made it easier on Pa if she'd been excited about it. When she died of pneumonia, in Ohio, it was like she gave up her life doing something she didn't want to do. I sometimes thought she gave up because she didn't want to try life this way."

Uley turned away so that he couldn't see the tears that were coming. "I've been mad at her for a long time for that. I've been mad at her for dying." Now that she was finally confessing it, the frustration she'd been carrying came pouring out. "I've been mad at her for ruining Pa's dream. I've been mad at Pa for making her do something she didn't want to do.

"Mostly, I'm mad at both of them for her not being around now. I've got so many womanly questions to ask her. I don't know how —" She looked up at him then, tears streaming down her face, like an innocent child begging for help. "I've had to decide so many things and *be* so many things."

"I see."

"And now I think I'm getting mad at God because He hasn't saved *you*."

Gently, he reached for one of her hands. Aaron held her hand within two of his own. "We're quite a pair, aren't we, you and me?"

"I suppose." She stood motionless, as perfectly still as a fawn in the wilderness, ready to run, not knowing if she should move and give herself away.

"Of all the things you had to be," he said quietly, daring finally to ask the question that had plagued him for many nights as he lay awake thinking of her, "have you always been . . . Uley? Is Uley your given name? Or is it something you and your pa came up with to complete the charade in Tin Cup?"

She smiled then, tears sparkling in her eyes like stars, and shook her head at him. "No. Uley isn't my given name. That came from a book. Pa and I were crossing Nebraska with a book about mining in hand. In it was a story about Uley Jacob, an old miner who'd come to Colorado and hit pay dirt even before he pitched his tent. Pa thought it would bring us good luck if he called me Uley, too. And it was such a funny name, something I thought you'd only call a dog or a mule. We laughed about it all the way across eastern Colorado. By the time we arrived here and it was time to introduce myself, it was funny and familiar. So I used it."

He was gazing down at her, a strange expression on his face. "Every time I turn around, I see something new in you. First it was all that beautiful taffy-colored hair. I look at you and think of it all jammed up inside that funny little hat and I can scarcely bear not touching it. Then it's the way I feel whenever our hands meet . . . as if it's forbidden . . . as if I'm giving secrets away because of what's happening inside me. Now I find I don't even know what your name is. Uley, I feel like I'm walking on a log, tottering, about to fall off. I don't know what to do about you."

"There's nothing to do about me," she whispered. "It isn't . . ."

He still clasped her hand between his own, and he could feel them trembling.

"Tell me."

"I shouldn't."

A week, only a week, remained before the trial resumed. The hours and their passing would stay with Aaron now. The ticking watch in his pocket would add constantly to the weight he carried within him.

Aaron took Uley's second hand in his own and held both of them against his chest so that she, too, could feel the moments slipping away between them. "I want to know your name," he said desperately. "I don't want to die next Friday and not know who you are, Uley. You, the person who trusts me."

The tears that had been glistening in her eyes now welled up and spilled over. Aaron's first inclination was to release her and wipe them away. He didn't. He stood before her, hanging on to her as best he could, letting them fall unhindered.

"I —" But she couldn't speak just yet. Her emotion ran too deep. She felt as if Aaron had broken down a wall within the very core of her. Just by caring, he'd released portions of the little girl she'd been, portions that had been buried deep within her since the day the black Ohio loam had landed in shovelfuls atop Sarah's makeshift coffin.

"It's okay," he told her, over and over. "It's okay, Uley. It's okay. I shouldn't have pushed."

But she shook her head. "No, I —" And then she laughed. It was a light little chirp that sounded like the warble of a bird. "I want to tell you. I haven't thought of it in so long. And, somehow, it didn't seem important to me anymore. But it is, isn't it?"

"It is."

She pulled her hands away, and this time, he let her go.

"My name, do you want to know my real name?"

When he realized she was going to say it, he felt his heart shove halfway up into his throat.

"My name is Julia. Julia Kirkland." Then she smiled up at him. "You like it? That's who I really am."

"Julia," he said, trying it on for size. "Julia."

"Ma always called me Jubilee when I was little."

"I like that," he said. "It fits you."

"Another reason I picked Uley. It sounded somewhat the same."

Old Croppy waited nearby, his nose lowered to the ground, his yellow teeth ripping at the dandelions and clumps of butterwort that grew among the trees up here. The pines towered above them, their lofty trunks reaching toward the heavens with nary a bend nor a twist, their limbs bearing bundles of pungent, fleshy green needles. As the wind picked up, the trees creaked overhead like old rocking chairs.

Somewhere in the wood, a nuthatch began to hammer away with its beak, the sound echoing throughout the thicket. *Rat-tat-tat. Rat-tat-tat-tat. Rat-tat.*

Uley and Aaron stood facing one another, facing what the world had done to them, what the future would probably bring.

It was Uley who moved first. With a choked sob, she flew into Aaron's arms. Aaron caught her against him, gripping her with such fierceness that he knocked the breath out of her.

That didn't matter.

Nothing mattered.

"Oh, Julia," he whispered. The sound of her name seemed to reverberate against the tree trunks that surrounded them. "Julia . . ."

"Don't stop holding me. Please, Aaron."

"I don't ever want to."

He savored her closeness, saved it in his mind so that he'd have it to draw upon forever.

However long his forever was going to be.

"Uley . . . Julia. Jubilee Kirkland." His voice was suddenly full of purpose. He knew what he was going to do. He let her go just long enough to trace one tentative finger across her cheek. "What would you say if I kissed you?"

Her green eyes glittered up at him like peridots. *Ought she to let him kiss her?* This was all so new that the thought made her joyous but it also made her struggle. What if she said "no"? What if he died, and they never had the chance again?

"Yes," she told him. "I would like that."

He cupped her face in his hands, and then slowly, without asking permission, removed her funny little cap. "If I kiss you, I'm gonna take this silly thing off."

She didn't stop him. She stood still and tall, only a breath away, waiting for him, anticipating it all.

He removed the hat and hung it on a nearby branch.

He turned to look at her. She stood before him, the essence of femininity, with all the burnished hair escaping from her bun waving in unruly wisps around her face.

She raised her hands to the back of her head.

"You want to see the rest of it?"

He swallowed. "Yes."

"Very well, then."

As he stood mesmerized, she completed the task for him, carefully pulling hairpins out of the smooth knot twisted against her neck.

"Here," he whispered breathily, not daring to move. Good grief, how he had dreamed of this moment. "I'll help you."

"You won't . . . know . . . where they are," she said, her heart ramming crazily against her ribs. "I'll do the pins. You just . . . watch . . ."

What she gave him today symbolized everything she wanted to give him in their future, a future that might never come. She'd never set her hair free before a man before. Since she'd stopped wearing pigtails, in Ohio, she'd only let it down in darkness, once to brush it and braid it at night, once to remove the braid and twist it back into a chignon before the sun first came up over the eastern mountains.

Aaron counted pins to keep himself sane, scarcely daring to breathe as he waited for the inevitable to happen.

Two pins. Three.

She held them between her teeth and smiled beguilingly at him.

Four pins.

"I can't lose these pins," she said with them still in her teeth. He was scared to death she would swallow one. Then they'd both be found out. "I'll have to put it back up before I get to the Gold Cup."

"I have a pocket. I can keep them safe for you here." He laid one hand over his breast, suddenly realizing that, when he'd indicated his pocket, he'd also rested his hand precisely over his heart.

I can keep them safe for you here.

Five. Six pins.

She took them from her teeth and laid them in his palm. They were still wet from her mouth. He jingled them once in his hand, then pocketed them.

Seven pins.

The seventh pin did it.

A tumult of hair escaped in a disorderly tumble, cascading down past her shoulders to lay against her breasts, the curls riotous as they encircled her forearms.

Aaron had never seen such hair.

Uley had never felt so beautiful, so cherished, so much a woman.

His eyes were dark now . . . almost the hue she'd often imagined the ocean would be during a storm.

Aaron reached for her hair, grasping it where it lay against her shoulders, combing his fingers through it.

"You like it?"

His voice was as coarse as gravel. "I do."

She held her breath.

"I dream about this hair, you know. I suppose it will be my last thought before I give way to the hangman's noose."

Don't talk that way, she wanted to say. *Don't think of such things.* But it was something they both needed to think of, something that — as the days passed by — became more and more of a threat.

Aaron gripped her forearms, pulling her toward him. She met his fixed gaze at close range. His eyes, which from a distance appeared a solid crystal blue, now bore faint speckles of navy and lines of rich silver, as he gazed down at her.

She stepped against him and lifted her face to his.

He brushed his mouth across her lips just once, as lightly as the flicker of a butterfly's wing beating against the breeze.

She felt the breath catch. Her eyes met his again, wide and mezmerizingly green.

Aaron's heart almost stopped as she followed his bidding without stopping to question him. Their lips met again, coming together delicately, slipping to a position where they fit together and then fit even closer.

"Aaron," she whispered against his mouth. "I don't know how to do this."

"You are doing just fine."

Her lips parted further, and she stilled, waiting for Aaron to teach her.

Her tongue tasted faintly of horehound candy as he encouraged her.

Here, in Aaron's arms, she felt as if she were viewing her life from some wonderful, pivoting angle. She wanted to wrap her arms around Aaron's neck and hang on to him forever. Yet, as reality came, she knew she couldn't. No matter what the outcome of the trial was. No matter what they felt for one another. She knew nothing of being a man's woman. She knew nothing of daily tasks in a home. No man wanted to marry a girl whose greatest talent was shearing off timbers and shoring up a mine.

Aaron had said so himself only an hour earlier.

A refined lady can be a prize for any man, whether she is his sister or his love.

He deserved a woman like Beth, a delicate woman with social graces and soft hands and irreproachable ways. Uley could never be such a woman. She couldn't even pretend to be. And she was desperately, desperately tired of pretending.

She knew Aaron felt her sudden uncertainty. He backed off a bit and touched her nose, cocking his face at her and giving her a quirky little grin. "What is it, little one?" he asked. "What's wrong?"

Uley took one step away from his arms. "Oh, Aaron. So many things, I don't know where to start."

"Don't you like this? Don't you like me kissing you?"

"Yes," she said, as she felt unwanted tears rising in her eyes again. "I like you kissing me. That's why I'm fearful of all this."

As she backed away a little more, he could have kicked himself. He'd gone and done what he'd promised he wouldn't do.

He'd gone and reached out to her, showing her his feelings, when he had no right to do so. He had no right to make her care for him now. "Uley. I'm sorry. I shouldn't have done it."

She touched his arm briefly, reassuringly. "I'm glad you did. Aaron, I *wanted* you to. Don't be sorry for it . . . please. Without this, I might never have known how it would feel. Thank you."

He looked at her in disbelief. "You're thanking me?"

She said, "Yes. Even though I'm telling you it mustn't happen again."

He said, "I know that, too."

Already she was struggling with her hair. "I'd best be gettin' back up to the Gold Cup. They'll think I've taken Old Croppy and left town." With one hand, she bunched her shiny dark red hair at her neck and began to twist it around to contain it.

Aaron watched, noting that she had hair that couldn't be easily contained. "I have a comb." He pulled it from his vest pocket and handed it to her. "I always keep one handy."

"Thank you again, Aaron Talephas Brown," she said, smiling. She took the tortoiseshell comb from his hand and began to run it through her hair's richly colored strands. The comb's teeth separated them into tiny, fine runnels. As she worked her way through her hair, it fell against her shoulders in a sleek spray, the curls combed into submissive ripples. She finished both sides, then continued around to the back of it, struggling with a tangle she couldn't reach.

"You want me to do that?" he asked, his voice coarse.

"Would you?" she asked. "I can't get at it. I'll never make it all go into the bun if I don't work through that tangle."

He reached for the comb.

She hiked up the knees of her breeches and settled on a stump. "There you go. How's that? Can you reach me?"

"Yes. I can."

He stood feet apart, brandishing the comb, looking down at the back of her head. Now, how did a man do something like this? Where did he begin? He was terrified he would hurt her. He passed the comb once through her luxuriant hair. It gleamed in the sun like burnished copper. It felt like fine satin beneath his fingers.

"Ouch," she said. "Aaron, you mustn't tug so."

He gulped, holding the comb up as if he

were a butcher trying to decide at which angle to begin slicing beef. "I don't know how to do this."

"Then we'll both have learned something today," she said, chuckling again. "When you get to the tangle, make the comb go sideways. Pull out the larger strands first, until the remainder of it begins to fall free."

"Okay. Here I go." He lowered the comb. He stopped, swallowed, raised it again.

"Come on," she said. Then she laughed. "I promise not to say 'ouch' again. I've frightened you, I can see."

"Yes, you did. I didn't want to hurt you." How he meant those words — in a great many ways that had nothing to do with the fact that her hair was tangled.

He brandished the comb once more and returned to his chore.

She sat silently before him on the stump, her sleek, rippling hair lying like a fan against her shoulders.

Silence surrounded them.

Chore, Aaron decided, was the wrong word to use. This was no chore. As he combed her hair, he thought of a million different nights he'd like to share with her, a lifetime of them, a couple sitting in a home, the husband combing out tangles for the wife, as the fire flickered a dance of light and shadow on the wall beside them.

Her hair, as it moved between his fingers, took on a thousand evanescent colors. As he worked the shimmering strands through his fingers, Aaron had the feeling that her hair was magic, that it was never the same color twice.

The silence around them faded as the forest filled with sound. The trees creaked in the wind. A lazuli bunting called from its song perch. *Sweet-weet-chew . . . chew-seet-chew . . .* Aaron combing was almost more familiar and intimate than the kiss had been. The comb crackled through her hair, and he followed it with his hand, separating the strands and pressing them down to smoothness.

At last, at long last, she caught his hand with hers to stop him. "That should be fine," she whispered.

"I suppose it is."

"I should go."

"Yes, you should." Reluctantly he pocketed the comb.

She gathered her hair at the nape of her neck and began to twist it up again. He watched as it went up, twisting into a knot the same shape as a plump biscuit pretzel.

She stopped and turned, cupping the

bun in one hand and extending the other to him. "My pins, Aaron. I need my pins."

"Oh, yes." He touched a hand to his breast pocket and felt them there. "Here." He poked his fingers into his pocket and pulled out three of the pins.

"I'll need them one at a time," she said.

He dumped two of them back in and handed her the first. He winced as she jabbed it almost straight into her head.

"Another, please."

He fished out another.

And so they went through seven pins, Aaron extending them, Uley jabbing them in with gusto. Then she placed the cap firmly atop the bun and wiggled it into place. "There we go," she said, satisfied. She stood and wrestled the cuffs of her knickers down around the tops of her socks.

He waited. How could anybody — *anybody* — mistake her for a member of the male gender? Aaron wondered. She was the most mysterious, intriguing, *feminine* woman he'd ever known. Not feminine in the way of lace gloves and a parasol and bustles billowing out yards and yards behind her. She was a woman in an earthy fashion, unaffected, and sensible in a way that would serve a man well. Aaron wanted to take her into his arms again so desperately that he could scarcely bear it.

"I'd best be going," she said. "Old Croppy's eaten enough butterwort to give him stomach problems for a week. They'll never forgive me up at the mine."

"Yes," he said. "You'd best get Old Croppy out of here. I'm sure they'll have missed you by now."

Still she stood before him. "You gonna wait for the next supply wagon when it comes in?"

"Don't know. There isn't much use for it. I don't think I can bear the suspense of waiting while that thing jangles up the road toward me. I'll probably just stay at Aunt Kate's next time. If Dawson Hayes makes it into town, he'll be able to find me." He clapped his hands once in front of him, then swung them nonchalantly back and forth.

"I feel the same way," she said softly. "I'm afraid to watch for it, too. I figure if I don't go down there and wait, Dawson Hayes will come in. That's how it works, isn't it? The water never boils while you watch it?"

"That's how it works, all right."

Uley had put off leaving for as long as possible. She gathered Old Croppy's reins and tugged the mule toward her. "Goodbye, Aaron," she said with one backward glance. "I suppose I'll see you around town."

My life's been changed because of you. I'm not who I was before you kissed me. I'm trying to figure out what it is that God wants from me now.

But she couldn't say those things. She centered her attention on the furry pack animal, which was still resisting her. "Come on, mule. We've got mining to do."

Chapter Twelve

Aunt Kate Fischer's business at the board-inghouse doubled while Elizabeth Calder-wood and Aaron Brown remained in her keeping. Elizabeth cheerfully carried plates to the men at every meal, setting the steaming food upon the table with a mitt while the fellows lining the pine benches watched her every move, like cats ready to pounce on a mouse.

"Thank you, Miss Elizabeth," they said, one after another.

"Right pretty dress you're wearin', Miss Elizabeth."

"Nice-looking meal, Mrs. Calderwood."

"Pretty thing like you shouldn't be workin' in a boardinghouse, Miss Eliza-beth. I've got enough gold to pay your keep. Wish you would let me."

She smiled at them all, graciously ac-cepting their attentions, knowing full well they'd act the same way around any woman as long as her arms and legs were in the right place and she didn't have two heads. She answered them kindly.

Aaron stood inside the kitchen, up to his elbows in dishwater, listening to the miners wooing his sister. As he swished a rag over a plate, he decided Aunt Kate had no idea how much extra money she was pulling in with Beth serving out there. The place was packed morning, noon and night.

Beth came back into the kitchen with a pile of dirty plates balanced precariously on one arm. As she turned to place them on the sideboard, he could see the white linen bow of her apron tied perkily at the back of her waist. She'd make some man a fine wife, he thought. She'd made Fred a fine wife. They'd been happy until Harris Olney started meddling in their lives. As she piled up the plates, they finished the conversation they'd started before Aunt Kate's noon crowd had come in.

"I don't see why you're askin' me all these questions about women, Aaron."

"Because you know these things," he told her, carefully polishing another plate and doing his best to look noncommittal. "I want to know what it means when a woman says she likes you to kiss her one minute and says she's afraid of that kiss the next."

"It means she feels something for you in

her heart, Aaron." She stopped where she stood and tilted her head at him like a sparrow. "No woman likes to be kissed by somebody she doesn't care about, Aaron. And often, when a girl starts caring for a fellow, it scares her a bit. Did a girl say she liked you to kiss her?"

He nodded his head.

"She said that it frightened her when you kissed her?"

"Something like that."

Beth tucked a stray wisp of hair behind one ear and grinned at him. "You've done it, then, little brother. You've made some young gal fall for you. I'd like to meet her."

"It isn't like that. You don't need to meet her. Nothing can come of it."

"Did you leave a sweetheart behind in Fort Collins that I don't know about?"

"No."

"Well," she said, filling three more plates and making ready to head back out the door to serve them. "It's clear you're sweet on *somebody*. Who is she, Aaron?"

At that moment Aaron would have liked nothing better than to tell her about Uley Kirkland. But he'd made a solemn promise never to reveal Uley's secret. "I can't say."

"Why not?"

"I just can't."

She shook her head at her brother, teasing him. "I can't stand here all morning and listen to a fellow pining about a love he can't have. I've got to get these lunches out, or those hungry men'll have my hide."

"They want your hide, all right," Aaron said, "and it doesn't have anything to do with lunch."

After she left, Aaron turned back to the dishwater. *I promised to keep Uley's secret all my life,* he thought. *That life may be over in four days. Or it may last another fifty years. How can I face any more months of feeling what I feel for Uley and not telling anyone?*

Even before the thought was completed, Beth, white-faced, came back through the door and leaned up against it as if to hold it shut.

"What is it? What's wrong?"

"Olney just stepped in," she said, her breath coming in short gasps. "Wants me to serve him some of Aunt Kate's 'possum.' Doesn't the good Lord know there's only so much I can stand?"

Aaron's hands stilled in the water. "Don't go out. I'll take care of him." He let go of the plate he was washing and turned to dry his hands.

Beth stopped him with an upraised hand. "No," she said vehemently.

"It shouldn't be a woman's job to handle it. It should be mine. I'm your brother. I'll protect your honor."

"You've done too much of that already. Do you know how sorry I am I got you involved in all this in the first place?" All the while they talked, she dished up a plate of barbecued goose, beans, carrots and corn bread. "I won't give the people in this town another reason to convict you," she said, pushing her way back out the door to the dining room. "He's just here to eat. I ought to be able to handle putting a plate down in front of him."

The lunch rush was over. For a moment, as Aaron listened, all remained quiet in the room next door. He heard the other men leaving. Then he heard Harris Olney say, "Thank you, Beth. Looks like a mighty fine meal. Did you cook it?"

"No," she answered tersely. "Kate cooks. I just serve the plates."

"Fred used to say you were the best cook in the state of Colorado."

"It isn't my place to cook here, Harris." She turned her back and started toward the kitchen.

"Surely you don't think I came in here to

eat this stupid goose filled with buckshot and covered with molasses," Harris began. "I came in here to see you."

"Well, you've seen me."

"I want to do more than see you. I want to talk to you."

"You're talking to me now. You've already gotten more words out of me than I care to emit."

"I want to know if you're stayin' in Tin Cup after Aaron hangs."

"I don't see how I can stay here, Harris," she said quietly, anger and hurt filling her eyes. "You've already personally done away with one man I loved, and now you're tryin' to do away with another. Just because you wear a star, you think you can do anything. I'm here to support Aaron, Harris. After it's all over, I don't want to be anywhere within two hundred miles of you."

When the marshal spoke again, his ire was palpable. "You'd do best to get rid of that attitude right now, Mrs. Elizabeth Calderwood. All you've got is Aaron's word against mine."

"Aaron is my brother, Harris. He's my own flesh and blood. I helped Mama bathe him when he was a baby. I know who I trust and who I don't."

"Ever the vixen," he said, leaning back and laughing much too heartily.

"Stay away from me," Beth said. "You're the murderer, not Aaron. We both know that."

"Dawson Hayes isn't coming to help your brother, Beth. I want you to know that."

She glared at him. "Why would you say that? What makes you think such a thing? Of course Dawson Hayes will come."

"Don't you think he'd have been here by now if he was on his way?" Harris asked pompously. "I'm the marshal around here." He toyed with his meal with his fork. "I make it my practice to know what's going to happen in this county."

"You make it your practice to manipulate things."

His eyes locked with hers. When he spoke again, it was in a seductive yet disdainful tone that thoroughly repulsed her. "I don't want to see you disappointed on Saturday. It will be easier to face it now."

This was too much for Beth. How she hated Harris Olney. How she longed for the moment when she and Aaron could bring him to justice. For the first time, she understood Aaron's fierce commitment to track Olney to the Western Slope.

Father, forgive me for disliking this man

as much as I do. "My brother could have killed you easily. But no. He had to do things right. He had to do it the hard way and bring you in. And look what he's gotten for being fair." She knew Harris well enough to recognize his discomfort. "I don't know what you're up to, Harris Olney, but you're not going to get away with it."

Olney laid his napkin beside his plate and rose to go. "We'll see about that, won't we?" He looked down at her as if he were chastizing a child. "I suppose I'll go somewhere else for my supper. Doesn't seem like I'm welcome here."

Three days before Aaron Brown's trial was set to resume, attorney John Kincaid sifted through the papers on his desk for the fifth time, doing his absolute best to find something, anything, that might break this case wide open.

Things did not look good.

Resolutely he pushed himself back from his desk and poked one arm into his suit coat sleeve. He finished with the other and did up the buttons. He had an appointment over at Santa Fe Moll's place of an unusual sort, an appointment that couldn't wait.

He helped himself to a cheroot from the humidor on his desk, chomping it between his upper and lower bicuspids like a dog carrying meat away to be buried, then settled his fine derby hat at a jaunty angle atop his crown.

If he could win it, this was the case that would make his career. This was the case that would have everyone calling for his expertise, criminal and law-abiding citizen alike.

If, he reminded himself again, he could win it.

The way things stood, he didn't have much hope of that. But Kincaid knew how to fix things. He wasn't going to rely on some old coot of a trapper who lived out with the Ute Indians. Nosiree, Bob. His law career was too important to leave to happenstance. It was time to take matters into his own hands.

Kincaid swung onto his horse and made his way directly to Ongewach's. He arched one booted leg over and off the saddle, slid down and jumped to the dirt. By the time he flipped the reins over the hitching rail, Santa Fe Moll was standing in the doorway waiting for him. "You're late."

"I got tied up in business this morning," he said, removing his derby.

She didn't move back from the doorway, but just stood there, clasping her emerald-green dressing gown around her. She took the cheroot from his teeth and kissed him full on the mouth.

He grinned down at her with teeth as white as pearls. "I believe we've got business to attend to."

"Ah," she said, laughing as the huge pine door swung shut behind them. "So it's business now, is it?"

"Yes, ma'am," he said. "Business before pleasure. However unfortunate that may be."

"Nothing's unfortunate with you, John."

He took his cigar out of her hand and placed it back in his mouth. "I need to hire the services of one of your girls on Friday afternoon, Miss Moll."

"Oh, really?"

"It isn't for me, Moll. Don't you worry. You know how I feel about you. There could never be anybody else."

"Yeah. I know."

"Answer one question for me, Moll. Has Aaron Brown ever been at your place?"

She thought back. "No. I don't think so."

"Has he ever come into Ongewach's? Has he ever gotten close enough that we could place him here?"

"Never more than to poke his head in the front door looking for somebody."

"I need somebody who'll be willing to testify in Aaron Brown's trial. Somebody who'll be willing to say he's been in. Someone willing to say she's spent time with Brown."

"Pick your girl. I'm sure any of them would be happy to assist you, John."

"I've already picked. I want Wishbone Mabel. Of all your girls, I think she'll have the most credibility on the witness stand."

"You tell her I said to do whatever you need. She'll accommodate you."

"I'm going to need to talk to her for an hour or two this afternoon."

"Fine. She'll keep track of the time. That'll be two dollars an hour, for today and tomorrow, too."

"Moll? You going to charge me for putting Mabel on the stand?"

"Of course I am." She grinned. "Business is business, isn't that what they say?"

On Thursday, the seventeenth of May, the supply wagon came in.

The crowd began to gather along Washington Avenue a good thirty minutes before Lester McClain and his mule team appeared through the trees. Shop owners locked their doors, discarded their aprons and waited outside for the arrival. Taking advantage of the crowd, Judge J. M. Murphy officially began his campaign for Gunnison County commissioner, lingering on the front steps of the town hall and shaking every hand. Harris Olney donned his best paisley vest, polished his marshal's star and trotted his horse up and down Grand Avenue, telling everyone in no uncertain terms that he meant to keep order should anyone cause a ruckus.

Contrary to her brave words about watched pots never boiling, Uley stood there, too, Old Croppy's reins in her hands. She'd worked shaft eleven all morning, driving the broadax in characteristic splintering strokes. But as 2:00 p.m. had approached, she'd known she had to get to town. This marked the third half-day's pay she'd forfeited during the past week, but it didn't matter one whit to her. This afternoon would mean the difference between death and life to Aaron.

She stood with the rest of the miners, waiting for this last-ditch possibility, waiting for one grizzly, toothless man, one rickety wagon and a team of mules.

Lord, she prayed. *This might be the last*

chance for Aaron. You've got to help him. Please.

At precisely 2:45 p.m., a shout went up at the end of the street, and then the wagon appeared.

"Yah, mule!" Lester McClain hollered as he snapped his whip into the air. "Get goin'! You mules are the slowest confounded animals I've ever had the misery of drivin'." As the vehicle clattered up the lane toward her, Uley could see wooden crates, barrels and unbleached muslin bags teetering in the wagon bed.

No man rode there except McClain.

Murmurs began passing from one observer to another. "Don't look like Lester's bringing any passengers over today."

"Don't see Dawson Hayes anywhere."

"There ain't anybody else in that wagon."

"Maybe McClain's got him hidden on the floor between the flour bags."

"I doubt that. A man couldn't ride back there. He'd be hit in the head with a barrel by now."

Uley felt her knees want to buckle beneath her.

He isn't on the wagon, she thought. *Dawson Hayes isn't coming.*

As Uley's hope abandoned her, it left

nothing in its wake but sheer defeat. It was over, then. She had no way to stop Aaron from hanging.

What are You doing, Father? Why won't You save Aaron? She had to wonder, *could it be God's will for Aaron to be taken?*

"It's a crying shame," Old Ben Pearsall said from right beside her. "That Aaron Brown was such a nice young fellow."

"Best be searching town for strong hemp rope," someone said. "We'll need to trim the leaves off the big cottonwood, too. Looks like we're in for a hanging Saturday morning."

Harris Olney didn't say anything. He reared his horse, throwing clouds of dust into the air as McClain began to unload his latest consignments. Judge Murphy strode down the steps of the town hall and waved his hat at the crowd. "Citizens of Tin Cup!" he bellowed. "The court of law will be called to order tomorrow morning at nine. We will come together to mete out justice at that time."

Miners swarmed in every direction. Uley followed, not knowing where she was going, not caring. She had to find Aaron, had to seek him out and stand beside him. Where would he be? All of a sudden . . . as if it were predestined . . . she found herself nose to chest buttons with him, right in the middle of Grand Avenue.

"Uley," he said.

"Aaron," she said.

John Kincaid sauntered up just then and tipped his derby at Aaron. "Well, sir," he said, rather gravely. "I suppose we have our work cut out for us tomorrow."

"Yes," Aaron said, his eyes remaining on Uley. "I suppose we do."

Everybody spied Aaron in the crowd at once.

"Sorry, young fella," Lesser Levy growled at him. "It's been nice having you and that sister of yours around this town. We don't often take to our criminals the way we've taken to you."

Ben Pearsall stood right behind Lesser Levy. "Best of luck in the trial tomorrow. I figure you'll need it."

Aaron shook his hand. "Thanks, Ben."

Aunt Kate was next in line. "I was shore hopin' to keep you and that Beth around a good long time."

One by one, the people of Tin Cup came and pumped his hand, telling him in small, uncertain ways that he'd earned their respect. They gathered around him — Pearsall and Aunt Kate, Levy and Kincaid,

Alex Parent and George Willis — anxious to speak to him, somberly wishing him well, even as they bade him a solemn goodbye.

Between Aaron and Uley, Old Croppy brayed and snorted at the air, shaking his ears and pawing as if in disdain of the entire proceeding.

"You got the night off tonight," Aunt Kate said. "I'm not gonna make you scrub greasy pans when you ought to be out enjoying your last bit of freedom." They all knew that, if convicted, he would spend Friday night in jail. And come Saturday morning, he would see his last sunrise.

"Thanks, Kate," he said. "I'll put it to good use."

Uley's eyes locked on Aaron's as he stood politely greeting people in the street. The fleeting expression on his face told her he was glad she'd stayed beside him. "Hello, Hank," he said, shaking yet another hand. "Thank you, Charlie . . . Hello, Hollis . . ."

The moment bound them together.

Aaron's gaze strayed to meet Uley's, seeing everything in her that no one else in Tin Cup could see. As he shook the fifteenth hand in a row, right there in the middle of the street, a thought crashed down on him like a boulder that might have come bounding down off Gold Hill.

Father, I can't help what's happening in my heart about this girl. I'm falling in love with her and I know it. Is this what You have wrought for me?

As Uley stood in the street beside him, knowing without a doubt that he needed her there, she felt like somebody had grabbed her innards with a fist and twisted them. The thought came just as unbidden as a snowstorm on a spring day.

I used to feel sad for Elizabeth Calderwood, knowing she loved a man who was going to hang. I didn't know I'd be thinking about myself. I didn't know I'd be loving that exact same man.

Neither of them spoke. Neither of them knew that the revelation had claimed the other's soul.

Around them, the crowd teemed in the street. Inside them, their hearts were filled with certainty and longing. Between them, the hours . . . the moments . . . ticked away.

Judge J. M. Murphy pounded the cup on the podium at precisely nine the following morning. "I hereby call to order this court in the town of Tin Cup, county of

Gunnison, state of Colorado, on this day, Friday, May eighteenth, to cast a verdict in the trial of Gunnison County versus Aaron Talephas Brown, who is accused of pulling a gun on Marshal Harris Olney."

Aaron felt like Murphy might never stop talking. He'd never heard such a long-winded introduction in all of his life. As if this trial needed an introduction at all. The jury from Pitkin had arrived in late last night, champing at the bit — Aaron was sure — to find him guilty. Mawherter had allowed them all to stay at the Grand Central for free — his revenge against Elizabeth, Aaron had decided, for making her place at the Pacific Hotel.

Everybody in town had been counting the hours, watching for supply wagons, waiting for Dawson Hayes.

This trial needed no introduction at all. He wished Murphy would just get on with it. *I'm innocent, Lord, but there can be no making them see it now. I'm praying for my own pride and I know it.* He'd done everything he knew how to do, and now, he figured, it was time to go on to glory.

As the attorneys prepared to make their final arguments, John Kincaid shuffled through his notes. He leaned over to Aaron, pulled his cheroot from between his teeth and grinned. "Smile, man," he said. "You're sittin' in that chair lookin' as glum as if the world's just ended."

"Hasn't it?"

"No," Kincaid said with certainty. "It has not. You see, I've been preparing for precisely this occasion. I figured a long time ago that Hayes wouldn't make it in. So I've got another plan instead."

"What is it?"

"Not tellin' you just yet. You'll know soon enough. I'm gonna call a surprise witness or two. You just keep your mouth shut and nod at everything I say. I intend to win this trial for both of us, Aaron Brown."

Aaron sat back in his seat, hope once more bursting into flame in his heart. Just what, he wondered, did Kincaid have up his sleeve?

As Aaron leaned back in the chair, he caught sight of Uley. She sat against the far wall, facing him, her face pinched and still. He managed to muster a smile for her. Then he turned away. Now that he knew where she was waiting, he wouldn't look at her again. He couldn't. She was the one part of Tin Cup that beckoned him toward life. I suppose I made a foolish decision, coming here, he thought. Even so, I suppose I'd do it again. Because doin' what I did, I did right. Guess I just did the right thing, only I did it wrong.

Seth Wood rose and approached the bench. "The prosecution rests its case, Judge Murphy. In light of the evidence already presented, I do not feel it necessary to call any more witnesses at this time."

"That's fine," Murphy said, with only a hint of his former zealousness. He, too, had come to respect Aaron Brown over the past three weeks. He'd been sure, when he made the decision to adjourn the trial for three weeks, that left to his own devices, the criminal would publicly prosecute himself. But that hadn't happened at all. And, the way people came and went up in the gold camps, Murphy almost felt that he was hanging one of his own now. "Kincaid? You got something for us? Or are we gonna end this thing?"

John Kincaid raised himself from the chair with both hands and strode purposefully toward the front of the town hall. He approached the bench, standing close to the potbellied wood stove, which sat idle this time of year, and whispered something in Murphy's ear.

Murphy's countenance changed somewhat. "What?" He leaned in closer. "Again."

Kincaid spoke further, while whispers of interest spread throughout the courtroom.

Murphy thwacked the cup against wood.

Kincaid pivoted to face the onlookers.

Murphy scowled at everyone, letting his expression quiet them, because he knew his words wouldn't.

Kincaid waited for silence, then began. "Your Honor, the defense would like to call two witnesses this morning. The first is a witness we would like to return to the stand. Mrs. Elizabeth Calderwood."

Spectators mumbled surprised pleasantries and stepped out of the way so that Beth could gather her skirts and proceed to the podium.

"Good mornin', Miss Elizabeth . . ."

"Lookin' mighty fine, Miss Elizabeth . . ."

Beth ascended the steps and placed her hand once more upon the Bible. When she'd been sworn in again, Kincaid directed her to her seat.

Aaron squirmed in his chair. Beth had told him nothing of this. He had no idea what surprises his sister and his lawyer might be about to deliver.

"Mrs. Calderwood," Kincaid said, "I suppose, of everyone in this lovely town, you are the closest of all to your brother, the defendant, Mr. Aaron Talephas Brown."

"I don't know," she said quietly, her bell-like voice singing out as every man in the place leaned forward to catch her words. "When I first testified, I would have told you that was certainly true. Now, to be honest, I am not sure of the answer anymore."

Kincaid smiled confidently. They had obviously rehearsed this show. "And . . . why is that?"

"Because Aaron has started to care for some woman very deeply while we've been here in Tin Cup."

"He has?" Kincaid said, glancing only once in Aaron's direction. "What makes you say that?"

"Because he's been askin' me some pretty hard questions about womenfolk, Mr. Kincaid."

Good grief, Aaron thought. What was Beth fixin' to tell everybody?

"Give me an example," Kincaid said, prodding her. "What sort of questions did he ask?"

"He wanted to know what it means when a woman says she likes you to kiss her one minute and says she's afraid of that kiss the next."

"Why do you suppose he asked *you*

these things, Mrs. Calderwood?"

"He said he asked me because I was a woman . . . because he figured I knew the answers to such things."

"What did you tell your brother when he asked these questions?"

"I told him it meant that woman felt something for him in her heart."

"Why do you think this, this *woman* . . . was afraid for your brother to kiss her?"

"Often, when a girl starts caring for a fellow, it scares her a bit. That's what I told Aaron."

It was everything Aaron could do to remain in his seat. What did this portion of his life have to do with his innocence or guilt? He began to fear that, in some unfathomable, impossible way, he'd given Uley's identity away.

He dared not cast a glance in her direction. She'd never forgive him, if this was what his loving had done to her. He'd never forgive himself, either. If it came out like this, he'd have soiled her in the miners' eyes forever.

The next question came, and Aaron went stock-still. "Did you ask your brother if you could meet this woman, Mrs. Calderwood?"

"I did."

"And what did he say?"

"He said, 'You don't need to meet her. Nothing can come of it.'"

"What do you suppose he meant by that?"

When Seth Wood sprang from his seat, Aaron found himself joyous to see the prosecuting attorney object at last. "Your Honor," Wood said tightly, striding toward the front of the room and raising an arm to indicate intense ire. "I'm sure all of us here find this very interesting. But I fail to see what evidence of Aaron Brown's love life has to do with whether or not we hang this man tomorrow. I've seen lesser men who were loved much more."

Me, too, Wood, Aaron wanted to shout. Let's get Kincaid away from all this.

"Your Honor," Kincaid said slowly, as if he were speaking to a roomful of school-children, "you will see in a moment that this line of questioning is entirely relevant. It has everything to do with the person I'm going to call to the stand *next*."

This time, Aaron cast his gaze across at Uley. Had she confessed? Was she in on this, too? What could she gain by revealing herself to them now? She'd already testi-fied against him. If he'd known it would come to this, he might just have let them hang him three weeks ago. But when he saw her expression, he knew she felt trapped, too. He shook his head briefly, desperate to communicate to her that he had no part in this. Then he turned his eyes downward, staring at the boot-scuffed pine floor as if it held the key to every confusing question his lawyer had raised in his mind.

Kincaid was prodding his sister further. "Mrs. Calderwood, I'll ask you the question again. What do you suppose your brother meant by telling you that you could not meet the woman he was beginning to care for?"

"I found it . . . odd. We've always been very close. In Fort Collins, before we both came to this point in our lives, he would never have hesitated to bring a girl home for me to meet. With the exception of one or two instances —" Elizabeth said meaningfully "— he has always trusted my judgment."

"What reason can you think of, then? Why doesn't Aaron want you to meet this woman?"

"I don't know."

"Could it be because the woman has a tainted reputation, Mrs. Calderwood? Could it be because your brother has fallen for someone that it might not be *proper* for you to meet?"

"I . . . I don't think he would . . ."

"Just answer my question, please."

Elizabeth was finding this very difficult. But she knew she owed it to Aaron to tell the truth. "Perhaps, Mr. Kincaid," she said, keeping her eyes on the attorney, willing to risk any embarrassment so long as it would save her brother's life. "Perhaps that is why. It is all I can think of."

"Thank you very much for the information, Mrs. Calderwood. You may come down from the stand."

Chapter Thirteen

❧

John Kincaid's question resounded in Uley's mind.

Could it be because the woman has a tainted reputation, Mrs. Calderwood? Could it be because your brother has fallen for someone it might not be *proper* for you to meet?

Why didn't he just ask, "Could it be because your brother has fallen for a gal who's fooling the whole town? Could it be that your brother has fallen for Uley Kirkland, the very member of this community who sprang into the darkness and stopped your brother's wayward actions in the first place?"

She felt stuck again, stuck and perhaps ready to be skewered. Perhaps she should tell Sam. Perhaps she should let her father know that she'd only followed her heart's bidding, that she and Aaron had only found each other because of that one rowdy night when she'd jumped out at him and her hat had come tumbling off. But then, she realized, her pa would see that she'd been fooling him, too. He'd realize that all this time she'd been getting to know Aaron, she'd been getting to know him as a member of the opposite gender. Will there ever come a time, she wondered, when I can make my decisions based on who I *am,* instead of who I am not?

Has Aaron told them? Has he broken his promise? After her revelation in the middle of the street yesterday, after her realization that she truly loved this man, she didn't dare glance across the room at him. Should I not have trusted him? Surely it hasn't come to this. But, perhaps, it has.

She'd never in her life felt so confused . . . so ashamed . . . so frightened. . . .

Kincaid dismissed Elizabeth from the stand.

Uley sat with her hands clenched together on her knees, fully expecting him to call her name.

The defense attorney waited until the room quieted again to call his next witness. He smiled slightly before beginning. Here came the coup de grace, the witness to ensure his victory.

"I call to the stand . . ."

Uley made ready to get up.

". . . to speak next on behalf of Mr. Aaron Talephas Brown. . . ."

Uley laid one hand on Sam's knee, as if to placate him before the unthinkable happened.

". . . Miss Mabel Cornelius."

Mabel Cornelius?

Uley didn't even know a Mabel Cornelius.

Up the aisle, from just outside the front door, where she'd been waiting to hear her name called, came Wishbone Mabel.

The judge swore her in, and then the defense attorney said, "Miss Cornelius, will you take the stand, please?"

Mabel gathered her skirts and mounted the steps, smiling prettily at the men in the room — most of whom were her customers — before settling herself upon the stand like a queen upon a throne.

Judge Murphy pounded his cup again, informing them loudly that they were in a court of law where a man's life hung in the balance and they had best keep their mouths shut.

It took several minutes for the din to fade.

Uley stared at Mabel.

Laura had said she'd seen Aaron at Ongewach's. Perhaps he'd gone for a tumble with a hurdy-gurdy girl and Laura hadn't the heart to tell her.

"Now, Miss Cornelius," Kincaid began, "I thank you very much for coming forward so this town could put an end to this nonsense. I don't think I need to tell you that I am about to ask you several difficult questions."

"Honey, I can answer difficult questions." Mabel smoothed the bodice of the very appropriate, very demure dress she was wearing. "I'll answer everything."

When Kincaid began his examination, the place got so quiet Uley could hear a fly buzzing outside the door.

"When did you meet the defendant, Mr. Aaron Brown?"

"About a month ago," Mabel said. "Aaron came into Santa Fe Moll's place and paid for my services the night before he first got thrown in jail."

"You say his given name as if you're familiar with it."

"I'm familiar, all right. He's been comin' up to see me since his sister posted bail for 'im. And I've been goin' down to see him, too."

He's been seeing Wishbone Mabel, Uley thought, and she believed it, no matter how badly she didn't want to, no matter how impossible it sounded. *That time he touched my hair and kissed me, he was probably comparin' me to that . . . that . . . soiled dove. . . .*

"You've been goin' down to see him?"

"I've been meetin' him at Aunt Kate's sometimes, early in the mornin'. That's the only time I could get away from Moll's place to go see the man I care about."

"Do you love him, Mabel?"

"Yes," the girl said quietly, her eyes riveted on Kincaid's, thinking about the money she was going to earn for her trouble. "I do."

"Does he feel the same for you?"

The fly outside the door buzzed by again. "Yes. I believe he does."

"During your times together, has Aaron Brown ever let you into his confidence about his personal matters?"

"Yes. That first night, before he got pitched in jail, he told me all his reasons for coming to Tin Cup."

Uley wanted to cry out. All the times she'd thought she knew him, all the times she'd measured his gaze upon her own and felt her soul answering, she'd been wrong.

"He told you he'd come to town to shoot the marshal?"

"No. If he'd told me that, I'd have talked

to the marshal myself."

"What did he tell you that night, Mabel?"

Her eyes finally wavered from Kincaid's. She took in the whole room with one glance before she said it. "He told me he'd come to Tin Cup to take Harris Olney back to Fort Collins with 'im. Told me he figured that's the only way fair justice could be done."

Harris Olney leapt from his seat and lunged toward the podium. "This is the most ridiculous fabrication I've ever heard. You shut up Hell, Mabel, I'm one of your best customers, and everybody knows it. You shouldn't be sayin' this stuff about me."

"Sit down, Olney," Murphy hollered. "If you tell another witness to shut up, I'll have you thrown out on your rump. You've already finished your talkin'. I don't want to hear any more."

Kincaid continued. "Why do you think the defendant told you about his plans, Miss Cornelius? Was he afraid to talk about it? Has he been afraid to talk about it since then?"

"Not a bit," she said. "He weren't afraid to talk to *me*. He asked me for advice, you know. We're real close. He talks about it all the time. He says he never intended to shoot anybody. He just felt real strong about bringing Harris Olney to justice back in Fort Collins. He told me the story over and over again, just like he told it to Elizabeth."

Uley found herself now in a trap of a different sort, a trap clamped upon her very being. These very words, a double-edged sword. Words which would free Aaron, but would also mean that he was not the sort of man who she'd thought him to be. Inside her, she wrestled with every possibility Mabel Cornelius's testimony set before her.

Now that she loved Aaron, what could she wish for?

Do I trust him? Do I really trust him the way he said he wants me to?

I don't know.

I don't know.

Did he look at other women, say the same words to them, touch their hair?

"Hey," Sam whispered. He'd noticed that her face had blanched to the same hue as cold ashes. "You okay?"

She didn't answer him.

Kincaid turned to the spectators. "There you have it, my fellow citizens of Tin Cup. I have researched heavily and have brought forth a second testimony attesting to the goodness of the defendant, Aaron Talephas Brown. We did not need mountain man Dawson Hayes. We've kept Miss Mabel Cornelius here as a surprise witness all along." He turned toward the jury and gestured grandly at them. "I suggest we allow the jury to come to its decision now, and put this innocent man out of his misery. I suggest you find the defendant, Aaron Talephas Brown, blameless of all charges brought against him."

It wasn't until Aaron scanned the far wall and found Uley again that he knew he had to take action against his own attorney. Ever since Kincaid had bellowed out Mabel's name, Aaron had figured this event for the circus it had proved to be. Except for one night he had poked his head into Charles Ongewach's looking for Lesser Levy, he had never laid eyes on Wishbone Mabel Cornelius, much less consorted with her. The only person in this valley he'd poured his thoughts out to was Uley Kirkland.

And, truth be told, he'd gone and given her his love, too.

Never mind that Kincaid's shenanigans grated against everything Aaron believed in. Never mind that Kincaid and Beth and

What's-Her-Name Mabel were coming close to clearing him. All he could see in his mind's eye was the white-as-china, full-of-pain face of Uley Julia Kirkland as she sat wordlessly in her chair, losing all her hope, all her faith, in him. And he wasn't gonna let that happen, not even to save his life.

He leapt from the chair so fast he knocked it over.

"No!" he hollered. "I can't have it, Kincaid. *No.*"

As he summoned up the words he knew he had to say, he supposed he was about to do the right thing wrong again. He'd die being honest like this. But just now, that honesty meant everything to him. "Mabel's lying. I never told that gal anything."

Mabel sprang from her seat, too, just the way she and Kincaid rehearsed it. "Don't say that. How can you, Aaron?"

"I don't know who has paid you, ma'am," he said, waggling a finger at her. "I certainly appreciate the effort you're makin', but I won't be acceptin' my freedom this way."

"Nobody's payin' me anything!" she screeched. "Now git back down in that chair and let this jury acquit you."

"Mr. Brown." Kincaid scowled at him.

306

"This is highly irregular."

"*You* are highly irregular," Aaron said. "I will not have this. Not this way." He would not let Uley think he'd spent even the shortest amount of time with Wishbone Mabel. For days, all he'd wanted was to tell Uley every feeling his heart encompassed for her. He'd rather die knowing he'd left her with that knowledge than live knowing she thought he'd betrayed her.

Judge Murphy rose from the bench, flapping his black-sleeved robe so that he resembled a cave bat. "Do you deny this, then? Do you call your sister a liar? Is this a diversion Mrs. Calderwood and Mr. Kincaid have constructed to save you from an almost certain fate?"

He fumbled for words. "Yes . . . but, no. . . . I . . ." How was he going to get himself out of this one? What was he going to have to sacrifice so that Uley's secret could remain intact?

For one instant . . . one long breath that seemed to hold the length of his life in it . . . he allowed himself to gaze at the back wall, where he knew she was sitting. "I will be honest," he said. "Call me to the stand, and I will tell you some of it —"

He saw Uley grip the arm of her chair like she'd grip a heavy pump handle. The look they exchanged would have been obvious to everybody . . . if everybody had known . . . if anybody had known the intensity of the kiss they'd shared, of the future they'd begun to long for.

You'll be satisfied, he tried to tell her with his eyes after he came forward. *Don't run from this. This is so you'll trust me.*

John Kincaid concealed his face in his hands, knowing full well he'd been defeated. "Okay," he said quietly. "If you insist, we'll get on with this."

"No." Murphy held up one hand to halt the defense attorney. "I'll do the questioning from here on out."

Kincaid acquiesced. "He's your witness, Your Honor."

Murphy came down from the bench and positioned himself to the front and to the right of Aaron. "Now, Mr. Brown. Suppose you tell us what's going on here."

Aaron found one specific pine plank to stare at, focusing on a knot the size and shape of a black bear's eye. "I have come to care for someone in this valley very much. For one . . . woman."

Uley felt as if a gigantic hand were clutching at her throat.

"My sister did not lie under oath, Judge Murphy."

"Where did the lying begin, Mr. Brown?"

Aaron gave a long sweeping gesture in the direction of Wishbone Mabel. "Mabel. Kincaid. I figure I know what you're trying to do. But I won't let you do it. I have to tell the court. Mabel is not the woman of my affections. She is not the one with whom I share stories the likes of these. If I was a lesser man, or perhaps *more* of a man, I'd let the jury decide my fate after hearing Mabel's story. But I will not let this continue in this courtroom. I would not have *her* hear Mabel's testimony and think it happened Mabel's way."

"Who is it you care for, Mr. Brown?" Murphy asked. He was completely confused, but he figured he'd at least have somebody else to call to the stand.

It's me, Uley wanted to sing out. *No matter what, it really is me.*

Aaron shook his head. "I can't tell you that."

"You can't tell me? Mr. Brown, surely you realize your life hangs in the balance here."

"Yes," Aaron said. "I realize that. Even so, I won't divulge it."

"I don't understand, Brown," Murphy said, as Elizabeth, in the fifth row, began to weep openly. "I don't see why this is so all-fired important."

Aaron's eyes journeyed to Uley's. He could see even from this distance, that her insides were being wrenched. He figured he knew everything she felt inside. "Ain't no sense in sayin' it out loud, Judge Murphy," he said. "Her deposition wouldn't clear me. Dawson Hayes is the only eyewitness to the events that occurred along the Cache la Poudre River. The woman I'm talkin' about . . . she knows who she is. I won't tell you her name. I made her an important promise once. I won't betray that promise now."

Murphy shrugged. "Is that all you've got to say for yourself?"

"It is, Judge Murphy."

Murphy paced across the front of the room once . . . twice . . . three times. Aaron figured he couldn't quite decide what to do. At last he clasped his hands behind his back and cleared his throat. The sound had the same resonance as an elk's mating call. He faced the Pitkin miners. "Distinguished members of the jury," he began in a blustering tone. "You have heard the testimony in this case. The outcome of this trial is in your hands. At this time, we will clear the town hall. You will remain locked in here until you reach a decision. We'll all be waiting on your verdict outside. Somebody just bang on the window and we'll come back in."

His expression somber, Murphy motioned for the spectators in the front row to follow him. One by one, the entire assembly filed outside and into the glare to wait. The group that had once been apt to murmur now remained hushed. The men milled about on the steps, eyes down-turned, occasionally thwacking a back or shaking a hand. Then the whispered questions began.

"What do you suppose'll happen in there?"

"What do you wonder they're thinking inside?"

"Figure it'll take all day?"

Even if it did, none of them would think of leaving.

Aaron and Uley met once, finding themselves standing face-to-face in the hushed crowd. Now, more than ever, Aaron knew he must be careful how he reacted to her in front of these miners. His impassioned speech in that courtroom might very well still give her away.

Their eyes locked.

Their hearts touched.

They cried out to one another, silently,

in pain and in hope.

I'll always trust you now, she longed to say. *I'll always know you did right.*

I knew you were afraid, he longed to say. *I don't want you to question what we've shared.*

At precisely one o'clock p.m., one of the Pitkin miners came to the rippled window and tapped on it with his fingers.

"They're ready for us," Charlie Hastings shouted.

"Verdict's in," Frenchy Perrault announced.

Judge Murphy pulled an iron key from his pocket, rotated it once in the lock, threw open the door and beckoned to everybody to find a place within.

The men filed silently to their places.

Three of them drew out a chair so Elizabeth could sit with her brother at the front table.

Uley stood beside Sam, gripping her father's arm. No matter what the jury's decision was, she could express no emotion at all. She dared not swoon in defeat or cry out in relief. Instead, she stood as still as a fence post, the room tottering unsteadily around her, as the fellow who'd tapped upon the glass came forward carrying a small card.

"Gentlemen —" he swallowed once, and

then his eyes lit upon Elizabeth Calderwood "— and the lady. Jury's done votin' and arguin'. We're ready to tell you what we've decided. We, the jury, do hereby say . . ."

Tension.

A whole room full of it.

". . . that because *this* lawyer —" here he pointed to John Kincaid "— could never come up with any eyewitnesses to attest to the defendant's stories, and *that* lawyer —" here he pointed at Seth Wood "— came up with a witness who saw the defendant with the gun actually in his hand . . ."

The shuddering and rumbling in Uley's ears might well have belonged to all hundred men.

". . . we find the defendant, Aaron Talephas Brown . . ."

Our Father, she prayed. *Don't let them do this. Please don't let them do this.*

". . . guilty of the charges . . ."

Harris Olney didn't waste any time. He took a set of handcuffs from his belt. They snapped around Aaron's wrists with a resounding clangor.

The miner's words came to Uley's ears in disjointed fragments that numbed Uley even before she fully comprehended them.

". . . to be hanged at nine o'clock in the

morning from the cottonwood tree by Willow Creek . . ."

Judge Murphy encircled Elizabeth with his arms and held her there while she wept, crying, "No . . . no . . . no . . ."

". . . around the neck until dead . . ."

The editor of the *Tin Cup Banner* ran past them all and down the outside steps. In three hours, the newspaper would have an extra edition proclaiming the event of a hanging at precisely nine the next morning.

Kincaid exited next, shaking his head. He'd almost done it. He'd almost saved his client. If only the fool hadn't found the need to be so altogether *honest.* If anybody asked him, he'd tell them he'd prefer a cheatin' man to an honest one any day. Cheatin' men you could predict and place a winnin' bet on every time. Honest ones weren't so easy to figure out.

Marshal Harris Olney took hold of Aaron's handcuffs and prodded him toward the door. Aaron passed Uley, meeting her gaze, then dropping it.

"It's gonna be nice not havin' to worry about you anymore," Harris said.

Aaron hung back, making Olney work for every step they took together. "You're gonna worry about me your whole life.

You're gonna wake up every mornin' with my blood on your hands."

Harris poked him along with the butt of his firearm. "That's fine by me. I've seen you come after me one too many times. Don't figure you'll be coming after me from your grave."

Late-May dandelions grew in sprigs around Tin Cup's business establishments, spiking open like clusters of tiny suns. Magpies flew past, their wings flickering white, their blackness shining jewel-blue as they searched for roosting spots in the willows. As Uley hiked toward the jailhouse for the first time in three weeks, the late-afternoon sun reflected against the creek, dull and golden.

Strange, she thought, how things of the soil and sky can proceed on such a day as this.

She opened the jailhouse door. Harris Olney was reclining in his chair, his boot heels atop his desk, picking his teeth. When he saw her, he swung his feet to the floor. "Don't tell me you're back again. You gonna stay immersed in this episode 'til it's all over, ain't you?"

"I need to see him."

"Sure beats me why. Beats me why you

ever got involved in this in the first place."

"Don't show me the way back. I know where he is."

She walked to the back room and stood on the threshold for a long moment, waiting, thinking of his words on the stand. *I have come to care for someone in this valley very much. For one . . . woman.*

He stood when he saw her. "Uley," he whispered.

"Aaron."

He came forward, clutching the bars with both hands in a gesture of need very different from the frustrated one he'd made the first time she came to visit. He stared down at her. "My, but you're a sight for sore eyes."

"I'm glad." She struggled to find words. None came close to describing the feelings or the predicament they shared. "You're good for my eyes, too."

He hesitated, searching for the words. "Funny how we're back at this place again, peering at each other with bars between us. Seems like it's the same as it was three weeks ago."

No, it isn't, Uley wanted to say. *Because I love you now. We can't go back three weeks.*

"Uley."

"I've got to tell you I'm sorry," she said, tears springing to her eyes, "for everything I did that got you here."

"No need to be sorry," he said. "You did what your heart told you was right."

But not anymore. My heart's not telling me it's right anymore.

"It's more than that, too. I'm sorry for all the doubts I had in my mind. I'm sorry for not trusting you. Today. When Mabel took the stand."

"Mabel did a good job up there. Any girl would have believed her, hearing how she talked."

"If you hadn't been trying to protect *me*, perhaps you would have let her finish it," she said.

"Perhaps. But perhaps not." He didn't want her to feel responsible for the choice he'd made. She meant everything to him.

He gripped one of her hands in his, pulling it forward, turning it so that he could examine the web of lines running across her palm. He traced the longest, deepest crease with one rough finger.

She closed her eyes against his touch.

"You know my words were true up there, don't you? You know you're the one for me, Uley. The only one."

"It's what I've been hoping for, for the

longest time," she whispered. "It's what I've been wishing for." She raised her palm, pressing it against the grainy stubble of his sprouting beard. She tightened her fingers against his jaw, knowing this might be the last time she ever touched him.

Her tears came now, finally spilling out of her eyes, tracking down her cheeks in rivulets. "I'm the one who did this in the first place, Aaron. If I hadn't been the one to stop you."

"You mustn't question the outcome of this, little one. It won't change anything."

"I wish," she said, very quietly, "that you could hold me."

His two hands gathered her own and tugged her gently toward the steel bars. "Almost," he said. "I can almost do it."

"Aaron . . ."

As he wrapped his arms about her as best he could, she pressed her hands against his cheeks, holding his face there, a breath away, a world away, grieving for him.

He pushed her slightly away then, searching her face, drinking in the color of her eyes one last long time, eyes the clear, green hue of the moss that grew on the rocks way above the timberline. "I'll go to my grave tomorrow thinking about how you let me touch your hair. I know a man's supposed to have his eyes on the Lord at times like this."

"Yes, you are."

"I figure the Lord won't mind me thinking about you just as I go. It'll be what gets me through, Uley. I want you to know that."

His words touched her heart in a strange, weightless way even as they filled her with sorrow.

"Don't say it."

"I have to say it. Anything I don't say now doesn't get said at all." He took her face in his hands. They stood together for long moments in just that way, hands to skin, eyes to eyes, man to woman.

A ruckus arose in the street outside the cell window.

Aaron didn't take his gaze from her face. "That'll be Aunt Kate Fischer and the others. She promised to bring me a last meal tonight. Roast beef and potatoes. She knows it's my favorite. She had to change her whole menu because of it."

"I should go. You won't be needing me with all those people in here, and a roast beef dinner, too."

He touched one finger to her chin. "I'll always be needing you, Uley. You remember that. Even when I'm with the angels up in heaven, I'll be wishing one of them was you."

She closed her eyes against the tears.

He had in mind to kiss her one last time. He had in mind to gather her close to him and take her mouth awkwardly with his own. But even as he thought it, he decided it wouldn't be the thing to do. He'd kissed her once . . . amid the lodgepoles . . . with his fingers and the breeze tangling through her hair. It was the way he wanted always to know her, as the woman pliant beside him, without these confounded bars shoving into their ribs. The memory of such a kiss would carry him on to eternity. It couldn't be duplicated now.

"Know what you've given me, Uley," he whispered. And with that his last dinner clattered in through the door.

Chapter Fourteen

Nobody in Tin Cup would donate a horse for the hanging. As the sun rose over the eastern mountains and splashed the valley with a palette of vibrant yellow, Harris Olney was still trying to round up a suitable animal. He sure wasn't gonna use *his* horse for a hanging.

When he'd contacted Sam and Uley Kirkland last night, Sam had told Harris in no uncertain terms that he didn't want *their* horses utilized for such an event. Jason Farley's horses were gone, all rounded up and ridden down the canyon to Gunnison to sell at auction. So the marshal settled for a mule donated by Carl Hord, just another old animal that had been brought in to work the mines, one that had probably walked a thousand miles if it had walked one of them. Old Croppy.

When the crowd started gathering beneath the ancient cottonwood, the sun had already ascended a third of the way, casting a brilliance down upon the primal colors of nature, blue sky, green willow, brown loam. The mule stood at the ready, a dusty brown ear flopping down over one eye, as serene as the donkey that had transported Mary and Joseph on their ardent, ancient journey to Bethlehem.

Uley, who'd been awake since long before five, knew she wouldn't see Aaron until Olney led him out of the jailhouse. The huge roast-beef dinner had marked Aaron's last onslaught of visitors. Aware that — at best — he held on to human sentiment in the valley by a slender thread, Olney had ousted Aaron's last callers from the jailhouse at eight p.m. He hadn't let anyone stay with Aaron into the night.

Elizabeth Calderwood waited now with all the others, Aunt Kate Fischer holding her hand and clutching a damp cloth to dab across her forehead should the woman swoon as her brother met his demise. The hemp rope dangled from the lowest, strongest limb of the tree, tied by the expert hand of Gilbert P. Hughes, the town's sometime undertaker. Hughes had worked long into the evening yesterday. He'd dug the seven-foot hole right beside poor Bob Wester up on Boot Hill.

At 8:45, Aaron vacated his cell. He waited, hat in hand, for the marshal to lead him outside. By 8:47, virtually everybody in town was waiting beneath the tree. The Pitkin miners were gathered together in a group, bearing the burden of their decision of justice. Five or six men had ridden up from Gunnison during the night to witness the event for the state of Colorado. Even as late as 8:50, the assembly remained quiet, the onlookers almost paralyzed by the shock of the events of past days. They'd come to a troubled, uneasy respect for this outlaw, one who'd come into their midst quietly with his sights, some said, set on righteousness. One who had fallen victim to a justice system more powerful than any man.

Despite the jury decision, today wasn't a moment of which they'd all be particularly proud. Though nobody would admit it out loud, the story of Olney's foul deeds had seriously eroded the faith some citizens placed in their marshal.

Just suppose Olney had been on the wrong side of the law and killed a man, Judge Murphy thought as he awaited the hour of execution.

Just suppose Olney was using his polished star to hide from what he'd done.

Just suppose they were hanging an innocent man.

Just suppose.

At 8:55 a.m., Olney led Aaron Talephas Brown from the jailhouse and into the crowd. He wore his best black suit, the one Uley'd seen when she rummaged through his things in search of writing utensils. She figured he'd decided to be buried in that suit after all.

As if he could already feel the taut rope around his neck, he hadn't fastened the top button of his shirt. The fine white linen fell open at the hollow of his neck, and the horn on his bolo tie hung at half-mast. At her first sight of him, Uley bolted forward, struggling toward him in the crowd, pushing her way past Charlie Hastings and Lesser Levy and Lester McClain.

She knew the moment his eyes found her in the mass of men. She felt his gaze upon her the way she felt the sun upon her face, warming and all-encompassing, life-giving, necessary.

She spoke no words to those she shoved past. She only moved closer and closer, knowing he needed to know she was there.

And need her he did, he thought as he saw her coming forth from the throng.

Life, he thought. *Not much of it left.* And he prayed, *Father, make me ready for this.* Adrenaline pulsed through his head. His arms felt as limp as Aunt Kate's apron strings. *Please comfort me, Lord. I can't do this on my own.*

Leaving Aaron standing before them all, Harris walked to Old Croppy and untethered the animal. He brought the mule forth and prodded Aaron with his gun butt in an effort to get him to climb aboard.

Aaron couldn't mount the animal because of his handcuffs. Olney lifted him from the ground and held him steady while he swung one suited leg over the velvet-dark line marking Old Croppy's spine.

As Olney gave the command and Hughes shimmied up the tree to lower the rope, Aaron closed his eyes, remembering last night, his long hours of contemplation in the cell. For the past half year, he'd been ruled by suspicion and outrage. This, he supposed, would be the ultimate lesson. Even as he prayed, begging God to be near, he didn't understand why the Father hadn't brought Dawson Hayes to exonerate him. He had wrestled with this long into the night, unable to grasp its meaning until, near dawn, he had made a quiet peace. It was out of his hands. Olney would find his just deserts in the world below, where the very air men breathed seared hotter than fire. His own anger had been spent in the stalking and defending and accusing. He had nothing left now except a silent gratitude for the richness of this past month . . . the stolen evening jaunt with Uley . . . the chase in the willows . . . the kiss . . . yes, even the first night, when she'd sprung on him and sent him to the dirt.

He'd spent hours thinking of Uley last night . . . as the summer night turned deep and cold . . . as the morning finally came fading into the sky with a color like peach ice cream.

He felt the bite of the noose for the first time as Olney worked it over his head, then settled it against the pliant skin where a closed shirt and a knotted tie should rest. He swallowed once . . . twice . . . his Adam's apple wavering up, then down, at the pressure of the rope.

He felt as if he were strangling already.

Hughes pulled the rope up tighter, adjusting it to the length that, Aaron knew, would properly leave him suspended, his body stretched full-length in the air, his feet dangling inches from the earth where Old Croppy now stood.

As if in response to the choking obstruction of the rope, Aaron opened his eyes and viewed the town around him, the makeshift, dilapidated buildings, the flaring sun, the dismal faces, the mountains that looked as if they truly had been chiseled out by God's hand. In those few moments, he saw life . . . life at its worst . . . life at its best. Everything around him seemed more pronounced, perfect, from the nutty smell of the rope that encircled his windpipe to the perfect shadowed Vs etched deeply in the cottonwood's bark.

Olney stepped back and slapped his hat against his knee. "Your time's come. You want anybody to offer up a prayer for your soul?"

"Yes." He leveled his eyes on his enemy. "I do."

"Now, where's that preacher? Talking big about staying in town, running church services here, when all he's needed for is to offer last words over this man's embittered life?"

Pastor Benjamin Creede stepped forward, brandishing his Bible. "I have come to do my duty before Christ."

Aaron mustered a smile. "Thank you, Pastor."

"Mr. Brown, do you know where you are going to spend eternity?"

He nodded.

Benjamin Creede's eyebrows shot up. "You do?"

"With Jesus Christ, my Lord."

A murmur surged through the crowd.

"Guess I don't have as much to talk to you about as I thought I did."

"They can bury me on Boot Hill if they want." The boldness in Aaron's voice made pain heave in Uley's bosom. *Oh, Father. Why this?* "I have made my peace."

"Very well, then. Let us bow our heads."

All over the crowd, hats came off in a show of respect for eternity. Stetsons. Wool caps. Bowlers. Even a beret or two. Every hat in the crowd came off, except one. Uley's.

It was everything she could do not to remove her cap and let her hair fall down once more for him. She stood before him, her back to the rest of the throng, tears of anguish coursing down her cheeks.

Don't you do this. Don't you do this, she berated herself. *It wouldn't do for a fellow to cry.*

"Heavenly Father, in the name of Your son, Jesus," Creede bellowed, "we ask that You receive the soul of this child unto Yourself. That You would comfort him and take him quickly, that You would use this desperate moment to promote Your own

328

goodness in the world, that You would bring all criminals to justice and protect all men who are innocent, that You would be among us and guard our hearts against any joy that we are about to see that would entertain us or bring us harm, that we would accept it as Your perfect justice, that You would ensure that Aaron Brown's spirit is, this day, in heaven with You —"

"Amen." Olney clattered the reins on Old Croppy. "Amen, already. Creede, that's about the longest prayer I've heard anyone pray and we don't have time for it."

"I beg your pardon." Benjamin Creede looked none too pleased at being interrupted. "Aaron Brown has time for it."

"Let's get this taken care of so we can go back to work in the mines. No sense these men losing valuable earnings just to listen to your prattle." Olney signaled them by raising his bowler into the air. Hats went back on.

When Olney moved toward Aaron, Aaron sat straight as an arrow. "I want my hat on."

"That's an easy enough request. Here. Let me put it on your head."

Aaron kept a tight grip on his hat band. "I don't want you to touch me. I want Uley Kirkland to put my hat on."

Olney backed off. "Okay. Uley it is. Uley! Come on up here and put this Stetson on this man's head."

"Me?" Her heart started pounding like a smithy's anvil. "He wants me to do it?"

"Git on up here, Uley," the marshal bellowed. "Time's a-wastin'. It's already 9:04. This scoundrel should have been dead and gone three minutes ago."

Timidly Uley made her way the rest of the distance to Old Croppy. Aaron peered down at her with eyes like blue water. He released his hat into her hands.

She couldn't reach to place it on his head.

He couldn't bend his neck to help her.

"Marshal." She cast teary eyes in Olney's direction. "I can't get to him."

"We've got him almost all the way strung up. I'm not gonna take him halfway down now."

"Lift me up, then," she suggested. "I can sit behind him and get it on. Croppy's carried loads at least the weight of two of us together."

"Wouldn't do that way." Olney wasn't about to give either of them an opportunity to cut the rope and ride off.

"It's a man's last request," Uley said. "You can't very well deny it."

Olney mumbled something unintelligible and signaled to Gilbert Hughes. "Lengthen that rope fer a minute, would you? We've got a man who wants to put his hat on down here."

Hughes took a long moment to undo the knot, tugging it over and through itself until it fell free of the branch. "There, Marshal."

"Okay," Olney growled as he grabbed hold of Old Croppy's bridle. "You can bend your head down now. Be quick about this. Come on."

Aaron pitched slightly forward, his shock of black hair falling straight over his brows. Uley'd have given anything if she could have raised one hand and run it along the freshly shaven skin of his cheek. She laid the hand that ached to touch him one last time on his knee instead.

He'd splashed on enough bay rum this morning to make a mule skinner sit up and take notice.

"Thank you, Julia Kirkland," he whispered. "Thank you for everything."

This nearness was all he'd wanted. In his heightened state, he longed to catch the fragrance of her one more time, the woman smell, the one that blended lye and flowers and female.

She took the Stetson in two hands and settled it upon his head, letting her fingers brush his coffee-black hair. It was already warm from the intense sunlight pouring down upon them.

"There you go," she whispered.

Between them, an eternity passed as, still, he leaned forward.

"The angels in heaven won't be as beautiful as you," he whispered. "You must live, and live well, for the both of us."

"I will."

"God bless you," he said, "for all that you've done for me."

"Goodbye." Her eyes dry with shock. "God go with you." She backed away from him then, keeping her face steady on him, wanting her love to be the last thing he saw when he departed this life.

Inside, her heart broke.

Olney adjusted the noose over Aaron's head, this time making it big enough around to fit over Aaron's Stetson. He cinched it tight. Then he called out, "Hughes!"

Once more Gilbert Hughes fastened the hemp to the branch, working it over and under and through, testing it to make certain the loop would hold a man's weight, making ready to counter-balance with his own. He tested it once more, then signaled down from where he sat in the tree. "All's ready, Marshal."

"Very well." Olney glanced about one more time, his eyes coming to rest on Beth, who was now sobbing openly, Kate Fischer supporting her with one burly black arm.

"We'll go on with it." He raised his bowler in one hand, making ready to give the signal.

Olney nodded up to Gilbert Hughes.

Hughes nodded down to Olney.

The crowd hushed.

Beth sobbed.

Uley held her breath, her eyes locked on Aaron's, her lips moving in a wordless prayer.

Suddenly, from up on Alpine Pass, came a cloud of dust and a thunderburst of hooves.

"What on earth?" Olney hollered.

"Who's that?" Gilbert Hughes shouted.

Olney recognized the rider first. His eyes took on the same steely hardness as lead bullets. He signaled for the hanging to commence. But Gilbert Hughes was too busy watching the approaching stranger. He didn't see Olney's signal.

The fellow coming in wore a white beard as full and long as Santa's and had hair that encircled his head like a tangled mane. Around his neck he wore a string of grizzly-bear claws. "Halloooo!" He saluted the miners, the long buckskin fringe along his sleeve waving like a flag.

Elizabeth's eyes went as big around as bucket lids.

"What's goin' on, fellers?" The man was huge. His massive round nose reminded Uley of a bull moose. "Figured I'd best get over here. Figured I might miss somethin' important." At that precise moment, the huge man spied Aaron atop Old Croppy, the rope firmly adjusted around his neck. "What on earth you doin' up there, boy?"

Beth stepped away from Aunt Kate. "Dawson," she said, in a voice so soft that not many around could hear her. "Dawson Hayes."

"Beth!" Dawson called, his eyes twinkling like stars. He swung his buckskin-clad leg over the saddle and hopped off his horse. Even though he dropped the reins, the animal stood where he'd dismounted. "Heard you were in these parts."

The pair stood staring at each other in amazement for a moment. Finally Hayes's massive arms wrapped around Elizabeth's tiny shoulders and they rocked each other back and forth. As the fellow greeted Beth, his eyes squinted shut in rapture, the skin around them a fretwork of lines radiating to his temples like sun rays in a child's drawing. "Don't it just beat all," he said, still swaying her to and fro. "Don't it just beat all. . . ."

"You got Aaron's letter," she said, weeping. "You got it and you came."

"Aaron sent me a letter?"

Beth moved out of his grasp and stepped back, just staring at the mountain man for a long moment. "He did. Three weeks ago."

Dawson Hayes pulled a single crumpled sheet of paper from his pocket and unfolded it. "I got a letter, all right. Delivered to me out in the wilderness. But it didn't have Aaron's name signed to it."

"It didn't?"

"Nope. See here." He held it up for Elizabeth to see, then folded it up again, holding it in a tiny square until he fished a pair of round, wire-framed eyeglasses out of a buckskin pouch and slid them onto his nose. He opened the letter again, reading it aloud so everyone who gathered close could hear the words.

Dear Dawson Hayes
Here — *blotch* — is sum money. No

need to come to Tin Cup. We —
blotch — do not need you.

Hayes glanced up at all of them. "Had a
crisp new five-dollar bill inside. I decided
I'd better come out here to find out why
somebody figured they didn't need me for
somethin'."

Judge Murphy angrily shoved his way
through the men. "Let me see that
letter."

Hayes handed it over. "I just couldn't
figure who'd have written such a thing.
The handwritin' ain't familiar."

"It is to me," Beth said, almost in a
whisper.

Murphy read the letter over once, his
brow furrowed with consternation.
"Where's the five-dollar bill?"

"I spent it fast. I bought me so much
chewin' tobacco, I didn't know what to do
with it all. I had to trade half of it away to
the Utes."

"That bill could have been used as evidence, Hayes."

Beth stood, still staring at the blotched
letter, her face empty of all color. "Mrs.
Calderwood," Murphy said in genuine
concern. "Would you like to sit inside?
Perhaps the sun is too much."

Then, surprisingly, she smiled. "We don't need the five-dollar bill, Judge Murphy. I know who wrote that letter."

"You know who might have done this? You know who might have wanted to stop Mr. Hayes from testifying on your brother's behalf?"

"Yes." She pulled open the strings of her reticule and began to rummage through its meager contents. When she found what she wanted, she pulled it out triumphantly. "I never *did* want to leave this in the safe down at the Pacific Hotel. I was too afraid somebody would try to sneak away with the bail money."

She handed Judge Murphy the two documents and waited triumphantly while he examined them.

The first, a sworn affidavit from Aaron and written in his own hand, promised the defendant would appear at the Tin Cup Town Hall on the scheduled date at the scheduled hour to attend the scheduled trial.

As Murphy read, the marshal abandoned his post beside Aaron, coming forward to join them, his eyes suddenly wild.

Murphy turned to the second voucher.

"That's my receipt," Beth informed him.

Murphy read it aloud. " 'I do hereby' —

there's a part here I can't make out — 'acknowledge receipt of $500 for the bail of Aaron Brown.' " He stopped momentarily and commented, "I've never seen such a bad example of penmanship in all my living days. Harris, didn't you attend primary school and learn how to handle an inkwell?"

Olney appeared rather agitated. "I don't see what this has to do with —"

"Let me continue." Murphy held up one hand and finished reading aloud. " 'The money' — more words I can't read — 'be returned to Elizabeth Calderwood when Aaron Brown arrives to attend his trial. Signed on this day, in the' — here's another blotch — 'year of 1882. Marshal Harris Olney.' "

"See what I mean?" Beth asked.

Murphy held out one palm toward the mountain man. "Hayes. May I see the letter you received once more?"

Hayes handed it to him, his eyes leveled on Olney's in undisguised enmity. "I heard you left Fort Collins in a hurry, Harris Olney. I figure I'm about the only man who knows *why.*"

Murphy stood with the document in one hand and the letter in another, casting his eyes from one to the other. "Olney —" he turned his eyes to his marshal "— it appears as if you've gone to great lengths to keep Hayes from appearing in my courtroom."

Olney burst out in audacious laughter. "You cain't prove a thing, Murphy. Just because there's blotches all over the both of them . . . just because the letters might look as if they're formed the same way . . . this . . . this doesn't determine a *thing.*" He swung in a wide circle, taking in everyone gathered beneath the cottonwood with the sweeping gesture. "Everyone in this town needs to have his head taken off and put back on straight. You're all startin' to believe in a man who tried to murder me. . . ."

"What?" Hayes roared, advancing toward the marshal with fists upraised. "That's the most preposterous thing I've ever heard! Is that why Aaron Brown's waiting on that muley animal to swing from a noose? You're tryin' to hang him for goin' after *you?*"

"He *did!*" Olney roared back. "The jury found him guilty in a court of law."

"In *my* court of law," Murphy pointed out. "A court you obviously tried to keep this key witness out of."

Olney lowered his head, looking like a

bighorn sheep ready to butt. "You don't know that."

A voice rose out of the crowd. "I do. I know it."

Hayes, Murphy, Olney and Elizabeth — all four of them turned toward Old Ben Pearsall, who was weaving his way toward them through the throng.

"I'm warning you, Pearsall," Olney hissed between clenched teeth. "Keep your mouth shut."

"Cain't do that, Marshal," he said. "I sat and watched you write that letter. I've spent all night talkin' to that there defendant, and I figure him to be a kind fellow, the sort who'd follow after what's right."

Murphy jumped in. "You saw Olney compose this letter?"

"I did. I didn't know the implications of it then. I do now."

John Kincaid extricated himself from the group and joined them. He waved one hand toward Old Croppy. "Perhaps we'd best reexamine the evidence, Your Honor."

"You stay out of this, Kincaid." Murphy's tone left no doubt as to his feelings toward the ungovernable lawyer. "You did about all the damage you could manage yesterday, don't you think?"

Hayes glanced from Olney to Judge

Murphy. "I've been tryin' to spare Elizabeth Calderwood, sir. But I'd best say what I know."

Murphy removed his derby and slapped it against his leg in consternation. "*Everybody* had best say what they know. What is it, Hayes? Out with your story."

"I'm the only livin' witness to this, Murphy. Marshal Harris Olney is a cold-blooded murderer."

"You're an eyewitness to this?"

"I am," he said. "I couldn't get to his side in time to save Fred. For that, ma'am —" he tipped his beaver cap at Beth "— I will stay sorry the rest of my livin' days. But I sure got close enough to identify your lawman there."

"What did you see?" Murphy asked as Aunt Kate moved to support Elizabeth once more.

"I was comin' up from the fort, ridin' my roan through the meadow, goin' for the river to water him before I made my way back to the Utes. I heard a commotion and knew I'd best keep myself hidden until I found out who was fightin'. I saw Fred Calderwood on the ground, Olney hittin' him with the butt of his six-shooter. I figured Olney couldn't shoot because he couldn't blame it on the Utes that way.

He's got a real creative way of gettin' rid of people standin' in his way."

"No!" Olney shouted, struggling to get to Hayes. But the Levy brothers were too quick for him. They grabbed him by the arms and restrained him. "You weren't there! You're lyin'!"

Hayes kept at his story. "I crept closer and closer, tryin' to get a good look at Fred without givin' myself away. By the time I got close enough to jump Olney, I could tell Fred was already gone. Olney sat and skinned a rabbit, fried him up and ate him — right there — while Fred lay dead. Then he flopped Fred across his saddle horn, bound him up like he was binding up a sick calf, and headed off toward Fort Collins."

"Where were you?" Olney screeched. "Where were you?"

"I was all around you, Olney," Hayes said. "You forget I live plenty of months out of the year with the Utes. I know everything they do about movin' through the brush without bein' detected."

"I've heard enough," Murphy said.

"Aaron didn't tell me," Elizabeth said. "I thought you saw Fred and Harris leaving the Utes together . . . alive."

"It was worse than that, Beth. I just

didn't want you to know, you bein' in the delicate emotional state of a widow just losin' her husband. Aaron and I decided it would be best not to tell all of it just then. That's why Aaron stayed so adamant about coming out here and bringin' Olney back, no matter how you pleaded with him. He knew I'd be willin' to testify as to what I saw."

Murphy hollered up to Gilbert Hughes, who was still sitting on a cottonwood limb, his feet dangling, waiting to finish his job. "Don't you think that man's been sittin' on that fool mule long enough? Get that noose off his neck."

Gilbert scrambled to release the knot again. "Yes, sir."

While the Levy brothers held Olney, Judge Murphy fished around in the marshal's back pocket for the keys to the handcuffs. He retrieved them and went to release Aaron Brown himself.

"Much obliged, Judge Murphy," Aaron said graciously as he ran one finger around the inside of his collar to loosen it. The imprint of the rope was red and raw around his neck.

"Something tells me you're gonna like what I'm going to do now, Brown." Judge Murphy walked back to Olney as Beth moved to support her brother. With the Levys helping, Murphy wrestled the marshal's arms behind his back.

Snap.

The handcuffs clinked shut around each wrist.

"This is atrocious!" Olney bellowed. "You cain't do this to me! I'm the marshal in this town!"

Calmly J. M. Murphy reached up and removed Olney's highly polished star from his breast pocket. "Not anymore, you aren't. Your law-enforcement days are through, Olney."

"It won't stick." Olney struggled with the Levys, but to no avail. "Hayes is just a crazy man who roams the canyon and lives with Indians. I'll take this all the way to the state government. Nobody in *Denver* will take his word over mine."

"That's funny," Murphy said, smiling slightly, "because I do. You've played me for a fool long enough." The judge turned his attention to the huge group of men gathered around them. "Now. Since I've got a prisoner here, looks like I need to appoint a new marshal to keep a vigil over things."

The men around him stood taller, all of them throwing their shoulders back and poking out their chests.

Murphy grinned and started toward Ben Pearsall. "I like somebody with experience. Pearsall, you're one of the ones who broke this case wide open. Congratulations." He pinned the shiny star on Old Ben Pearsall's chest, and Ben stared down at it, his mouth agape. "You think you can handle this job? Can you handle the prisoner?"

Ben straightened, the glitter of the badge already reflected in his eyes. "Yes, sir, Judge Murphy. I can handle the prisoner just fine."

He started off in the direction of the jail-house, following the Levys, who were already transporting Harris Olney to his new quarters.

"Hey, you forgot something!" Murphy called out.

Ben turned to see the judge holding up the huge ring of metal keys he'd retrieved from Olney's belt. "You'll be needing these."

"I sure will."

"Lock him up, Marshal Pearsall," Murphy said.

"I sure will," Ben said.

"Hey!" Hughes climbed down from the cottonwood, the rope gathered in his hands now. "You want me to go up to Boot

Hill and fill in the hole I just dug?"

"No," Murphy said. "Leave that hole be. I figure we'll have somebody else to bury up on Boot Hill real soon."

Chapter Fifteen

The first thing Aaron wanted to do as he climbed down off Old Croppy's back was to fall headlong into Uley's arms. Only problem was, he couldn't do it.

Like it or not, a promise was a promise.

She waited just below him, peeking up from beneath the brim of her hat, her eyes sparkling like the glassy green sapphires that occasionally turned up in the rubble from the Gold Cup Mine. Her eyes spoke of everything they'd shared, every hope still to come, as he slid down off Old Croppy and landed on the ground beside her.

"Meet me," he whispered, as everyone else came to slap him on the back. "Tonight at nine outside the Gold Cup. It'll be dark, and no one will see us."

She nodded. "I'll be there."

They met just after dusk, Uley strolling up the mountain as if on her way to fulfill some purpose, pausing when she saw a profile standing against the looming dark mouth of the mine. Even without seeing his features, she knew Aaron by the way his Stetson tipped cavalierly to one side. She knew him by the way his broad shoulders jutted out like the *T* of a crossbow, by the way his lanky legs came together quickly when he heard her approach.

She stopped before him, pausing just long enough for him to know she waited. He gripped one of the lodgepoles that lined the porch and swung himself down.

"Uley?" he asked. "That you?"

"It's me."

Aaron strode toward her, his face still totally shadowed in the darkness.

He reached her with the lantern he carried and peered down at her, wondering if she knew how beautiful she looked with all that sweet golden glow shining on her skin. "Uley," he said, just gazing down at her. "I thought tonight would never come."

"It almost didn't." He reached for her with his hand.

She took his big fingers in her small ones and smiled up at him. It was a smile that made his soul lift with possibilities.

They walked beneath clouds etched with the silver filigree of moonlight. Uley was well aware that Aaron was comfortable with silence, unlike most people. They

348

could both go through long stretches of it without floundering around, trying to fill it.

Night sounds encircled them, the unearthly, spectral hoot of a great horned owl observing them both from the highest point of Hansen Smith's barn, the vibrant croaking of the frogs, loud and heralding, the muffled voices rising in discord, blending to harmony.

Strange how ten minutes of silence with the wrong person could be devastating, Uley thought. Ten minutes of silence with the wrong *man.*

Strange how ten minutes of silence with the right man could be wonderful, right, peaceful and filling.

As if sensing the buoyancy of her heart, Aaron stopped where he stood and swung her about. This time Uley's face remained eclipsed, Aaron's reflecting the gold from the flame inside the lantern glass. The disarming scent of bay rum wafted between them. For the first time, Uley realized that Aaron hadn't found the time to go back to the jailhouse and gather his things. Everyone had been so busy celebrating with him, celebrating *for* him, that he probably hadn't gotten any time to himself at all. Even now he wore the perfectly tailored dark suit, the white linen shirt and the horn bolo he'd chosen to hang in.

At this moment, the reality hit Uley full-force. At this very moment, he might now be buried beneath clods of dirt up on Boot Hill. At this moment, he might be gone from her. She'd known she'd never get through the ordeal if she faced the reality of Aaron's hanging. So she'd hidden the defeat, the love, away within her. She'd kept a close rein on all her feelings — until now.

The emotion hit her so fiercely that she felt her knees wanting to buckle. "Oh, Aaron," she cried, the tears rising in her eyes and clogging her throat. "To think what they might have done. To think what they were *going* to do."

"But they didn't, little one," he whispered. "They didn't."

"But they came so *close.* And we just all stood there and *watched.*"

"I was a murderer, remember?" Tears rose in his eyes, too, beautiful, cleansing tears of forgiveness and misplaced contrition. "You thought so, too."

"I did." What could she say? If she'd known, she'd have done things differently. She wouldn't have been so quick to condemn him. She wouldn't have been so fast to rush out at him in the road, to testify against him in a trial that had been more a farce than an act of justice.

"Uley." His eyes, almost navy in the dusk, reflected glimmers of light, spots of white and gold and yellow bound with the blue, like firelight coming from within.

The tears coursed down her cheeks. "I don't . . . I can't . . ." She couldn't speak, though she tried over and over again. "Just think, if I'd, they'd, if Dawson hadn't, hadn't come, or Beth, or Harris. If I'd —"

The only way Aaron knew to calm her was to do what he'd been wanting to do all evening anyway. He grabbed her against him, tucking her against his chest with a force that knocked his own breath away, even as she continued.

"I just, if you had had, I thought —"

"Hush and let me kiss you."

"I just —"

It was the last sound she uttered. She clung to him now, as he lifted her face to meet his, found her wet skin with his lips, in the darkness, skin that sparkled like stars from the moisture there, felt her seeking him with her lips.

They found one another.

Her mouth was as wet and salty and slippery as the tear-soaked skin of her face. As the night encircled them, their mouths slid desperately into place, both of them tasting the water and the tang of Uley's tears.

It wasn't enough. One kiss, one caress, one groping, desperate holding in such a darkness, could never be enough to fulfill either of them or to serve as a balm for what they'd both experienced.

Aaron kissed her again, harder than the first time, turning his face sideways to give her the full force of the kiss, and she returned it in a fervid attempt to dash away the pain of this morning, the days, the weeks, all the time that they'd both fought to persevere.

He drew away momentarily, found her mouth with his thumbs, lightly brushing its corners with each one.

Her breath fanned his chin with sudden warmth. He lifted her up to him again, this time gently, this time testing her mouth as she raised up on tiptoe. No iron bars stood between them now.

"You're here," she said softly. "You're really here."

"So are you." He took her mouth again in a slanted, wide, all-encompassing kiss. She felt her heart hammering against her chest and her spirit welled with thankfulness. *Oh, Father. Look at what You've done.*

She wrapped her hands around his neck, her fingers clasping together in his hair, pulling him down to meet her.

Just suppose she'd never known this feeling.

Just suppose Aaron had never come into her life.

Just suppose she'd gone on forever not knowing this poignant aching inside.

Encircled in Aaron's arms, a woman took shape and was born. The joy she found inside seemed as adventurous as exploring some newfound vein of gold on the mountain.

What had happened to the child she'd been? What had happened to the young girl who'd thought she could stand beside her father and live a life such as this? That idealistic youth had vanished beneath this man's kisses, beneath this man's touch. In her place stood an expectant, radiant woman.

He saw it, too, as he angled away from her. "You're beautiful," he told her.

"Do you know," she told him, "how many times I've wanted to be beautiful for you? Do you know how I've wished to stroll down the streets with a parasol like Beth's? With skirts like Beth's? With hair hanging down my back for you, hair like

Beth's hair? I wish I could be pretty."

"You don't have any idea how I like you the way you are. With your knickers and your hat."

He felt her go quiet. He knew, suddenly, his last sentence had been the wrong one. It didn't matter how he measured her beauty. It mattered how *she* measured it herself. It mattered that she be able to walk down Washington Street unfettered, unscathed, unblemished.

It couldn't happen.

Not here.

The miners wouldn't forgive her for the way she'd deceived them.

She'd laid her forehead against his chest, and she was crying, her sobs muffled.

"What can we do?"

"There isn't a thing."

He couldn't leave Tin Cup, not now, not when everything he'd fought for was finally nearing fruition. Word had already reached him that Ben Pearsall, enjoying his first addictive taste of power as Tin Cup's marshal, had announced he would set up a speedy, decisive trial for Harris Olney and that Otto Violet would serve as prosecutor in the case. Dawson Hayes even planned to stay, with a gold pan in hand, to placer his way up Willow Creek.

Thanks to Aaron, John Kincaid had taken down his shingle and was moving to a different camp. Judge Murphy proclaimed the entire business now under Gunnison County's jurisdiction. Because Olney had been hired by the county, had served as marshal here for a great many months, and had done his best to hang a man he knew was innocent, Murphy wanted every aspect of the investigation and the trial to take place in the community. He'd probably have to bring a jury all the way from St. Elmo or Aspen. He'd already used everybody he could from Pitkin.

"I can't leave until it's over," Aaron said.

"I wouldn't ask it of you. After everything Olney tried to do, I'd love to see your testimony put him right where he tried to put you."

"You can't tell them about yourself," he said. "I wouldn't ask that of you, either."

"Walk me home, Aaron." She took one step back from him, holding his two hands in her own, hands that lay so large and gentle and strong within her own. In the air, everything still waited between them, the questions neither of them knew how to answer.

I promised to keep her secret for a life-

time, he thought. *I figured my lifetime would be over by now. Now I face more years of loving her and not telling anybody about it.*

As they walked back, the silence hung heavier and higher than the Continental Divide, an impassable boundary between them.

Moll hadn't lost her talent with figures. As a half-dozen of her girls waited at the top of the stairs and she sat at her desk beside the door, she scribbled names upon her ledger and realized that, as a result of the hoopla surrounding Aaron Brown's trial, her profit for this month looked somewhat scarce. She'd be down to nothing this week if not for the Pitkin miners who'd walked through the front door searching for a little feminine companionship. The girls, who had painted their faces heavier than usual and donned their fanciest, frilliest dresses, stood whispering in a cluster, as intrigued by the outcome of the trial as everyone else.

"Get to thinking about where your next meal is coming from. Can't live on gossip, girls. I want to see you fluffing up those skirts and wearing your prettiest smiles, want to see you *attracting* men, not standing around *talking* about them."

Laura gripped the wooden rail with both hands, doing her best to steady herself. As long as her friends had been discussing the outcome of Aaron Brown's hanging and chattering about happenings in town, she'd been able to hide from anyone who might come in, asking for a companion. But when Moll raised her eyes and began bellowing how she wanted them to stand, everything would be lost. Someone would walk in and choose her for sure. And Laura didn't know how to explain what was happening in her heart since she'd prayed and asked Jesus to take over in there. She felt uneasy, her heart a heavy pendulum clanging against her insides, whispering over and over, *You are mine, beloved. You don't belong to yourself. You don't belong to this.*

And yet she did.

How does a person go about changing her life on the inside when everything's the same on the outside?

Tin Can Laura had no idea.

Just as she had thought, the door banged open and in stomped a man wearing a cowhide jacket almost as big around as the animal it had come off of, his Levi's legs the same circumference as milk pails.

The man's grizzly beard cascaded over the snaps of his dirty brown long johns. "Hey." He clomped toward Moll. "Got a gal in here for me?" He glanced around the room for the spittoon. It waited, burnished and ready, on the floor beside Moll's desk. Evidently he didn't see it. He hauled off and spat a wad of tobacco clear across the room. He watched in fascination as it slid down the wall, leaving a trail in its wake. "Didn't anybody tell you that you need a spittoon in here?"

"We've got a spittoon. It's right here, if you would have looked to see it. Although I'm glad you didn't aim in this direction. It would have been frightening, Mr. . . ."

"Mortimus. Henry Mortimus."

"Yes, Mr. Mortimus. You may have your pick of the girls at the top of the steps. They're all ready and available."

Laura was trembling in her shoes. *Lord, please don't let him pick me. Please. I just can't do this anymore. And not with him.*

Last night, she and Uley had been poring over Scripture in Uley's Bible and Uley had showed her the one that read, "All things work together for the good of those who love the Lord." That seemed all well and good when they'd been discussing the events that had led up to Mr. Brown's exoneration. It did not seem so easy to accept here.

The detestable man surveyed them. His scowl turned to a frown, then the frown turned into interest and amusement. He never did come close to a smile.

"I see the one I want. That one. Right there." He pointed at Laura. "The young one with the feather in her hair."

"You've picked Laura." Moll gave a nod that showed she was pleased. "A good choice. That one's been managing not to get herself picked much lately."

As he started up the stairs toward her, his boot steps made sharp blows against the wood. As Laura's belly filled with dread, she tried to figure why he seemed so familiar. Whoever he was, he did not look pleasant.

"Hey, you purty little thing." He took her by the arm when he reached the top of the steps. "Didn't have any trouble picking you, all dressed up in red. Red's my favorite color."

He smelled like he hadn't seen soap in a month.

"You ready to sit and talk for a while? You ready to make friends?"

As Laura led him to a room and shut the

door, her mouth went as dry as a chunk of dirt from the Gold Cup. She leaned her head against the door and prayed. *Please, Lord. Protect me.*

But why should He protect her from something she'd chosen to do herself? Why should He come as her rescuer when she knew she didn't deserve it?

"Gonna be a rich man someday," the horrid man bragged to her. "You ought to be feeling lucky, getting picked by someone with such promise as me. I came all the way over from Pitkin. Did you know that, little red lady?"

Ah. It began to make sense. Laura had forgotten about the Pitkin miners in town for the trial. That would explain why she recognized his face. He went back to her earlier days.

With one dingy hand, he reached and pulled her close to him. He buried his face against the flesh of her shoulder.

Oh, Father. Show me what I'm supposed to do.

At first she thought the pain came from the man's huge, prickly beard. Perhaps a wiry strand was poking into her. But she should have known better. Poking beards didn't hurt like that. Henry Mortimus was biting her.

"Ouch!" She jumped up. "You can't do that to me."

"I can, too. I'm paying for companionship, aren't I?" He followed her across the room.

"No, you can't." She hated the quaver in her voice. "Please, mister."

Henry Mortimus stopped stalking her across the room and stood straight up. "Now, you don't have to go goody on me. You're nothing but a hurdy-gurdy girl. I pay Moll, I can do anything I get a mind to."

He stopped.

She followed his eyes to the tin can sitting on her dresser. His eyes shot back to hers.

"That there your tin can?"

"Yes."

"Laura, it is? Your name's Laura?"

She squared her shoulders, swallowed hard. Who was this man?

"It is."

"Tin Can Laura?"

"The very same."

She didn't like the contempt in his eyes. "Well, I'll be. I been looking fer you a long time, little lady."

The bite on her shoulder had not drawn blood, but throbbed like a hot brand.

"Think back two or three years, Laura Wilson."

She flinched at his use of her given name. Around her, no one knew it.

"I'm sorry," she said. "I don't remember."

He spat another wad of tobacco across the room, this time not even bothering to look for a spittoon. "You were my favorite girl to call on in Pitkin, Laura. That is, until you got to feeling like you were too good for the likes of me. I saw you one night through the church window, I did."

She gasped. No one in the world was supposed to know how she'd come to learn to play the piano in Pitkin.

"I saw that fancy preacher teaching you to play 'Oh, for a Thousand Tongues To Sing.' Just about laughed my eyeballs out. Hurdy-gurdy girls got tongues, all right, but the tongues they got are made for kissing, not for singing praises to God."

"You hush up."

"I wouldn't figure God wants a tarnished dove singing about him to folks, now, would you?"

"I'd always wanted to learn to play the piano," she said haughtily.

"Seems to me you were doing more than learning piano playing. You were laughing up at that man like a wife sharing a secret."

Laura didn't care what Henry Mortimus thought about her. She *did* care what he thought about the man who'd been pastor of the Pitkin Congregational Church.

"He was doing what every preacher does for his flock, Mr. Mortimus. He was telling me that, no matter what sort of work I do, the Lord died for all my bad choices."

"After that day I seen you at that piano," Mortimus growled at her, "I knew why I'd been getting those feelings from you every time I stepped into the place."

"What feelings?" she asked almost frantically. She didn't remember sending any feelings out to him. She couldn't remember him at all.

"Just like today," he said. "Acting like you're too good for what you're doing. Acting like you're too good for *me*."

"I'm not acting that way." She backed away from him, feeling for the edge of the bureau with her hand.

"You're my gal for the next hour."

"No. I don't think so."

"See here." He pulled a pouch from his pocket and opened it so she could see the gold dust. "My money's just as good as the next fellow's."

She scooted sideways, out of his reach.

"I've had enough of you playing coy, Tin Can Laura. It's been fun watching you pretend to be a lady. But I'm getting bored with it now."

"No, Mr. Mortimus."

"You come here."

"I don't think so. Please."

He grabbed her arm, wrenched it behind her back.

"Won't do what you want me to do. I don't care what Moll says."

"Yeah. That's what I thought. That preacher, teaching you piano. He went and put notions in your head, didn't he?"

"This doesn't have anything to do with my piano-playing days. It has to do with what's going on inside my head.

"I belong to the Lord."

"A girl who's done what you did? Thinking God would care about what happens to you?"

"Yes."

"Trust me, little red lady. The Lord doesn't want anything to do with the likes of you."

Laura felt sick. *Maybe he's right. Maybe I've been fooling myself, thinking it would make any difference.*

Even though he still had a grip on her, she'd made it to the door. She struggled with the handle with her free hand.

"Hey!" he bellowed. "What do you think you're doing?"

The bolt wouldn't give. Laura jerked frantically, trying to pull it through the metal ring that held it secure.

"You get away from that door."

"You take your hands off of me."

He spun her around.

"Please."

"You begging?"

She kicked him and twisted herself free. One of her slippers came off in his hand. Leering, he flipped the shoe across the room and dove after her other foot.

She landed a blow square on his nose. Blood sprayed from it.

"Confound it." He cupped his face with his fingers. "Look what you've done."

"I'll bloody more than that —" she squinted at him with all the friendliness of a wolverine on the attack "— if you don't figure out that I mean what I say."

Her words baited him. He crawled forward on his elbows and went for her skirt. The satin gave way with a rending tear. As she struggled to wrap the fabric around her again, Mortimer climbed up and caught her around the waist. "You haven't changed, have you?" He jerked her head backward by the hair and spun her toward him. "You're the same snotty little thing who thought she was too good for her britches over in Pitkin." He hauled off and slapped her hard across the face.

Father, if You're with me, show me what to do.

Then suddenly, she knew. She didn't have to be treated this way ever again. It wasn't what a loving Heavenly Father would ever want for her. She would never again have to deal with the likes of Henry Mortimus. She kneed him in the groin. When he doubled over in pain, she ducked away from his arm. She pummeled the door with force she didn't know she possessed, desperate for someone to help.

Mortimus grabbed her away from the door, shoved her against the wall. When she heard the crack Laura didn't know whether it was her head or the pine planking behind her.

"Open up in there! Laura, you okay? This is Charles Ongewach, mister. You open this door."

"You're nothing but a dirty bird."

Laura was fast slipping toward incoherency. From outside in the hallway, she could hear someone ramming the door.

The wood around the bolt began to splinter.

"You almost got it," she heard Moll shout.

"Again! Come on!" She recognized that voice as Peter Sturge, a fellow who Charles must have brought in off the streets to help because he'd always been too shy to come in here.

The wood shattered. The bolt fell to the floor. From somewhere far away, Laura thought she heard hinges squeaking, a door yawning open. There was a glint of Ongewach's gun, a voice growling, "You unhand her, man."

She felt herself being bundled inside a quilt, felt Moll rocking her back and forth on the bed as if she were a hurt child. And the woman's voice crooning, in a tone she'd never heard before, "There you are. We come to get you, Laura. There you are."

Chapter Sixteen

Moll shook Laura's dress free of wrinkles. She shook her head at the rip in the skirt. "Going to make him pay for a new working dress for you when Ben Pearsall lets him out of jail. It's a crying shame what he did to this dress."

Laura sat on the bed, her legs curled beneath her, a demure flannel nightgown buttoned up to her chin. She didn't speak.

"In the morning, we'll find Doc Gillette. I want him to look at those bites."

Still Laura said nothing.

"Guess it's too much to wish that Mortimus fellow has rabies. He acted like a dog gone out of his mind. I'd like to find some reason to shoot the nasty coot and put him out of his misery."

Laura fingered the pearl button at the hollow of her neck.

"You did the right thing, signaling us and all. We can't have customers thinking they can come in here and do this."

"Yes."

"Nasty shiner on your eye, too. Ought to be the talk of the town now that the murder trial's over."

"Yes."

"Ain't it something how Pete Sturge came running in to help you? Charles went bellowing out the door that Laura was in trouble, and you should've seen the look on that young Pete's face. He come barreling in here like a bull out of a rodeo chute. Ain't it something?"

Silence.

Moll snuffed out the tallow candle on the wall. "Tomorrow will be another day, won't it? We'll get somebody up here to fix this door." She let herself out. The door, though shut, wouldn't fasten all the way. As Laura's eyes adjusted to the darkness, a ribbon of light lay across the fancy dress still hanging on the wall peg.

I'm not wearing that horrid thing again as long as I live.

I don't care what anyone does to me.

I'm not going to be Tin Can Laura anymore.

The room stopped spinning. Slowly she stood.

She paused, holding her breath, when she heard somebody coming up the stairs.

She wouldn't take time to dress. There

was too great a possibility that Charles or Moll or one of the other girls might come back up to check on her. She pulled her yellow calico down off the peg and laid it out on the bed.

She stooped beside the mattress and ran one flat, outstretched hand beneath it. After three passes, she found what she searched for, a leather pouch not much different from the one Mortimus had displayed, filled a third of the way with gold dust and coins.

She untied the strings and opened the pouch. She picked up the tin can beside her bed and shook it. It had been a slow night. She didn't have much to add to the pouch. She dumped the evening's earnings from the can and left it sitting empty beside the bed.

The pouch she tied up neatly and hid within a pocket of the calico dress. That was all she gathered to take with her. Joe was nowhere in sight. But even if the cat had been curled up at the foot of her bed, where she usually stayed, Laura couldn't have taken her. Ever since the spring storm, that cat meowed louder than a cow bawling. Joe would certainly give her away.

Laura draped her shawl around her shoulders, shoved her bundled yellow dress up beneath one arm and climbed out the upstairs window.

Uley sat on her bed, braiding her hair, with Storm purring contentedly from the lap of her nightgown. A pounding came at the window, loud enough to make her flinch and make Storm stop her purring. "Uley! You gotta help me! Quick!"

Uley recognized Laura's shrill whisper. She pushed the cat off her lap, ran to the window and threw open the curtains. "Laura? What is it?"

Even in the moonlit darkness, Uley could see Laura's distended nose, the bruised, cut skin surrounding her eyes. She ran to the door, unfastened it and met her friend in the side yard. "Who did that?"

"Nobody you know. Just a customer."

"You've got to see Doc Gillette."

"No. I don't. Moll was planning to take me tomorrow, but I'm not gonna go. And if *you* take me, then Moll will come here looking."

Uley took Laura by the hand and led her inside. "Here. You lie on my bed. I'll put a warm cloth on you. We've got warm water on the stove."

"That'll make it feel better."

Storm was waiting on the bed for Uley

to return. Laura climbed up on the covers and stroked the animal sadly. "I had to leave Joe behind." Finally she allowed herself to cry. "She'd have been caterwauling all the way down the street. Moll would have caught me sneaking away for sure."

Sam came to Uley's room. "What's going on in there?"

"Laura's here, Pa," Uley told him. "She's hurt real bad."

"I'm not, either," Laura said as she climbed into Uley's bed and covered herself with the quilt. "It's just sore in my heart is all. But I'll heal up." How well Uley knew the truth, though. Heart wounds often went much deeper, took longer to heal, than bodily ones.

Sam pushed open the door to see his daughter stroking Laura across the forehead with a warm cloth.

"That hurt?" Uley asked when Laura winced.

"Don't ask that question. It ought to never hurt when a friend's workin' on you, should it?"

"Even so," Uley said softly, "sometimes it does."

Sam sat on the bed beside them. "Does anyone know what this man did to you?"

"Yeah. They all do. He's locked up in the

jailhouse right now. It isn't as bad as it looks. He just knocked me around, is all." Laura grabbed Uley's hand and sat straight up. "I'm not going back to that place, Uley. I can't do it."

"You'll stay here with us," Sam said. "We'll take you in. Some decent man in this town'll give you a job and you can start a new —" But both Laura and Uley were shaking their heads at him.

"It won't work that way, Pa."

"Joseph Devendish down at the bank is looking for somebody. Maybe he'll give her a job."

"No." Uley stood up and went to hug her father. "Nobody'll hire her because she's a hurdy-gurdy girl. We've already tried once without telling anybody. The men in this town may be rough themselves, but they're awful ready to judge everybody else, too."

"They'll look down their noses at me like I'm something rotten." Laura gathered Storm up next to her, finding little comfort from the cat's nearness. "I think they'd rather not have any money at all than have me counting it or givin' it out at the bank."

Uley had long since illuminated the lantern. She walked to the mirror hanging over the bureau and gazed at her own face. It was the first time in months she'd looked upon herself with candle-light flaming and reflecting in her own eyes. Always, she'd gauged her feminine appearance by filtered moonlight. Because of her friend's need, she saw herself now, saw who she'd become. Uley made her decision, the one she'd known was coming, the decision that would end her charade.

Can I be myself in front of You, Lord, the same way I was able to be myself with Aaron? Would You give me the strength to let go of my own plans and accept Your plan for my life, Lord?

She turned to face the two of them. "I've been promising a long time that you and I could go to Aunt Delilah's place, Laura. I think the time's come for you and me to start things over in Ohio."

Despite her injuries, Laura practically leapt from the bed. "You mean it? You'd go with me? You'd take me there, Uley?"

"Yes." Uley turned back to the mirror, thinking of Aaron, thinking of everything she longed to give him, everything she kept hidden away. Aaron deserved everything a woman who loved him could give him. He deserved a woman like Beth. "I'll go with you to Ohio."

Sam rose from the bed. "Uley? You want to go back?"

"Yes."

"If you do, I'll take you."

But Uley shook her head at him, her thick red braid flopping against her shoulder. "There's no need, Pa. I'll travel as a fellow, just the way I've been living these past years. Everybody'll think me and Laura are married. We'll get on without any trouble at all."

"I never wanted it to be that way."

"You don't have any choice, Pa. You and Ma came here to find a fortune. I won't let you give it up now. Not after all of us have sacrificed so much. There's a supply wagon leaves here tomorrow. If we're on it, Moll won't be able to stop Laura."

"But you'll need supplies. And money to pay your passage."

"I've got the money." Laura reached for her yellow calico, held up the leather pouch. "Lesser Levy made sure of that."

"I'll come back to Tin Cup someday, Pa," Uley said. "But things will be different next time. I'm sure of it."

Even so, Uley knew she wouldn't be back soon enough for Aaron. He wouldn't wait for her return. He'd proven himself trustworthy to her time after time again.

Uley knew that, above all else, he needed a woman in his life who could stand beside him right away, the kind of woman who would make him feel like a treasure.

Uley could never be that woman here in Tin Cup.

He'll forget me soon. But I'll never forget him. Not for a minute. I will love him always.

"Uley," Pa said. Then he used her real given name. It was the first time he'd allowed it to escape his lips since she was fourteen and they laughed about it on the Overland Trail. "My dearest Julia."

She took her father's hands and held them. "I know."

"How can I let you do this?"

But she found no words. She shook her head at him, tears pooling in her eyes. "Laura's my friend, Pa."

Laura wrapped her shawl around her shoulders and came toward them both. "It's asking too much, Uley."

Uley shook her head. "It's more than that, too. Pa and I both know it. And so do you."

The lantern light flickered in the unshed tears in her father's eyes. "I've known this had to come ever since I took her away from Delilah the first time. It just wasn't proper, what we did."

"It might not have been proper, but it was right, Pa. We were family. We still are. And Ma gave up everything for what you dreamed of."

"Don't I know it." Her father gazed out the window toward the silver-lit moon beyond, his features softening in sorrow and love, as if he were gazing upon his wife's face one last time. "Don't I just think I know it." He turned to his daughter. "You're gonna be needing her things."

Harris Olney was beginning to have regrets about how he'd built his jailhouse. He hadn't exactly made the place easy to break out of. Now, why had he worked so hard to build heavy iron bars? It made it so a man had to stay put. Only trouble was, he'd never figured the man having to stay put might be himself.

He had no idea of the time. He only knew that dusk had dropped into deep night. He stared out at the black sky, grumbling, "Sure not gonna let it end this way."

He'd already examined the dirt floor and the pine wall. He figured going at it that way would be hopeless. He could dig himself out if he had seven more nights and something inconspicuous to put over the hole. The problem was, he didn't have that long. The way public opinion seemed to be against him these days, Olney figured he only had about three nights — at best.

The other option he considered was bribing Ben Pearsall. As marshal, he'd taken his share of bribes. Harris Olney figured that in time Old Ben would succumb to the temptation of easy money. The problem here was, he'd be approaching him on his first full day as marshal. That wouldn't sit well with him. Pearsall was still proud of that new shiny star. It would take something or somebody mighty potent to make Pearsall forget he was wearing it.

Nope. Bribery wouldn't work, either.

The timing here was all wrong.

Olney lay on the squeaky cot, trying his best to get some sleep. He could see straight up out of the window, straight up out at freedom.

He figured he'd done the wrong thing.

He figured he should never have let his longing for that Cache la Poudre treasure get tangled up with everything he'd started feeling for Elizabeth Calderwood. He'd killed a few men in his life, but never one of his friends. When he'd been alone in the wilderness with Fred, he'd looked at the spindly man hunched over the fire and he'd thought, *He's the only thing standing in my way. He's the only thing keeping me from all that money. And he's the only thing keeping me from Beth.*

It used to be, when he gazed up at the stars, he saw Beth's eyes. Now he saw Fred's, glaring down at him from a spot way above heaven. He guessed he'd always see them there. But he didn't feel sorry for what he'd done. He didn't feel remorse. He'd gone after what he wanted, and he'd go after what he wanted again.

Tonight, what he wanted was to get out of this jail cell.

He had no idea what time Ben Pearsall brought the second prisoner in. He heard a ruckus in the front office, a medley of irate voices that he couldn't quite make out.

"You ain't got no right to keep me here. I ain't under the jurisdiction of this county."

"When you spit, sir, please use the spit-toon."

"I'll spit anywhere I please. You cain't hold me in Gunnison County. You the new marshal, ain't you? I saw you appointed this morning. You're as green behind the ears as a sapling in springtime."

Ben marched to the holding cell with a huge, bearded fellow ahead of him.

"You just test me," Pearsall snarled as he unlocked the cell door. "You just see how green I am."

Pearsall shoved him inside and slammed the door shut.

Harris Olney sat up on the cot. "Welcome home."

"Hey!" the new prisoner bellowed. "There's only one cot in here. I need one, too. I've got to get sleep. I've had a bad night."

Marshal Pearsall stood outside the cell, his hands planted firmly upon the butts of two gleaming six-shooters. "You're under the jurisdiction of Tin Cup, Colorado, Henry Mortimus. In Tin Cup, we can only afford one cot. Never had two prisoners at the same time before. You two fellas are just gonna have to share."

He turned to walk away.

"I don't say's how I like Tin Cup's hospitality," Mortimus roared to his back.

"Good," Ben said, without looking back. "Once I get rid of you, I won't have to worry about you ever turning up here again."

Harris waited until he heard Ben settling in at the desk before he staked his claim. "I helped build this jail." He lay back down again, doing his best to appear settled. He knew he wouldn't sleep tonight. But, even if he couldn't, he sure was going to pretend it. "I'm not giving up this cot."

"If I had my gun," Mortimus said, "I'd just have to shoot you."

"Well, you don't have a gun, so you're out of luck."

"This town is the most mixed-up outfit I've ever seen," the bearded man said.

"So, what're you in here for?" Now that Olney had claimed the cot, he relaxed a bit.

"Nothing important," Mortimus told him, squatting on the ground in the corner and groaning because he couldn't get comfortable. "You'd think with all the gold in the hills over yonder, the *government* could afford two cots."

"They've never had two prisoners before."

Mortimus eyed Olney. "You're the old marshal, ain't you?"

"I am."

"I'll tell you right now, I don't like people who think they're better than me."

"Guess that means we don't like each other, then."

"Guess that's what it means."

They stared at each other for a minute, like two prize bulls assessing each other across a pasture.

Olney finally broke the impasse. "You didn't say what you were in for."

"I roughed up one of your tarnished birds, that's what I did. I found one I knew from a long time back, and I didn't much like her attitude."

"Which one?"

"Ain't telling you. I figure you've murdered plenty of men yourself. Ain't giving you a reason to murder me, too. Everybody in that place got so *upset.* One fellow even *calf-roped* me. I cain't figure why everybody would put so much value on a two-bit red-dressed hurdy-gurdy girl."

Olney sat up, thumping his two boots onto the floor. "Red-dressed? Was it Laura? Tin Can Laura's the only one who wears that color over there."

"Yep."

Olney started getting red in the face. "You roughed up Laura?"

"See what I mean?" Mortimus asked. "Nobody cares how we treat them over across Alpine Pass. Then I get over here, find her and there's all this fuss."

"You keep your hands off Tin Can Laura."

"She roughed me up pretty bad, too. About broke my nose, she did. Hit me with her fists and kicked me. That's why I'm wishing for that cot. Parts of me are hurt purty bad."

Harris Olney grinned. It was a great, wide grin the likes of which nobody'd seen since Aaron Brown had come to town.

"Tell you what." He moved away from the coveted canvas contraption and motioned to it with both arms, the very picture of the genteel host motioning a guest to his best accommodations.

Mortimus eyed him suspiciously. "Why don't you get a good night's sleep on this thing?"

"What're you doing that for? You're sure experiencing a change of heart."

Olney clapped him on the back. "I'm not going to sleep, anyway. No sense wasting the nicest bed in the house."

"You want something out of me, don't you?"

"What makes you think that?"

"Because I know fellows like you. I know fellows who don't give up their position unless it serves them some good."

"Well, you got me figured right." Olney sat down in the corner of the cell and stretched his legs, letting out a rush of breath as he did so. "I *do* want something."

Mortimus didn't sit down. "I guess you'd best tell me what it is."

"I want us to help each other."

"Help each other with what?"

"I've got unfinished business to attend to," Olney explained, a good deal of sarcasm in his voice. "I've got to be away from this jailhouse sometime tomorrow morning. I figure you have about as good a reason as I do to want to bust out of this place."

Generally, summer thunderstorms didn't rumble into the high mountains around Tin Cup until the end of an afternoon, boiling up over the Divide, fueled by the intense midday sun. The rain usually fell fast, cooling and cleansing everything in the valley with thick, settling drops. Fifteen minutes later, as quickly as the afternoon rains gathered and fell, they dissipated.

But today's storm came in a different fashion.

Everybody who knew the weather said that if a storm hit before ten in the morning, it'd last the rest of the day. This storm crescendoed down into the valley just after daybreak, thunder echoing across the gold hill before most of the guests at Aunt Kate Fischer's had even finished their breakfast.

Aaron donned his Stetson and a jacket, knowing full well he'd be soaked by the time he completed his morning errands.

Beth walked into Aunt Kate's kitchen, her apron bow tied prettily at the small of her back, carrying a pile of dirty breakfast plates. "You going out in the rain?"

"Figure so. I'm planning to talk to Otto Violet. I need to get him to begin proceedings before Harris Olney can escape from that jailhouse." Aaron had other plans, too, but he wasn't going to tell Beth about them. Yesterday afternoon, he'd passed the window at C. A. Freeman's and seen a lace parasol on display. He'd lain awake all night, wondering how much it cost, wondering if he dared purchase it for Uley. This morning he'd decided to examine it.

Not that he cared a fiddle bow to a fence post whether Uley Kirkland carried finery such as that. She seemed everything wonderful to him just the way she was, as unaffected and fresh as dawn. But he wanted her to be happy more than anything, wanted her to have everything her heart desired. He'd seen the flashes of pain that often came into her eyes. Before the day was over, Uley would have her parasol. He didn't care if she had to hide it beneath her bed for the rest of her living days.

Beth stood before him. "You getting tired of serving men their breakfast? You can go back to Fort Collins, you know. You don't have to stay here waiting on me now."

She set the pile of plates down on the washboard and flicked soapy water at him. "You think I'm going to miss all the excitement?"

"You're getting me wet."

"You'll get wetter outside."

"But the water'll be coming down from the sky, not straight on into my face." He turned to go.

Beth stopped him. "Aaron?"

"Yeah?"

"I'm sorry about saying you were after Wishbone Mabel. I thought it would help things at the trial."

"It would have," he told her, "if I'd have let it stand."

"I know. And I thought . . . I just didn't know." She hesitated. She didn't know exactly how to say it. "From all the questions you asked me . . ."

"Certainly. It made sense, didn't it?"

"Sounded to me like you were getting

sweet on somebody. When John Kincaid talked about Mabel, it seemed to fit together. But after that trial and what you did there, I can't make anything fit together anymore."

Aaron stood in the doorway, holding his hat on his head with one hand, trying to decide how to explain it to her. But he couldn't. He had a promise to keep. "There's twenty hungry men out there waiting on you to come back with plates full of eggs and sausage. I figure you'd best quit worrying about making everything fit and get back to serving breakfast. There isn't much going on here that will ever make sense."

She turned her back to him, picking up the filled plates and aligning them along one arm. "I guess you're right," she said huffily, halfway mad again because he hadn't confided in her. She pushed her way back through the door.

Aaron sighed. He checked his hat to make certain it remained settled on his head. Then he hurried outside, head bent against the pelting rain.

Aaron walked past C. A. Freeman's window on his way to the attorney's office. He didn't stop to peruse its contents. He'd examined the display at great length last evening. With his eyes closed, he could name half the items arrayed there. Instead, he kept his appointment at Otto Violet's office, happily recounting the events of the past month that had led to this day, while Mr. Violet took notes.

"We have a fine case here," the attorney told him. "A fine one indeed." Violet surveyed Aaron over the desk. "I can honestly tell you, young man, I am sorry I did not agree to take on your case the first time. If it had been handled properly, the right lawyer could have made a name for himself politically in Colorado. It was quite a show."

"A show I didn't know if I'd survive or not," Aaron noted.

"But you did. You did." The lawyer chortled. Their eyes met meaningfully. "I can only thank you for giving me this case now and not keeping it from me as retribution for my past mistake."

"Everybody makes mistakes," Aaron said. *Thank you, Father,* he prayed, *that Your Son Jesus died to cover all of mine.* Victory felt good this morning. Life felt good this morning. "Luckily, this morning I am in a position to absolve you of your mistakes the way I have been absolved of mine."

"Yes," Violet said. "Luckily."

"Good day, sir," Aaron said, tipping his soggy Stetson before he stepped out the front door into the muddy street below. The rain slackened to an intermittent drizzle as he headed toward Freeman's. He found the dry goods store, its window abundant with examples of finery, and walked inside.

"Morning, Calvin!" he called out in a loud voice.

"Who is that?" Calvin Freeman stopped sweeping and waddled toward the front of the store, tucking his chin so low to see through his spectacles that his eyes almost met his eyebrows. "Oh, Mr. Brown. It's good to see you alive and well this morning."

"Thanks, Calvin. It's good to *be* alive this morning. I'd like to examine the parasol in your window, please."

Calvin Freeman's eyebrows, once so close to his eyes, now shot up in arches the same shape as a miner's pickax. "The parasol?"

"Yes. Please. It will be a gift."

Freeman waddled toward the window, pushed other items aside and retrieved the item of interest. He carried it to Aaron and laid it on the wooden counter.

Aaron didn't touch it. He knew that, if he did, he'd be all fumble-fingered. How did one even go about opening such a thing? He had absolutely no idea.

Calvin Freeman didn't touch it again, either. "It's the finest parasol available anywhere," he said. "Manufactured in St. Louis, with a handcarved mother-of-pearl handle and metal grommets. The lace is . . ."

But Aaron didn't hear another word. He was picturing Uley standing before him, her hair down around her shoulders, spinning the parasol high above her head.

"Mr. Brown?" Freeman asked. "I say, Mr. Brown? Can you hear me?"

"Oh, yes, I . . ."

"I asked if you'd like me to open it for you."

Aaron almost agreed just so he'd have a moment to recapture his wits. But there was no need. He'd known he wanted this for Uley ever since he'd spied it. "No, thank you, Calvin. I'm sure the young lady will know how to open it, one of those good things a woman can always teach a man. I'd like you to wrap this up for me, please."

Chapter Seventeen

At exactly the same moment Aaron was looking at the beautiful parasol upon the counter at C. A. Freeman's and agreeing to pay for it, Uley flipped open the dusty trunk that had been hidden beneath the bed since the day she and her father had arrived in Tin Cup.

"Are those your mother's things?" Laura asked, poking her head over Uley's shoulder.

"Yes." Uley's voice filled with reverence. "They are." She lifted the first item out of the trunk. It was a tiny tussy-mussy, all tied together with gathers of lace and ribbon, still smelling faintly of roses and spring clover. Uley sniffed it, closing her eyes, remembering. "Smells like she's standing right here in the room with us."

"Maybe she is," Laura said. "Maybe she's watching you the way the angels watch."

"I figure she is," Uley answered. "I figure she's been doing that for the longest time."

Uley laid her hands atop the pile of belongings, willing herself to go on. The only thing she'd taken from this spot in the years she'd been in Tin Cup was the beautiful silver-handled brush she kept in the bureau. "I know Pa figured on going to pay for our passage this morning so he wouldn't have to look at everything in this trunk. He hasn't been in it since the day he buried Ma and we packed it all away."

"She must have been real pretty," Laura said. "Look at all the fancy things she wore."

"She was, all right." Uley lifted a pink checked calico skirt and draped it across the floor. "But I always figured she just looked so good to me because I loved her so much."

"You going to wear that?"

"Do you think it'd fit me?"

"Everything looks to be about your size, Uley."

Uley stood and held the skirt to her waist, surprised to find that it hung just to the ground, and no more. "It does, doesn't it?"

She knelt to her knees and gingerly lifted out a simple blouse with an agate cameo still attached to the collar.

Next came a hat, a lovely wide-brimmed

one made of leghorn straw, the wheat braids fine, yellow and flat as the braided rug that lay before the wood stove in the corner. On it sat an assortment of fruits. If the ornaments hadn't been made of paste, their perfect lines and brilliant colors would have made them prime candidates for blue ribbons at a county fair. "She wore this to church the last Sunday before we left on the Overland Trail," Uley whispered. "She had the fruits put on down at the millinery. I remember her saying, when she put this hat on, the Book says that a 'life should always be measured by the Godly fruit it bears.' And I remember Pa teasing her and saying, 'Sarah, if there was anymore fruit heaped on your head, then *I* wouldn't be able to bear it!' "

Both girls sat quietly smiling for a long while.

"Have you cried over your ma going?" Laura finally asked. "When mine died, I did."

"So did I, Laura, but not enough. Me and Pa both cried. Then I figured I had to be brave. I figured I had to act like a fellow on the journey, too, or Pa'd turn around and take me back."

"Well, he didn't. And look where it's gotten you."

Uley peered into the trunk again, her eyes watery. As she unpacked the remainder of her mother's trunk, the tears which she'd held so long at bay began to flow, warm and free at last. It surprised her that something could feel both sorrowful and healing at the same time. Still sniffing, she unloaded the last dress, a bright emerald chintz, with puffed sleeves and tiny covered buttons that ran all the way from the scalloped collar at the neck to the gathers of the skirt. "She wore this one to parties. I used to watch sometimes while Pa would help her get into it. It has tape ties, so many of them I had trouble counting when she put it on."

"It's got a bustle, doesn't it?" Laura breathed. "I saw a lady with a bustle once. She'd come to Pitkin all the way from Denver."

"When Ma stitched it for herself, she said it would be the most fashionable thing she ever owned."

Laura gripped Uley's arm, her eyes as big around as the paste cherries that adorned the leghorn hat. "Uley. Put it on. I'll help do up all those buttons and tape ties. Together we ought to be able to figure out how it's supposed to go."

She held up the acres of green cloth.

"I'm not taking this one with me. It's too special to Pa."

"It doesn't matter if you're taking it with you or not. Just try it on."

"You think I should?"

Laura nodded, grinning, her cheeks as bright as persimmons.

Uley fingered the chintz. *Did she dare?* As soon as she asked that question, Uley almost thought she heard something say, *Do it, child. Take every blessing I have to give you.*

First came the buttons. No less than twenty-six of them ran up the front of the bodice. As Laura and Uley both worked on them, Laura from the bottom up, Uley from the top down, the bodice tightened nicely around her, the cloth shimmering like rocks catching sun at streamside as the dress took shape around her middle.

Next came the tape ties. "I have absolutely no idea what to do with these things," Laura said, poking them up and under, trying to find where to secure them.

"Here." Uley reached beneath the skirt and affixed one just the way she'd seen her ma do it once, leaving a loop of cloth that bunched out at her hip and hung like fine drapery.

"That's it. You know how to do it!"

"But that's just one. There's more. Lots more."

Together they poked and prodded and giggled until they found every one of the trusses.

"This goes here."

"No, that's backward. Try this."

"That's right."

"What about this one?"

"Maybe this one goes there."

"No, this one."

"There. It's fastened."

"It's backward."

"No, it's right. See? What do you think?"

Uley stood before the mirror, her hands lightly resting one on top of the other at the bodice. She stood motionless, the color rising in her cheeks, her eyes perfectly reflecting the glimmering green of the chintz.

"Oh, Uley," Laura said, sighing. "Just look at you!"

Outwardly, Uley didn't move. Inside, her heart had taken flight. She'd never imagined she could look this way. *This is me! This is really me!*

The dress fit perfectly. Uley stared in the mirror. A stranger seemed to stare back. And the stranger was her.

This is who You intended me to be, isn't it Lord?

She paused as she thought of Aaron, wishing he could admire her in this dress, wishing he could see her this way. *But he never will, will he, Lord? Oh, Father. I've made so many mistakes.*

How could she leave on the supply wagon this afternoon? How could she disappear from his life and never share a walk with him again, or a joke, or a kiss?

If Aaron could see her now, he'd know everything she needed to give him, everything her secret bound her not to reveal. Sometime during the years she'd hidden away, she'd grown into the woman she'd dreamed of becoming.

She closed her eyes, picturing him. This was what she would carry with her now.

A memory of him, a memory of what he had given back to her.

The thought of doing without Aaron in her life was not a new one. She'd lived with it during the weeks since she'd met him, knowing he faced trial and conviction and hanging. She'd steeled herself to face the possibility, knowing she'd live through the ordeal because she had no other option. But this afternoon, when the supply wagon pulled out to cross Alpine Pass and she was on it, the choice would be her own.

Loving Aaron Brown had given her the

impetus to begin finding herself.

Now, to become the person she'd found, she had to leave Aaron Brown.

The door swung open just then and Uley whirled to face it, the skirt whirling about her in waves.

Sam Kirkland halted the moment he saw his daughter. He stood framed in the doorway, his silhouette dark against the dreariness outside.

"Hello, Pa," Uley said very quietly.

Sam just stood there, his hat in his hand, rainwater dripping off every part of him, his face gone pale.

Uley knew she shouldn't have donned the dress. She scurried to the other side of the room to grab her sweater and knickers. "I'm sorry, Pa. I shouldn't have tried it on. But it was the last thing in the trunk, and I . . ."

He took one step toward her. "Oh, girl. You're the very picture of your Ma. Do you realize that?"

She shook her head, sending curls spiraling down around her neck.

He grabbed her elbows. "I've never seen anyone so beautiful. So grown up. So like a *lady*."

"Am I?" She felt herself blushing.

"You must take that with you."

"But I couldn't. It was Ma's."

"I sat with her at fireside and watched her make every single one of those stitches. I saw her laughing across the room during every holiday when she wore it. I know how happy she would be to see you in it now."

"You think so?"

He nodded, then pulled her into his arms, holding her close for one long, poignant moment. "I know so."

He released her then, holding her at arm's length, and she thought his eyes were watery, too, but she couldn't be certain. "I brought you supplies. You'd best get them packed away with that dress. Lester McClain likes to stay right on schedule. He won't wait for you. I sent word to Delilah this morning. If the mail is as trustworthy as the government says it is, she'll be expecting you both to arrive Friday next."

"We're really starting a new life." Laura's cheeks, too, had gone rosy with joy.

Uley stepped out of her father's embrace and headed for the bed. "Best be getting everything into the trunk, then."

But Sam was still staring at his daughter. "You look just like her, you know that? You look just like my Sarah. God blessed us both when he blessed Sarah's womb with a child so beautiful of heart." He stood exactly where she'd left him, arms dangling at his sides, both hands fisted into knots.

When she turned back to him, tears were streaming down her father's face. "How can I let you go?"

"I'll be back someday, Pa," she whispered. "You just wait and see."

"Oh, but I'm going to miss you until someday comes," he whispered back.

In the end, of course, Henry Mortimus got the cot at the jailhouse. He lay on it now, hunkering like a mountain, snoring louder than the thunder outside. Marshal Ben Pearsall banged on the bars with one fist, balancing two breakfast plates on the other. "Wake up in there," he hollered. "Never seen prisoners sleep as late as this."

Olney, who was on the floor, rolled over and opened one eye. "Shut up, Pearsall. You're interruptin' my beauty sleep."

"Ain't no amount of beauty sleep going to help you," the new marshal said.

It was hard to imagine how their talking could not wake up Mortimus. The man was still snoring loud enough to drown them out. Even so, the Pitkin prisoner gave a moan and flopped over toward them, smacking his lips in an odious fashion that made even Olney cringe. "What time is it?" he growled to Ben.

"It's plumb near nine o'clock."

"Confound it, Pearsall," Olney said, rolling over and raising himself to his knees. "I just got to sleep three hours ago. This here's got to be the hardest floor in Gunnison County."

"We made it that way on purpose," Pearsall said, gloating. "We wouldn't want anybody getting too comfortable in there."

Olney managed to stand, though his knees and elbows were still stiff. "Shut up, Pearsall. I helped build this jailhouse, too, if you'll recall. We didn't do nothing unusual to this floor."

"Must be it's just your conscience making it seem hard, then. They say that'll happen to a man."

Mortimus sat up and rubbed his eyes like a baby just waking up from a nap. "What you got there?"

"It's breakfast, is what I got. From Aunt Kate Fischer's. Each plate's got eggs and ham, fried potatoes and gravy. Got two biscuits apiece, too."

That was all it took to get Henry Mortimus up and clenching the bars. "I'm ready."

"I'll just bet you are. Stand back, boys, so I can unlock this door."

They did exactly as Pearsall instructed them, both of them acting like model prisoners.

"Sure looks good, Marshal."

"Jist look at them biscuits."

"It's been a month since I've eaten ham cooked up like that."

"Sure is a full plate."

Pearsall backed out and locked the cell door behind himself, sighing with relief as the key clicked in the lock. Prisoner-feeding time was always a bit dangerous. Harris Olney had taught him, as deputy, to be careful. Not that Pearsall expected Olney to try to make a break for it. But no one knew anything about that other fellow in there. Now that Pearsall found himself in charge of everything, it seemed he had a thousand things to remember. "You two behave yourselves today," he warned. "I don't want to have to waste time breaking up any fights. I'm mighty busy getting everything organized."

"What do you mean, *organized?*" Olney asked. "I had everything organized just fine before you took over."

"Not how I like it, you didn't. It's my office now."

The minute Pearsall waved goodbye to them both and returned to the front office, Olney crouched low on the ground again, his joints miraculously cured. Henry Mortimus grabbed Olney's plate and started eating off both of them.

"That's a sorry thing you've done," Olney muttered, still trying to see Pearsall around the corner, "talking me out of my cot *and* my breakfast."

"I figured I'd better get while the getting's good. This may be the last meal we both have for a while. Besides," Henry said, his mouth stuffed full of buttery biscuit, "you owe it to me for helping you escape like this."

Olney snorted like a bull. "Oh, yeah. As if you weren't going to reap any benefit from it yourself. Now shut up and let me concentrate on Old Pearsall in there."

The two men quit bickering long enough for Olney to make his assessment. The only sound in the cell for several long minutes was Henry Mortimus smacking through his very ample meal.

"Well?" Mortimus finally asked, his mouth still full. "Is it gonna work?"

"Yeah. It'll work, all right. He's doing just what I expected."

"You think he thought we were asleep

when he came in here?"

"I reckon he did," Olney answered. "He isn't smart enough to think anything else."

"You think he doesn't know we were up all night figuring how to break out of here?"

"Shut up, would you? Quit asking questions, Mortimus. I trained the man. I tested him just then. If he'd have thought we were up to something, he never would have unlocked that door and brought those plates in."

"Sure beats all how you think you know everything, Olney."

"It doesn't beat all. I *do* know everything. You just wait until this afternoon, when we go after our plan. You'll see I know what I'm talking about."

"Yeah," Mortimus said dubiously. "I'll see."

If fresh gossip was going around, Elizabeth Calderwood heard it as she tidied things at Aunt Kate Fischer's, cleaning up after the afternoon meal and making ready for the onslaught of men just before suppertime. What she heard today made her dish rag pause in the middle of the wooden table. She glanced toward Charlie Hastings.

"Yep. I heard Sam Kirkland say it as plain as day. He wanted two passenger tickets on the supply wagon going out this afternoon. He *paid* for them. I can't figure it. Everybody knows Sam isn't leavin' town."

Alex Parent leaned in. "No. But I bet I know who is."

"Who, then?"

"Nobody's seen Tin Can Laura over at Santa Fe Moll's since last night. I heard she got roughed up by one of the miners that came over from Pitkin. And you know Uley Kirkland's been sweet on that hurdy-gurdy girl for a long time now. I figure Tin Can Laura and Uley Kirkland are running off together."

"No!" Hastings hollered. "Can't be. Those two wouldn't run off together in broad daylight."

"I don't know," Jack Strater commented. "You know Uley. Such a fine, upstanding member of the community. He wouldn't think he had anything to hide."

All three men glanced up to see Beth.

"Sorry, ma'am." Alex Parent looked contrite when he saw her there. "We shouldn't have been talking about it with you here. It ain't right, discussing a woman of ill-repute around a real lady."

405

"No, ma'am," Hastings agreed, coloring. "We shouldn't have been talkin' about that hurdy-gurdy —"

Strater clobbered Hastings on the shoulder. "Shut up, will you? There you go serving it right up."

Beth's cheeks turned as red as a cardinal's wings. She went back to scrubbing the tabletop.

Alex Parent scooted over until he sat right next to Beth. "You know, even though Kate's business has doubled since you started carrying plates, it isn't fitting for a woman like you to have to work so hard."

"This isn't hard work," Elizabeth replied, as she folded the rag over, found a clean spot and kept right on going. "Scrubbing tables is easier than the work I was doing on the farm."

"Even so, I could take awful good care of you, Beth Calderwood. For the third time, I wish you would consider my honorable proposal of marriage."

"Thank you, Mr. Parent. I am honored every time you make the request."

"What about my proposal?" Hastings added. "Are you still thinking about that one? I'd make you a fine husband, Elizabeth."

She'd finished scrubbing. "Gentlemen." She managed to include all of them in one winning smile. "I'm not ready to marry anyone. I am still grieving deeply for my own dead husband."

"Yes, ma'am." Parent nodded, his brows furrowed. "I'm sure you are. I'm willing to wait as long as need be."

Jack Strater stood at her elbow, his face serious. "Miss Beth. I haven't mentioned this to you. I've been afraid to. But, if you ever get around to considering all these proposals, I'd like you to consider mine, too."

"Thank you, Mr. Strater." It seemed there was no end to it. And, really, it flattered her. She waggled her rag at all three of them. "This *work* won't get done without me. I'd best go about my chores in the kitchen."

Just after dinnertime, Uley placed the last pair of britches upon the pile. Hated as they were, her eyes still filled with tears when she looked at them lying there.

"I guess we're ready, Pa. I can't think of anything else we need to put in."

Laura sat cross-legged on the bed. "I wish we could take Storm."

"Me too, but Pa needs a good mouser here."

"Here's some pasties you can take," Sam said, his hands trembling as he handed them to his daughter. "I'm sure you'll both get hungry before you reach St. Elmo." They'd just finished a big meal, but it wouldn't last them very long on the journey.

"Is it time to go?" Laura asked.

"No," Sam told them. "With what you went through last night, I think it best to wait until the last minute. You two ought to try to get out of town as quietly as possible. We don't want Santa Fe Moll trying to catch up with you." Sam pulled out his watch and snapped it open. "I figure we ought to get down there to meet Lester McClain no sooner than three o'clock. By three-fifteen, you two'll be headed on toward your new life."

"Our new life," Laura echoed, sighing, her eyes cast somewhere far atop the mountains out the window, picturing a future for them as rosy as a calypso orchid. "Oh, Jesus, thank You! Our new life!"

"Oh, Pa." Uley grabbed hold of Sam, sending her cap askew, revealing hair held straight back from her face by Laura's tortoiseshell combs.

"You've grown up so much, honey," he whispered against her shining hair. "I'm so proud of you, little one."

"Oh, Pa." *How can I be so sure of something and have my heart breaking at the same time?*

She held on to her father as tightly as she knew how.

At precisely 2:30 p.m., Harris Olney winked at Henry Mortimus and began to execute the plan. "Oh," Olney moaned at the top of his lungs, holding on to his belly. "Help, I think I'm gonna *die* in here."

Mortimus peered out between the bars, trying to see into the front office.

"Aw, it hurts." He added some curses to emphasize his pain.

"You're gonna have to yell louder than that," Mortimus instructed. "Pearsall ain't comin'."

"Shut up," Olney hissed between clenched teeth. "He'll come. He's a sound sleeper. It takes a few minutes for sounds to register around that man." He hollered again. "Oh, *help* me."

"He ain't comin'."

Olney eyed his cohort, whispering fiercely. "Get over here, Mortimus. Stop staring out through those bars. I'm hollering for help. You've got to look like you're worrying about me."

"I wouldn't worry about you if you were getting gored by a herd of stampeding oxen. I'd say good riddance."

"Get *over* here."

"I don't care what kind of show you put on —" Mortimus spat a wad and let it roll down the wall just beside Olney "— he ain't comin'."

"He *will*. He always gets his heaviest sleep of the day right after he eats a big meal from Aunt Kate Fischer's."

"This ain't gonna work."

Olney bellowed as loudly as he could manage. "Oh, *help!* My belly hurts something *awful!*" Olney sprawled out on the cot, writhing in feigned pain. "I'm gonna *die* in here."

Mortimus heard the squeaking of a chair out in the front office. "You know, that might have done it."

"Get *over* here," Olney snarled. *"Now."*

Mortimus went to the cot and stooped over. "Sorry you're feeling poorly," he said. "Ain't nothing I can do, though."

From out in the front office came the sound of slow, groggy footsteps.

Olney bellowed a string of curses, then added, "Ain't never had anything hurt as bad as my belly hurts now."

Pearsall leaned against the doorway,

scrubbing at his eyes with clenched fists. He'd forgotten to put his Stetson on. "What seems to be the problem in here?"

"This fellow's sick, says he's going to die," Mortimus volunteered.

Pearsall took one step toward them.

Olney clutched his stomach and thrashed violently about upon the cot. "Must be something I et. I'm not going to make it, Pearsall."

"You can't die in here," Ben Pearsall said reasonably. "We've got to keep you alive so we can hang you."

"Now that makes a lot of sense," Mortimus commented.

"Please." Olney squeezed his belly and writhed. "At least come in here and give me a look-see. I don't wanna go on feeling like this."

"I'm not an idiot." Pearsall took three more steps toward his prisoners and squinted into the cell. "I can recognize an attempt to escape from my jailhouse when I see one. Ain't no way I'm opening that door and coming in there."

Olney lay still for a minute. Then he let go of his middle and rolled toward the new marshal, grinning slightly, the anguish gone. "Confound it, Pearsall. I should've figured I couldn't outwit you."

"That's right." Pearsall squared his shoulders proudly. He'd been waiting for their breakout attempt, and it looked like he'd just foiled it. "You can't outwit me." He shook his head at both of them, then turned to go.

That was when Mortimus pounced.

He came at Pearsall from the opposite corner of the cell, gripping the new marshal's neck through the bars with rope-thick fingers. "Got you!"

Pearsall didn't make a sound. He couldn't. Mortimus's clenched fingers completely blocked his windpipe.

"Ah!" Olney roared. "Foiled our breakout attempt, did you?"

Pearsall's face puffed up like a sick trout. He struggled with his arms, trying to propel himself across the room. Despite the iron bars, Mortimus had a clear advantage.

"Me and Mortimus here —" Olney stuck his mouth as close to Pearsall's ear as he could manage "— are in the mood for killing."

Pearsall thrashed about.

"Luckily," Olney continued, "we ain't in the mood to kill *you.*"

Pearsall's face was slowly turning an unhealthy color of blue.

"All we want," Olney explained, "is that key ring hanging out of your back hip pocket."

"No."

"You were right, Olney," Mortimus said, paying no mind to the death grip he had on his captive. "He *did* bring his keys with him."

"I told you he would. Idiot's so proud of them, he has them dangling out of his back pocket like fishing bait. Thinks he has to swagger around with them on his hip instead of keeping them safely stashed on the wall."

Pearsall couldn't speak.

"Bad move, Pearsall. How many times did I tell you to keep the keys on the wall? How many times did I give you the reason for that?"

Still, Pearsall struggled.

"Now, either way we do this is just as easy for me," Olney told his former deputy. "You hand me those keys and I tie you up, or I kill you and get those keys myself."

"No."

"What?" Olney asked, enjoying the marshal's discomfiture. "I can't hear what you're saying."

"Look at him," Mortimus said, chuckling. "Face is the same color as my gun

413

barrel. Blue as a snail."

"Stubborn fool. I figured this. Knew you'd be so proud of those keys, that you'd be carrying them around." Olney began to stretch. He reached with one arm.

Pearsall's knees began to buckle beneath him.

"Now," Mortimus bellowed.

Olney snatched those keys as quick as a fish snatches a fly off water. "Got you!" He dangled the iron ring proudly from his hand just as Pearsall hit the ground, unconscious. "Hurry!"

"Get them in the lock. Fast, before he comes around."

"He ain't coming around for a while. That fool Pearsall. I thought he was going down with his keys."

"Unlock it."

"It's this one."

Olney used it and the door swung open smooth as butter. Within moments, the two prisoners stood free.

Mortimus started for the door. "I'm leaving."

"Oh no you don't. You've got to help me tie him up. He comes to and you're still here, they'll hang you right beside me. He'll say you tried to kill him."

"I almost *did.*"

"There's rope in the front room. Hand-cuffs, too. You guard him. I'll get what we need."

Within seconds, Olney was back, toting a chair, a length of sturdy rope and two sets of cuffs. "Pull off his boots, Mortimus."

Mortimus complied. "Phew," the big man bellowed as Pearsall's boot hit the floor. Mortimus gripped his nose, holding his nostrils shut. "That's the gamiest-smelling foot I've ever been this close to."

"Shut up and help me lift him. A man's foot isn't supposed to smell like a spring day."

Once they got Pearsall settled in the chair, Olney snapped one set of handcuffs around Pearsall's ankles. He snapped another around his wrists. Then they bound him with ropes, gagged him and locked him inside his own cell.

"That ought to hold him," Mortimus said.

"It'll be at least forty-five minutes before anybody figures out he's not where he's supposed to be." Olney walked to the front room and manipulated the knob on the safe door. The tumblers clicked. The safe swung open. Inside lay their two holsters and their two guns. "Here you go. Best take this firearm and clear out of this town with it."

"What're you gonna do now?" Mortimus asked.

Olney didn't answer for a moment. He buckled the holster around his hips. He slid his six-shooter from its leather sheath, casually turning its barrel in the light, examining the sleek, cold metal.

At last he turned to Mortimus.

"My freedom isn't gonna last long. I've got about forty-five minutes to pay a man back for something mighty big I owe him."

"You going after somebody?"

Olney grinned evilly. "Let's put it this way." He held his gun high, turning it again, admiring the barrel as it glinted in the afternoon light. "See this gun? I got this gun so I could enforce the law, see? Now I aim to use this same gun to break it."

Mortimus buckled his holster on, too. "Well, whatever happens, I ain't sticking around for the party."

"Ah, it'll be a party, all right." Olney chuckled. "Now. Where do you suppose I could find Mr. Aaron Talephas Brown?"

Chapter Eighteen

Aaron sat on the front porch at Aunt Kate Fischer's, his Stetson on the step beside him, trying to figure how to best give a white lace parasol to a lady. He balanced the contraption in both hands, supporting the length of it, his fingers open, as if the lace might lift out of his palms and take flight of its own volition.

"What's that?" Beth climbed down the porch steps and sat beside her brother. Her black high-top shoes aligned with his muddy brown boots.

His face went red. "It's a parasol."

"I can see that."

Silence. He didn't volunteer any more information.

"Who's it for?"

"Beth. Don't ask me. I can't tell you."

"Aaron." She leaned toward him, exasperated. "You've always told me everything. I'm so curious about this, I can't sleep nights."

"You're going to have to stay curious,

Beth. I just can't say."

She gazed into the afternoon sky. "I wish you'd tell me who it is you think you're sweet on."

"Looks like it's clearing up," he said, following her eyes, desperate to change the subject. "The rain should be over soon. I wonder if it snowed up on the pass?"

"That reminds me," Beth said. "You aren't going to *believe* who's taking the supply wagon out today."

"Who?"

"You've got to promise you won't tell. It's two sweethearts running away together."

"Who? What two sweethearts?"

"Tin Can Laura, the hurdy-gurdy girl. I heard it all this morning. Uley Kirkland's been sweet on her for the longest time. They're leaving town together today."

Aaron felt as if his gut had just been jammed into his throat. "What?"

Beth went on, oblivious of the effect her words wrought upon her brother. "Tin Can Laura's running away from Santa Fe Moll's place, and I figure Uley's taking her away to marry her and start her in a new life. Everybody's talking about it. But everybody's being quiet because Moll's out looking for Laura. I figure everybody I've talked to wants that girl to get away."

Aaron leapt to his feet. The parasol clattered to the ground. "Uley? Uley's leaving?"

"That's what they're saying all over town."

"When? How?"

"I already told you. On the supply wagon this afternoon. Lester McClain's taking them. It should be about time for them to get away now." She peered up at her brother. "Aaron? What's wrong?"

"This afternoon? Beth   " he grabbed her arm to help her up "— I've got to get down there."

How could she do something like this?

The parasol lay forgotten on the wooden step. *She didn't even want me to know. She didn't even tell me goodbye.*

"Aaron? What is it?" Beth didn't understand. "What's wrong?"

"Don't ask." Aaron stormed up the street for ten paces, letting his anger propel him. "I just can't say." Then fear took over and he began to run.

What if he couldn't stop her? What if she was leaving to get away from *him?*

He sorted through possibilities in his mind, not liking any of them. He had to get to the supply wagon before Lester

McClain headed over Alpine Pass with his passengers.

Aaron sprinted around the corner just in time to see McClain and Sam Kirkland lifting a wooden trunk with brass latches onto the rear of the wagon. He shoved through the crowd, searching frantically for Uley. He didn't see her anywhere.

He didn't know what else to do except holler her name. "Uley! Uley! Where is —" *She. Where is she?*

Aaron spied Laura across the road, walking toward the wagon with a knit shawl draped over her head. "Laura!" He bolted forward. "Where's Uley?"

"She's coming. Right there."

Aaron spun in the direction of Laura's pointed finger. Here she came, up the street, bundled for a journey.

Uley saw him and hesitated. *Oh, Father. It's the only way, isn't it? Only I never meant for Aaron to get hurt in the middle.*

He raced forward and grabbed her arms, his face already gone rock-hard with anger and grief. He didn't care who heard his words now. "You weren't going to say anything to me?"

"No, Aaron. I thought it best this way."

"Do you mind telling me why you're doing this?"

She looked up at him, her face etched with her own intense pain. "I think you know, don't you? I have to go, Aaron," she said. "It's the only way things can be fair for the both of us."

He stared down at her. "I found out about this from Beth. Everybody in town's talking about the two *sweethearts* running away. That's ironic, don't you think? When it should be us?"

"I can't stay."

"I don't want you to go."

"I have to."

"I'd like to know why, Uley. And I'd like to know why you have to go this way."

"I have to help Laura. And I have to help myself." Tears pooled in her eyes. "It's the right thing, Aaron. I've prayed about it, and this is the only possibility that's come. It may not be easy, but it's right."

"Tell me. You tell me why it's right." But already, in his heart, he knew.

"Because I have to do it, Aaron. I have to find out who I am."

He couldn't very well argue with her reasoning. He knew how desperately she needed to disappear into a cocoon and be born again as a butterfly. She was right, and he knew it. But it killed him to think of her leaving.

"I didn't, didn't know how to tell you. Early this morning, when we'd decided, I should have told you." She was choking on the words. "Should have, Aaron, only I couldn't."

He asked, already knowing that she would never do this if she didn't have to. If he loved her, he ought to want what was best for her. "You weren't planning on seeing me again."

With tears sliding down her face, she nodded. As if to etch the details of his face on her memory forever, Uley reached up with one hand, fingers outstretched, to curve her palm around the length of his jaw.

"Oh, Aaron," she said, her eyes reflecting every bit of the anguish in her heart.

He saw every part of the pain he knew she felt. Knowing they shared it didn't make accepting it easier. "Me too." He whispered his next words. "Don't look back toward me, Julia Kirkland. Go out and become the person you've dreamed about." *Oh, Lord. Give me the love for her that helps me let her go. Give me a love for her that wants her to have these things.* He couldn't ask her to come back to him. She wouldn't be the same person then. And he was certain she might see

422

things differently when the time came.

I release her to You, Father. Take away all of my holds on her. Your ways are so much bigger than my ways. Help me to accept that.

"I will," she said, sniffing, her expression full of gratitude and something more, because he had released her to be who she needed to be. "Oh, Aaron. I will."

Just then, a menacing voice growled out from the crowd behind them. "Why, fancy meeting you here, Aaron Brown."

Aaron released Uley.

"Turn around, you yellow-belly. I'm not going to go after you from the back the way you went after me. I'm going to shoot you right straight on, the way a man should."

Aaron slowly turned around. "Harris Olney."

"One and the same."

"You can't do this."

"I can and I will. Put your hands up, Brown. I don't have any qualms about shooting you in cold blood. Any man who tries to stop me is going to beat you to the grave."

"You're supposed to be locked up."

"Ha! Everybody was feeling safe about that, too, weren't they? Putting a man like

423

Old Ben Pearsall in my place. I built that jailhouse, and I taught Pearsall just about everything he knows. It wasn't hard to bust out, Brown. I didn't even enjoy it none. It was all just too easy."

"Maybe you shouldn't shoot me, then." Aaron stalled for time. "Maybe you won't enjoy it if it's too easy."

"Oh," Olney said, offering up a sharp cackle of sarcasm, "I'll enjoy this no matter how I do it. Take your last breath, Brown." Olney leveled the gun at Aaron, holding it steady. He licked his lips, wetting them in anticipation, then placed his forefinger on the trigger.

The sudden motion from Uley Kirkland proved enough to distract Olney. "Aaron! Get down!"

"You. Why are you always around when trouble starts, Uley? A man would think you'd learned by now."

"Seems to me I'm not the only one around, Olney." She stepped toward Aaron.

In an instant, fire belched from the six-shooter. Aaron felt an impact. He stumbled back. But the rush of pain hadn't come.

Aaron rose on all fours and moved toward Harris, gripping a knotted tree limb

424

that lay in the street. He leapt up, roaring with rage. He rushed Olney with the branch. He smashed it toward his head before Olney had the chance to bring the gun around. Olney deflected the limb's blow. The six-shooter flew from Olney's fist.

Aaron threw his fist into Olney's fleshy stomach. The blow found its mark. Olney's stomach felt like a cow's udder filled with milk. Olney doubled over.

Charlie Hastings grabbed Olney and wrenched his arms behind his back. "You're finished, Olney. If this jail won't hold you, I'll ride you down to Gunnison tomorrow, where you can't do any more damage."

Aaron disdainfully backhanded the grime from his own face. It wasn't until he looked down to wipe the dregs off on his pants that he saw the front of his shirt.

The sweet, cloying scent filled his senses. Its identity began to register.

Blood.

Blood covered his shirt. Sticky, congealing, still warm, blood not his own.

He pivoted, remembering the odd feeling of impact, the movements of the woman who'd run to shield him in the street. "Dear God, no . . ." he prayed. Uley was the one who'd hollered and made that shot veer wild. Or maybe it hadn't veered wild at all. "Uley? *Uley!*"

She didn't answer.

Sam Kirkland knelt in the dust, his head bent low, tears running down his face, leaving great dirty streaks, as Uley lay bleeding in his arms. Aaron ran to them, sick with dread.

Sam lifted tortured eyes to Aaron. "Uley's been hit saving you, Brown."

He knelt beside them. "Uley?" He gripped Sam's arm as the crowd began to move in around them. "Let me have Uley, Mr. Kirkland. I'll find Doc Gillette."

"You know Gillette ain't in town, boy. He never keeps his office open. He's always up on the hill, digging for gold. We might as well not have a physician in Tin Cup."

"It's worth a try, Kirkland. He might be here today, by some miracle, or some blessing." He didn't know it, but tears were streaming down his face as well.

Sam nodded, extending his arms, and Aaron gathered Uley's crumpled body against his. When he saw her face, he swallowed to fight back a sense of impending doom. She lay heavily against his chest. He knew she was almost gone.

"Wait. Here," Sam said gruffly. He ripped away the front of his own garment and used the linen to stanch the bleeding. "Maybe that'll help."

Aaron stood with her cradled in his arms, shouting futilely: "Doc Gillette? Is Doc Gillette in this crowd?"

When no one answered, he started running toward the doctor's storefront office. "He won't be there," someone hollered at him. "He's never there except in the evenings. He's always up prospecting."

Aaron didn't listen. He just kept running and praying. *Lord, don't let her die. Please, God. Save her!*

A small group of men began to follow him up toward Spruce Street. He reached the physician's office and banged on the front door. To his utter amazement, he saw movement in the back room.

"He's there!" he shouted. Then, to Uley: "Hang on, little one. We've got a doc in town today. Things are going your way."

The men behind him took up the cry. "He's there!"

Dr. John Francis Gillette, beard flowing down past his chest, came forward at what seemed a plodding burro's pace to open his front door.

"Uley Kirkland's been shot, Doc," Aaron said the minute the door cracked open. "We're going to need your help."

427

Gillette fingered his long, elegant beard. "You'd best bring him on in here. Lucky kid, Uley. Today I've taken a toothache, and I didn't much feel like digging."

Aaron placed Uley's dead weight on Doc Gillette's long, narrow examination table while the other men filed in and took seats in the waiting room.

"Hope he can save that kid."

"Uley's such a fine citizen."

"Don't know what we'd do without Uley Kirkland."

"Can't feel much of a pulse," Gillette said. He removed the cloth Sam had torn from his own clothing. It was already soaked with blood. "Now," Gillette instructed, "I've got some tedious operating to do here. My hands are a sight more sure when I don't have somebody looking over my shoulder."

"But I could help you," Aaron suggested, desperate to remain by Uley's side.

Gillette carried over a thin tin tray containing bandages and surgical instruments. "I don't need your help. Now get on out there and sit on a bench with the rest of them."

"I want to be here."

A pair of scissors paused in midair. "The longer you hem and haw, the longer I'll wait before doing what I need to do."

Reluctantly Aaron backed away. "You sure? You sure I can't?"

"Get out of here, mister. I've got enough on my hands trying to save this kid's life."

Aaron backed through the door just as Gillette began cutting Uley's shirt away. The scissors began to snip the bloody fabric and Gillette began to pry the shirt from the wound.

Aaron sat down beside Jasper Warde. He'd lost his hat somewhere. He had absolutely no idea where it had gone. He buried his face in his hands. How many times must he face losing Uley in one day?

Dear God, he prayed, *I can let her go where she needs to go. I turned her over to You so she could live, Lord, not so she could die. Please, please, Father.*

Aaron had never felt this helpless. A clock hung on the south wall of the room, its pendulum nudging to the right . . . back to the left . . . marking off the moments in an agonizing, torpid tempo.

Actually, only three minutes passed. Then Dr. John Francis Gillette bellowed from his operating room. "Good grief! Good *grief!*"

Every man hurled up out of his seat. Gillette slammed through the door and pressed his back against it.

"Who knew about this?" Gillette bellowed.

When the physician first yelled, Aaron thought the worst had happened. He figured Uley had gone on to meet the Lord, the one he'd just been bargaining with, pleading with. But then he saw Gillette's astonished face, and he felt his heart stop.

"Who knew about this?" Gillette shouted, mopping his face.

Aaron had been so concerned about her life, he hadn't even thought of it. Uley had been found out.

"That, that, *person,*" Gillette hollered, the stark realization fully registering on his face. "That ain't a *boy* I'm operating on in there. Uley Kirkland is a *gal!*"

His announcement was met with momentary stunned silence. Then everybody started whispering at once.

"No."

"It cain't be."

"Think what that gal's been doing."

"Think what that gal's been saying."

"Think what *we've* been saying."

"Uley Kirkland? A *gal?*"

At that moment, the front door swung open. Sam Kirkland barged in. So did Tin Can Laura.

"Where is she?" Sam asked, forgetting the charade in his moment of anguish. "Where's my daughter?"

Hollis Andersen spoke up first. "Your, your *daughter* is on the doc's examination table, probably getting her just rewards for fooling us all so long."

Gilbert Hughes poked an accusatory finger at Sam Kirkland. "We thought Uley was one of us."

"Yeah."

Laura piped up then, unable to believe the doubt and the betrayal she read on their faces. "Uley's the only friend I got in the world who'll help me," Laura blubbered, sounding every bit like a calf bawling. "Doc, you've got to save her."

"Let me in there to see my daughter," Sam roared.

Gillette motioned for Sam and Laura to follow him. "I don't like it much, but I'll finish the surgery with you in attendance. I think, given the circumstances . . ."

Aaron didn't need an invitation. He followed Laura and Sam. They gathered around her, standing together, Uley's imperfect but loving family, as Gillette drew out his big iron tweezers and went digging for the bullet. Aaron knelt beside Uley. Her hat lay to one side now, all her beautiful, wispy hair tossed in knots around her face. He clutched her hand. "Crazy girl," he whispered. "Always stepping in the way of something. You've been strong enough to handle everything else and you can be strong enough to pull through this, too."

Lester McClain's supply wagon left an hour later than usual that afternoon. He took no passengers with him. He left the old trunk sitting on the front steps of the town hall, knowing some kindly soul would fetch it to Sam Kirkland so that the man could claim it. The poor man had enough on his mind right now without worrying what to do about his daughter's trunk.

Charlie Hastings stood watch over Harris Olney at the jailhouse all afternoon. "I don't want you getting yourself tied up with any more ill deeds," he said as he brandished his Winchester.

"You ain't even gonna bring me any supper?" Olney asked pitifully.

"No. I'm not going to give you any more chances. This town's seen enough of you to last a long time."

At six that evening, Hastings saddled up two horses and tied the prisoner to one of the mounts. "I was going to wait until morning to do this," he told Olney as he led him outside and bound him to the saddle. "I changed my mind, though. Don't even want you spending another night in this town. The sooner we get your rotten hide out of Tin Cup, the better." As Hastings rode out of town, he saluted Ben Pearsall. "I'll be back from Gunnison in three days."

"We'll be waiting." Pearsall waved back. "I've got plans to deputize you."

Upstairs at Ongewach's place, Santa Fe Moll was lamenting her misfortune at losing one of the establishment's best girls. She'd known when Laura missed breakfast this morning and her room turned up empty that something had gone amiss. But the men in this town could be just as close-mouthed and stubborn as they were greedy. She and Charles conducted a thorough search, but it was obvious that any man who knew anything had opted to keep his trap shut. And just after dinnertime, Moll realized where Laura would be.

She'd be with Uley Kirkland.

Moll considered marching right over to the Kirklands' and bringing Laura back home. But when Moll thought about it some more, she decided she'd just leave well enough alone. In a way, she envied Laura. She envied her having her youth, a

433

sweetheart, a chance to start life over.

Wouldn't do to be making any heartfelt decisions about this, she reminded herself. She wasn't a heartfelt sort of woman. But something odd had softened her heart, something that felt unfamiliar. She decided to make the decision on behalf of business, instead. If every fellow in this town was going to protect Laura, who was she to do any different? She could always find another hurdy-gurdy girl.

The sun was just beginning to set over Tin Cup that evening as Sam, Laura and Aaron waited futilely beside Uley.

"Come on, Julia," Sam whispered to her. "Jubilee. I'm here."

"I'm here, too," Laura whispered. "I ain't leavin' without you. And I sure hope you ain't leaving without me."

"You do this for yourself." Aaron gripped her hand. "Not for me. You've got so much to look forward to. So many of your dreams —" His voice broke. He couldn't go on.

Laura stood behind him, doing her best to comfort him, her small hand lying on his broad shoulder. "She asked me one time what it felt like when a man you loved came close," Laura said. "I figure she was

434

talking about you."

Dusk deepened into nighttime. They kept no track of time. Aaron stroked the hair now displayed in tendrils around Uley's pale face. Her breathing remained terrifyingly shallow. "She's everything I've ever wanted in my life. You know that? She had all these notions she had to be a fine lady before she'd be right for me. But I wanted her just the way she is. Muddy boots and britches and all."

As the morning sun began to rise over the Saguache Mountains, Laura noticed Aaron doing his best to keep his head erect and his eyes open. "You need to sleep, Aaron," she told him. "You had quite a fight with Olney. I'll bet your body's aching."

"I don't want to leave her, Laura."

"Some things're just part of nature, Aaron. You have to rest now so when she wakes up you can sit with her."

"What if she starts waking up before I come back?"

"I'll send somebody over to Aunt Kate's to get you. You go sleep now. I'll stay right beside her."

If Aaron had been in better shape, he might have argued his point with Laura.

Instead, he nodded and headed out the door, almost too tired to see straight. As he plodded up the front steps to Kate Fischer's boardinghouse, he heard a commotion inside the likes of which he'd never heard at breakfast. What was everyone so all-fired excited about?

The minute he walked inside the door, he figured it out.

The place quieted.

He felt every eye upon him.

So that was it.

Every single man in this place was airing his views about Uley Kirkland.

If it had been any other morning but *this* morning, Aaron might have let it pass. If it had been any other time but *this* time, he might have walked right on up the stairs and fallen on top of his wrought-iron bed in defeat without figuring he had to make a speech about it. But his frustration and his fear and his exhaustion overtook him. *Lord, help me find the words to set her free.*

"You're fine ones to talk here!" he hollered, his anguish clearly showing itself in his voice. "Uley Kirkland has saved my life at least twice since I came to this town. You know her pa wouldn't let her come with him if she came as a gal. He knew all the fellows in this town would give her so much attention, she'd never find the chance to breathe with all of you hovering around her. Just like you've done to Beth ever since she got here.

"Uley tried to figure out some way to tell everybody, but she knew you'd talk about things just the way you're talking about things now. That's why she was leaving. She was going back to Ohio to become the lady she wanted to be. I'm not going to question her motives in this. And I don't think any of *you* have the right to do it, either. Uley's given an awful lot of herself to this town. Why don't you think about that?"

As the question hung in the air, Aaron trudged up the stairway and slammed the door behind him.

The dining room remained silent for at least thirty seconds behind him.

Joseph Devendish, owner and president of the J. G. Devendish and Company Banks, rose from his seat, placed one hand over his breast pocket and spoke eloquently. "Gentlemen. We must examine our hearts here. All this time, I figured Uley Kirkland was out to find Tin Can Laura a job because those two were sweet on each other. Now I know the truth. We have been watching a loving heart in action, when perhaps none of us have seen a true loving heart before. We have been seeing a young woman standing on the faith she tried to share with us, and none of us would listen."

A murmur of assent moved through the room.

"They were doing their best to change and to impress upon the other to do what is fair and good. And, I'd like to do something here that will help them both."

"What?" several fellows hollered at Devendish. "What can you do to help?"

"I'm going down to Doc Gillette's office right now and offer Laura a job," he said. "I believe a young lady like that deserves a chance, don't you?"

Chapter Nineteen

Devendish strolled right straight into Doc Gillette's office and offered Laura Wilson the very thing she'd always dreamed of, a chance to support herself in a position that not only would sustain her living but would also give her an element of respect.

"You would do this?" she said, staring at Devendish. "You'd step out and do something like this for me?"

"I believe this is the way things are supposed to work," he said. "Uley Kirkland's stepped out over and over again on your behalf. When one person sees another doing a good deed in the name of the Lord, it encourages him to try his hand at charity, too."

Just then, Doc Gillette came to the door and beckoned to Laura. He fingered his beard. "She's tossing and turning in here. I figure she's trying to come around. You want to be here when she comes around?"

Laura jumped from her chair. "I've got to get word to Aaron." *Oh, Father. Thank*

You thank You thank You. It's like Uley said. You bring about good for those who trust You.

"I'll let him know," Joseph Devendish offered. "I've just come from Aunt Kate's, and I'm going right back. I'll get him down here as quick as I can."

Laura didn't know quite how to act around this man. He was proving savior and friend all at once, and just when she needed it the most. She wanted to throw her arms around him and tell him he'd given her something more valuable than all the precious metals men searched for up on Gold Hill. Instead, she shook his hand. "You will not regret your decision, Mr. Devendish. Thank you from the bottom of my heart."

The minute Joseph Devendish came into Aunt Kate's and tromped directly up the steps to Aaron's room, everyone in the place knew what was happening. Half of them made it down to Doc Gillette's before Aaron did. And so it was, when Uley opened her eyes and tried to focus on something, that she saw her father's face and Laura, plus practically every one else in the entire town.

Doc Gillette had never had so many

menfolk all crowding into his office at one time. As if in silent apology for the reaction they'd had when they first found out about her identity, many of the miners had brought gifts. Charlie Hastings presented her with a tiny green bottle filled with sweet-smelling rose water. D. J. Mawherter set a basket down beside her bed filled with pinecones and crushed needles from the lodgepoles up above town. It permeated the entire room with its tang.

"I just figured it'd make you feel more comfortable —" Mawherter alternately clutched his hands in front of his belly and then locked them together behind his spine, obviously uncertain how to conduct himself around her "— what with you having to stay indoors for a while and all."

Uley tried to sit up, wanting to acknowledge them all, but she couldn't. The pain in her shoulder seared through her like a hot brand. "Where's — ?" But she couldn't finish her question. It took too much effort to complete the sentence.

Calvin Freeman, proprietor of C. A. Freeman's Miners' Service Depot, opened the box he'd brought and removed a flannel nightgown with flounces and ruffles set around the sleeves and hem. Uley took the feminine garment, the first garment she'd ever possessed that was truly her own, without saying anything. She smiled gratefully at Freeman as she bunched it around her face and held it against her skin.

As the men pushed in around her, Aaron fell farther and farther back.

He'd brought nothing but himself. The last he'd seen that silly parasol, he'd left it lying on the step at Aunt Kate's. He felt a myriad of emotions as he watched Uley awaken to this new life, to these old acquaintances who were hovering around her in a new way. He felt afraid for her still, and humbled, as she lay stricken and pale.

He'd put her here.

She'd saved his hide one more time.

And he didn't figure he had any claim to her anymore. He'd certainly told God as much, and he'd meant it from the depths of his soul. He wanted everything that was good for her. Besides, from what he could see, he had a lot of competition now.

Oh, Lord, he prayed. *If it's Your will, You have to help me stop loving her. I can never do that on my own.*

Doc Gillette brought his shotgun out of the cabinet and started herding men away from her bedside. "Get on out of here," he said, holding the gun aloft so that they could all see it. "I worked for hours to save her from a bullet wound, and now you're going to kill her with attention. She isn't up to all this right now. Get on home, all of you."

Still they pushed in around the bed.

"Miss Uley, we never knew."

"Miss Uley, we didn't see."

"Uley, we just thought you couldn't grow whiskers!"

Gillette was right. Uley just lay in bed, too weak to speak or ask questions, clinging to the frilly flannel nightgown as if it meant everything in the world to her.

And just now, Aaron supposed, it did.

He wanted more than anything in the world to get to her side. But still, she hadn't asked for him.

"Let me through." He did his best to elbow his way past. "I'm the one Joseph Devendish came to get in the first place. Let me through."

"Hey," somebody growled at him. "I'm in line, too."

"Wait your turn like everybody else, Brown."

"But I'm —" He stopped. What was he to her, anyway? What could he say?

Doc Gillette kept waving the gun barrel in the air, warning everyone away. Aaron

443

supposed he didn't stand a chance. Now that every man in Tin Cup would want to court her, and she'd made it plain she was wanting to leave, Aaron figured she wouldn't want him anymore. She could have her pick of any man in Gunnison County.

As he left Doc Gillette's office, still hatless, he knew the time had come to stay away.

It took precisely two days for everyone in Tin Cup to start calling her "Miss Julia." The following week, in Wednesday's edition, the *Tin Cup Banner* had this to say:

On Monday afternoon some twenty-five to thirty gentlemen visited our new and estimable young lady of Tin Cup. Julia Kirkland is feeling much better and is able to move her arm without too much pain. Upon the occasion, several presents were given, and many were the congratulations offered. The afternoon was quite pleasantly spent in social discourse.

Laura began working for Joseph Devendish and surprised everyone, including herself, with her aptitude for numbers. In no time at all, she was able to decipher interest paid on time deposits. One morning, while she took deposits at the window, she glanced up to find herself nose to nose with Santa Fe Moll.

"Hello, Moll," she said, red-faced, as she did her best to count Moll's huge take from the night before.

"Hello, Laura."

"It looks like business is good over there."

"It is good. But not as good as before you left us."

Now, what was she supposed to say to that? But, much to Laura's surprise, Moll leaned forward and touched her with one gloved hand. "Don't you say anything. I figure I know what you've been through. Every girl has dreams. I had them once, too. If I'd've had a chance like yours, why, I'd have taken it, too."

"I meant to leave town where you couldn't find me."

"I figure it'll be harder for you to find a clean slate with the fellows here, Laura. I admire you for trying."

Laura figured the total amount of the deposit in question and filled out the corresponding receipt. She handed the paper across the counter to her former employer without further ado. "Sometimes the easiest way isn't the best way," she said.

"Thank you, Laura," Moll said. And that was the end of it.

That afternoon, as she did every afternoon, Laura walked to Sam Kirkland's cabin to visit Uley. That afternoon, as she did every afternoon, Uley sat propped up in bed, surrounded by gifts and exhausted from the attention of the miners who'd visited her, wearing the nightgown with the ruffles, her hair hanging in one rope-thick braid down her back. That afternoon, like every afternoon, she turned desperate eyes toward her friend's, gripped Laura's hand and asked, "Have you seen him? Did he come into the bank today?"

Laura shook her head sadly. Indeed, she hadn't seen Aaron since the morning Joseph Devendish had offered her a job. "I don't know where he's hiding himself."

"Why doesn't he come, Laura?"

Laura hated it, seeing her friend hurting like this. "I don't know, Uley," she said. "I really don't know."

It didn't take Beth long to notice that Aaron was hurting.

"You haven't eaten a decent meal for a week, Aaron Brown," she chided him.

"You ought to be relaxed and happy now that the trial's over. You ought to be celebrating instead of pacing the floor like a mountain lion every night. Ever want to know how loud your boots are when you circle your room a hundred times an hour? I could swear there's a corralled bull in there instead of just a man who can't sleep."

"I'm sorry," he said grumpily. "I'll try to stomp lighter tonight while I'm pacing the floor."

She glanced at the lace parasol he carried in one hand. "What are you carrying that thing around again for?"

He halfway hid it behind his leg, the very picture of a child caught playing with something he shouldn't. "Well, I don't know."

"I never did figure why you bought that thing in the first place. Up until Uley, I mean Julia, Kirkland came to light."

She paused, momentarily weighing her own words about Uley, then staring at her brother as if seeing him for the first time.

"Aaron! Aaron Brown! That's it, isn't it! That's what's got you storming around here like meat on the hoof. It's got to be her, doesn't it?"

He didn't let his sister go on. "Don't talk

about it. I don't want to discuss this."

Beth took one step toward her brother. "Look at me."

He wouldn't meet her eyes.

"Aaron, look at me, why don't you?"

"I don't want to talk about this with you, Beth."

"She's the one, isn't she? She's the reason you asked me all those questions about women. Aaron, how long have you known?"

"Long enough to get myself into trouble over it."

Finally, he faced her eye-to-eye.

"Since the day you met her?"

"Yes. I promised her then I'd keep her secret. That promise kept me from telling you, too, Beth, and I'm sorry for that."

When Beth took her brother's arm in her hand, her touch was feather-light, a gentle expression of the warmth and support he needed. "A promise kept is the sign of a strong character. And now, you fancy yourself in love with her?"

He nodded.

She smiled, her head tilted, the remembrance of her own love with Fred softening her face. "I'm happy for you, little brother."

But Aaron's face remained dispassionate

and pale. "Save your congratulations for someone else, Beth."

"Why? I don't understand." She put her hands on her hips. "Why aren't you down there with her, Aaron Brown? Why aren't you hovering at her bedside?"

How could he answer that question? How could he admit he was afraid?

I figure things change. I figure she'll see me different now that she enjoys the attentions of every fellow in Tin Cup.

And, besides that, Aaron feared something more.

When she'd taken that bullet for him, she'd been on her way to Ohio without telling him goodbye. Although he hadn't contested her decision to go, he was still reeling from the despair her decision had caused him.

He wondered if she still needed to go.

None of this could he voice to his sister. He told her only one thing.

"I figure it's her turn to come to me, Beth." He'd just purchased a new doe-colored Stetson from Calvin Freeman. He plopped it on his head, angling it forward toward his brows. He'd also purchased a tin gold pan. "I figure I'll spend some time up on the gold hill trying my luck," he said. *I agreed to let her go, Father. I made*

Doc Gillette gave Uley permission to get out of bed the following week. She walked around the room carefully, supported by Laura on one side and Sam on the other. After that, the doctor made her climb right back beneath the quilts. Two days later, he checked on her progress again. This time, he informed her that she could dress and walk about the house. Three days later, he noted how healthy and beautiful she was beginning to look. Her cheeks glowed like the autumn rosehips that were already beginning to dot the brush. Her hair shone like chintz, glimmering at all its folds.

But even Doc Gillette noticed that she didn't look happy. He heard her ask Laura Wilson, "Have you seen him at the bank? Do you know why he hasn't come?"

He heard Laura answer, "No, Uley. I don't know why. I ain't seen him still."

"I think it's time," Doc Gillette said, "for you to get out and take a walk in the Tin Cup air. The aspens are starting to turn gold out there. It'll do you good to see them, young lady."

He couldn't believe it. She'd been in bed and inside the house for weeks and even the suggestion of a walk outside didn't bring any anticipation to her eyes. "Yes, sir."

He sat down beside her. "Is there anything else I can do to help you, Miss Julia? You know all of us would do what we could to see you happy. You've got fellows in this town who'd give up their gold mines for you. Remember that."

"I don't want anybody's gold mine, Doc." She'd had enough of those to last a lifetime.

"Get out for a while. Take a ride on your horse if need be. Mull things over. If there's anything I can do to help, tell me."

"I will," she said. "Thanks, Doc."

After he left, she did what he'd told her to. It *did* feel good to stretch her neck back as far as it would go and peer up at the sky. But, even so, the translucent blue in the heavens above her only made her picture Aaron's eyes, the last desperate sadness she'd seen in them, and the intense betrayal.

She'd known all along how deeply her decision to go to Ohio would hurt Aaron. She'd also known she didn't have any other choice.

Her horse waited tethered up beside a tree. She considered riding him, but then thought better of it. She was wearing a

451

skirt now. She had no idea how to get a skirt draped over a saddle. She settled, instead, for scratching him on his supple, velvety nose while he snorted hot air across her fingers. "Things're going to be different from now on," she said, voicing her disquiet to the animal, "and I don't rightly know how to handle it, boy."

At that precise moment, she felt someone's eyes upon her. Uley glanced up.

Beth Calderwood stood in the middle of Willow Street, nervously fidgeting with the strings on her reticule.

"Howdy." Uley waved, her heart almost stopping.

Beth took two steps toward her. "Hello."

The usual pleasantries did not come. Instead, the two established ladies of Tin Cup stared at each other for a full minute before either of them spoke another word.

Uley spoke first. "You're so beautiful, Beth. I've been watching you for the longest time, just wishing I could be like you."

"Is that why you were going to Ohio? So you could become like me?"

"Yeah." *Because I thought Aaron deserved someone like you. Because you're such a proper lady. And you're his sister.*

Beth took one more step toward her. "I

452

can teach you things. You don't have to leave, you know."

"I'm not aiming to leave anymore."

"You're not?"

Uley shook her head. "No."

That was all Beth needed to hear. "Will you go to my brother, then? Will you tell him that? He's been hurting something awful."

The tears Uley had needed to shed for days finally rose in her eyes and spilled out over her cheeks. "He's been staying away. I've been waiting and waiting. How is it that searching for the Father's path can often leave others hurting?"

"Ah," Elizabeth said. "I do believe that your own journey set Aaron off on an important journey all his own. Him, the one who always tried to control things."

Uley didn't wait to hear anymore. She untied her horse's reins and did her best to swing up on top of the animal. "I hate skirts. They're all I ever wanted. And now I can't ride in them worth a fiddle without strings."

Beth ran up to help her. "Here. I'll teach you to sit sidesaddle."

"I don't have time to learn it right now, Beth. Will you teach me tomorrow? I've got to find Aaron."

Beth grinned. "Aaron's been stomping around his room at night like an ox trying to break out of its yoke. I'll sure be glad to get some sleep again." She took Uley's hand momentarily. "I care for my brother, Julia Kirkland. I see he cares for you, he needs you very much. You ride that horse any way you know how."

"Do you know where I might find him?"

"He's up on Gold Hill, prospecting in the creek."

Uley dug her heels into the horse's flanks. The animal bolted. Her skirts caught the wind and billowed out about her. Her hair, unfettered, bounced in taffy-colored curls against her back. She reined the animal toward the trees and kicked him again, lying low on his back as he sprang into a full gallop. The freedom of her hair and the running horse and her tripping heart filled her with joy.

At first, when she entered the clearing, Aaron didn't see her. He knelt at the creek's edge, his attention focused on working a shallow pan in circles.

She dismounted and tethered the horse. "Aaron!" she called. "Aaron Brown!"

Aaron thought his visitor was Beth. He left the pan on the ground and rose, shading his eyes. But the woman sprinting toward him was no one he knew. She held her billowing pink calico skirt with both hands and ran, her curls hanging in dark ropes around her shoulders. "Aaron. It's me. . . ." she called.

And that's when he knew.

"Uley?" he bellowed. Had she really come? "Uley!"

His breath caught in awe as he identified her. He'd never seen anyone — *anyone* — as fair and beautiful as the coltish girl racing toward him through the high-country meadow.

It became perfectly clear that she had every intention of launching herself at him again. He already knew the damage she could do. He'd been knocked off his feet by this woman more than once. But today he chuckled and braced himself as she flung herself at him. Today he was ready for all the blessings the Lord wanted to throw at him.

He caught her in his arms, swinging her around and pressing her against his chest.

"I'm not going away," Uley finally managed to get out.

"I've found some gold, enough to build a cabin and stake a claim up here."

"You did? Aaron, that's wonderful!"

"You must tell me what you want, what

you believe the Father is leading you toward now. But, if you would have me, I'm wanting to make it our home, Miss Julia Kirkland. Would you be my wife, share it with me? We need a good reason to bring that Pastor Creede back to town."

She gazed into his eyes, happy at last, happy beyond measure. "Yes," she whispered, cupping his face in her hands. "Oh, yes."

The only thing left to do, Aaron figured, was to kiss her. So he did. He kissed her with a yearning just as rich and wild as the Continental Divide country that surrounded them. And when he set her down to stand in the meadow grass beside him, Aaron knew full well they'd stand together like this for a lifetime.

"I love you."

"I love you, too."

It almost seemed too sweeping to take in.

Aaron scooped her up into his arms and held her there while she clasped her hands around the back of his neck.

"Tell me more," she urged him.

"I'll show you," he said. "I'll show you where we'll build the cabin. I'll show you where we'll build our life with the Lord together."

He kissed her once again, a signet of all their tomorrows. Their path together had not been easy, but they had trusted the Father to guide their ways. Their world had been righted because they'd sought the Father's power, not their own. Their love for each other would only be surpassed by His own. Aaron carried her through the autumn-ripe grass toward the creek that would run beside their home.

Discussion Questions

1. Uley made the choice to accompany her father to Tin Cup without praying about the consequences first. What other choices do you think she might have had?

2. When Sam and Uley rescue Tin Can Laura from the blizzard, Uley realizes that Jesus spent time with women very much like Laura. Are there any women from the Bible who remind you of Laura? Does Laura remind you of anyone you've known in your own life?

3. Do you think Aaron Brown made the choice to pursue Harris Olney because of his own pride or because of God's calling?

4. After she accepted the Lord, Laura had a difficult time "becoming a new creature" among the residents of Tin

Cup. This happened because the miners wouldn't *allow* her to change. Search your own heart. Is there anyone in your life whom you aren't allowing to change? In what ways can you approach this situation differently?

5. In what ways is Uley's deception of the miners in Tin Cup similar to Laura's sins. In what ways is it different?

6. There are several spots in this story where Uley could have blamed circumstances on herself. She could have looked backward, being angry with herself, instead of trusting the Father in spite of her mistakes. Is there a place in the plot similar to an instance in your life when you might have been tempted to blame yourself for something that happened instead of trusting the Father for the outcome?

7. At what point in the story does Aaron Brown truly turn himself over to God? On what do you base your answer?

8. Joseph Devendish, owner and president of the Tin Cup bank, was the first person besides Uley who let Laura step forward into a new life. What convinced him to do that?

9. Toward the end of the story, Aaron did not seek out Uley because he was certain she wouldn't want him now that she had so many male admirers in Tin Cup. Do you ever hold yourself back in your faith this way, thinking that there are other people more worthy than you to approach the Father?

10. In what ways is this story of the 19th-century West relevant to your own life and faith life?

A Note from the Author

Dear Readers,

When my parents married in 1954, my mother had never vacationed outside Texas. My father took her to Colorado for their honeymoon. This began a longtime love affair between my family and the mountains. When I was little, I used to mark off the hours on a chart before we would hop in the car and drive toward Tin Cup. In college, I worked at Holt's Guest Ranch. I rode horses to the lily pond. Just like Uley, I spent plenty of time at the Tin Cup Town Hall and, yes, I've even been to a wedding there! I've prowled around those hills outside the Gold Cup, and my poor little dachshund, Annie, got a porcupine quill in her paw while exploring an old ramshackle cabin.

It was so much fun imagining the characters who had once walked these streets, thinking about the lives of the miners and the girls at Santa Fe Moll's place. This story satisfied me when it was released the first time. But now that I've heard the Father's call to write books that draw readers toward Him, the opportunity to "redeem" and rewrite this project seemed like a gift. How many chances does a person have to redo the work of our hands, which we had meant for our glory, and offer it up to glorify our Heavenly Father? I am grateful beyond measure to Joan Marlow Golan at Steeple Hill for giving me this opportunity. I offer this story to you, in His name. I hope you will love Tin Cup as much as I do.

Deborah Bedford

P. O. Box 9175
Jackson Hole, WY 83001
www.deborahbedfordbooks.com